EXTREME

EXTREME

a novel

JOAN GELFAND

Blue Light Press * 1st World Publishing

San Francisco * Fairfield, Iowa * Delhi, India

Blue Light Press
www.bluelightpress.com
bluelightpress@aol.com

1st World Publishing
PO Box 2211
Fairfield, IA 52556
www.1stworldpublishing.com

First Edition
ISBN: 978-1-4218-3651-5

Library of Congress Control Number:
2020934935

We all have three lives. Public, private, and secret.

—Gabriel Garcia Marquez

EXTREME

1

AFTER FRUITLESS circling of the Purple, Coral, and Lime parking lots, Hope surrenders. She drives underground, winding four levels down into the bowels of Palo Alto's small Civic Center garage. She surrenders, but not before considering several vacant red, blue, and yellow spots, as tempting to her as any gooey dessert. "Employees only," "Electric vehicles," and "Disabled" parking spaces sit empty as a tossed Starbucks cup. It was tempting. But not today. Anything can happen in the five minutes it takes to run into CVS, including a beat cop under pressure to get his numbers up. When did parking in downtown Palo Alto at three P.M. become an Olympic event? Did the student population at Stanford just increase by a factor of ten? WTF?

Leaving the underground lot, Hope steps into daylight as harsh as the brightness after a matinee, a brutal transition from fantasy to reality. Today is very real. Today, Hope's fantasies are about work, even if FearToShred is its own movie.

Today there are questions to answer: Does the young company have legs? Why did Arthur turn down an eighty million dollar offer to sell it to Datex, his former company?

FearToShred hasn't gone public yet. That's a good thing for her as a potential employee, but a fact which had blocked Hope from getting the boatload of intelligence she wanted for the interview. *Crunchbase* was little help. She could call around, but sleuthing would sound an alarm that she's leaving Manuserve.

Hope squints. The sun is bright, but that's nothing new; the sun has been bright all year. She slips on Ray Bans, as integral to her outfit as her Apple watch or Blahniks. All of California has been steamy, smoky, and stuck in an endless summer. Is it November? August? January? Who can tell?

University Avenue and the surrounding roads are an obstacle course rife with a nonstop parade of joggers, cyclists, and mothers and nannies pushing baby strollers. The fires have been creepy. Hope's yard has deteriorated to a dusty grey; her showers are bullet short. One dry winter has turned into three. The water company's banned watering of lawns; abusers are ridiculed on the front pages of the press. Northern California blames Southern California. Tony golf courses of the wealthy are under civic scrutiny. All while California's economy shoots into the stratosphere.

With Google and Facebook gobbling up tech veterans, startups were desperate for talent. Which was why Hope wasn't surprised when Arthur called. Her name was one of the few raised when recruiters, hiring managers, and CEO's played the "who's innovating" game at meetings and cocktail parties. While Hope had been hiding out at Manuserve, collecting a fat paycheck and doing banal B2B, her reputation was still out there, reaching far and wide. What she and Doug had pulled off at Topia had been the stuff of urban legend. Topia was one of the very first companies to break through from geeky to a global audience. Yes, Arthur knew who she was even if she'd been heads down the past year.

Despite the severe lack of rain, today the world is fresh and new. Gardenia and jasmine scent the air; the breeze whispers "possibility."

Through the glass doors and up the wide aisle at CVS, Hope heads for the cosmetics to suss out a chintzy replacement lipstick for the MAC she accidentally left on her desk.

A wall of options waits like a chorus line of Vegas dancers. Hope checks her watch: thirteen minutes to pick out a shade that telegraphs, "serious, smart, perky." She assesses the check-out line. Decent. Two cashiers, one auto pay, and only a few customers standing in line. Hope sets her phone alarm for ten minutes.

Five foot eight, Hope weighed in this morning at 136, not her best weight ever but she's been busy. A thick lock of auburn hair stretches midway down her back. Her legs are long and slim. She woke up feeling good in her skin. A sexy wake-up call from James in bed this morning didn't hurt. She'll get back to 129, her fighting weight, soon.

Lipsticks. Maybelline, Cover Girl. Hope frets. Her go-to shade is Diva by MAC, but CVS doesn't carry the upmarket brand. Firecracker. Too wild. Ruby Woo. Milf. Hot Passion. Not for work. Ah, wait. Monte Carlo. Rich. Smart looking. She rubs a sample on the back of her hand. Possible. With a clean Q-tip she swipes her lips. Deep. But wait. There's American Doll. Looks like Diva's poor sister. Same shade, cheaper packaging. She wipes off the Monte Carlo with a moistened towel from a handy dispenser, swipes a fresh Q-tip.

With a hint of Monte Carlo adhered to her lip she creates an impromptu blend of the two shades. Perfect. Pursing her lips in the small makeup mirror mounted on the wall, wondering if her cheeks have flushed or if it's the lighting, she catches sight of Doug Wiser.

Hope swings her hair in front of her face, kneels down low to fumble with her Coach slouch bag. She's searching for her credit card when his warm hand alights on her shoulder.

"Hope!"

Hope looks up guiltily, her head uncomfortably level with Doug's crotch. Unfolding herself to full height, the single button on her pencil skirt pops.

Doug throws his arms around her in a cozy bear hug.

This is Doug? Doug Wiser? In skinny jeans and Nikes? This is Doug, clean shaven, bed hair and cheekbones? This is Doug in CVS at 3:10 P.M. holding a pregnancy kit and a bottle of vitamins? This is Doug who asked Hope (kindly) not to call because he "was lost?" A whirligig of thoughts spin. Her phone alarm buzzes. How is she? She's tense. And worse, she's ruffled by running smack into her ex in CVS a half an hour before an interview.

"I'm great!" Hope half smiles. "I'm just on my way—I'm late actually!" Hope nervously juggles the two lipsticks.

Doug's gaze lingers on her torso, taking in the whole of her. When her eyes finally meet his, he's looking at her the way a parent looks at a child accomplishing a new feat—a climb up the monkey bars, a ball caught. Or was that condescension? He, calm. She, frazzled.

"Go. We'll talk later."

"Totally," Hope promises, proffering a fingertip touch to Doug's exposed forearm. "Sorry to rush off."

At the check-out counter, she grabs a package of safety pins. It's been over a year. She's missed him. She thinks about Doug almost every day. Ahead of her on the line, a small woman with dark glasses holds the leash of a service dog, a beautiful short-haired golden that reminds her of Gracie, the first and last dog she owned. She peeks in her makeup mirror, checking the aisle behind her.

He's gone.

Hope exits the automatic doors, hurries toward High Street. Did she really just crash into Doug in CVS holding a pregnancy test? In all of her fantasies, in all the past year of secret dreams and fears, the last place she would meet Doug Wiser was in the lipstick aisle of the University Avenue CVS.

Now, she's got to rock that interview. Her nerves are jangled, and her button is popped. She suddenly tumbles a notch from Ninja-warrior Hope down to disheveled working woman. She checks her Apple watch: 3:25 P.M.

Slipping into Philz, Hope orders a green tea and scoots into the restroom to replace the popped button with a safety pin.

Perfunctorily repaired, she snags a tiny table. Creating lists, a habit she developed in college when she was juggling a late shift at Oscar's Burgers at night, parts modeling when she got the gigs, five classes, and an endless parade of reading and homework assignments, calms her. It's a habit she's never bothered to break.

She taps out a list of questions on her tablet: Arthur rejected an eighty million offer from Datex. Why? Was there a back-up offer? Was he hoping to create more value? Was Arthur passionate about FTS, or was he just in it for the money? She scratches out the last question—too forward.

At 3:35, her pre-Doug equilibrium nominally restored, Hope walks the two blocks to High and Homer. Past Serenity Yoga, Brew News Beer pub, Bucca di Beppo, and the Party Store. Yes, she really did just see Doug for the first time in a year. But it wasn't a reunion, was it? Reunions are planned. Hope erases the interlude like she'd erased the lipstick on the back of her hand.

Halfway across High Street, her iPhone rings. "Doll?"

"James?"

"That was sweet this morning. You good?"

"Yes. Listen, I'm running late," Hope's stomach churns. "Catch you later?"

"No prob. See you tonight?"

"Yes. No. I'm not sure. I'll call."

"Hope . . . we have that dinner tonight. Remember? John's out from New York?"

"Yup."

Three forty-six. She hadn't told James about the interview because she did not want to listen to a lecture on the fallibility of startups.

Outside FearToShred's frosted glass doors, she sneaks a peek in her tiny makeup mirror. Gone is the high cheek color of this morning; she looks pale, spooked.

2

Automatic doors swing open to FearToShred's sun-splashed lobby. Hope is two blissful minutes early.

Mounted on the wall behind a worn, recycled slat wood desk, FearToShred's logo—a silver X as two crossed skateboards—is spot lit. *Thrasher* posters line the walls, the images a dizzying display of once-in-a lifetime tricks: a lithe skateboarder, aloft, board floating on thin air, an upside down androgynous snowboarder mid-mountain, an extreme biker caught mid-spin, half-pipes, Maverick-sized waves, a history of iconic dares.

Tugging at the hem of her black skirt, Hope shakes off her tense morning. Skirt or pants? Black or yellow? Monotone or patterned? Matchy-matchy or mismatch? This morning, rifling her well organized, color-coded closet, she panicked while the digital clock's numbers clicked like time-lapse photography. She tossed a shirt on the bed, a belt, then a jacket. No. Black pants, grey button-down shirt. No. No outfit was right for slipping surreptitiously from her stodgy corporate office to an interview at a startup. After her two o'clock meeting, she'd told her assistant, Carla, she had a "doctor's appointment." The lie was an easy one.

She knew FearToShred's workforce would be decked out in t-shirts, or at best, button-downs with the tails out but she couldn't go quite that far. Finally, she chose a black pencil skirt, an ecru colored crisp shirt and an unstructured charcoal blazer.

At the far end of the lobby an Italian wool sofa, slate grey, two tastefully placed Breuer chairs, retro white-glass-globes and pink lava lamps, a mashup of Web 2.0 and reimagined toys, furnish the waiting area. Startups could acquire an entire office on fire sales from companies gone bust or moving their production offshore.

Hope holds tight to her supple Italian leather briefcase.

References, resume. All were impeccable.

"Hope Ellson to see Arthur McKnight."

"I'll tell him," the young receptionist answers in a loose British accent that could be Aussie. "Sign in, would you?" She points at an Envoy tablet. "It takes your photo and prints your badge."

The cloying sweetness of tuberoses arranged in a tall, blue glass vase overwhelm Hope like a walk down the perfume aisle at Nordstrom's. Is it the beautiful young receptionist's birthday? A gallant gesture from a geek in hot pursuit? Whatever. The spiky platinum-hair-with-blue-streaks gatekeeper, she of few words and pale skin, looks glamorous in their shadow. Directly behind the receptionist, a wall-sized video screen looms, looping highlights of the latest FearToShred challenges. Hope studies the heart-stopping video clips of FearToShred's most extreme challenges. She recognizes many of the stunts from the site's You-Tube channel: A surfer executing a perfect ollie on a longboard. A Heli-skier racing down virgin powder. A scene from *Free Solo*, the climber Alex Honnold captured on his final successful climb by the National Geographic team. As the clips roll, audience upvotes are tallied. The upvotes boost a team's score. A stream of emojis float over the clips as they play out, showing fan "likes" even "loves" as viewers rank and vote. And then the Oscar statue fades in. Hope had heard that the company had made a deal with the climber. Maybe Arthur would spill.

The receptionist is composed given the buzz generated by the screen just behind her. Perched gracefully on her ergonomic chair, she's a heron, balancing a diffident stance. Or is that a whiff of Euro disdain?

Either way, her fashion sense is pure Northern California: dangly hammered gold earrings, an orange cotton scarf wrapped around her thin neck and countless jangly bracelets. Hope can hear the HR recruiter: 'Edgy but educated.' Well, they got their girl. Hope slips the nametag into the plastic holder and settles into the chair farthest away from the desk. She scans her work e-mail, catching a grimace gathering around the receptionist's red-lipsticked mouth. Was that Indie Flick Mat? Or Firecracker? Hope hates job interviews, the cool assessment of strangers that begins in reception. Getting the job done was one thing; being the outsider always made her tense.

Across from the reception area, a wall of framed articles lauds FearToShred's successes: "Skater Brats Win Big." "Gnarly Win for Shredders." "On the Boards: Skater App Hits Big with Real-time."

Hope studies the articles from *Pando Daily*, *The Next Web*, *TechCrunch*, and *Boing Boing*. Jeff Price and Julie Tang are everywhere. She scans for details, anything she may have missed in her scrupulous research. Was the technology tight? The strategy realistic? The framed articles don't reveal anything new. But that's PR, always telling you what you already know.

Four ten. In her research, she learned that McKnight had raised a 10M A round on the idea that skaters, boarders and cyclists were hot to film themselves acting out FearToShred's dares: catapult over a creek or river, surf the Big Island at dawn—wearing a fluorescent tee and ski goggles. The challenges often required setup, a videographer, lighting designer, and crew. It was all about being discovered.

Hope notices the receptionist eyeing her calves. Was her skirt wrong? Too short? Could she see the safety pin under her short jacket? This morning in her sexy, post-orgasmic mood, the idea of exposing a hint of thigh seemed like a wise choice. Why not? She had pampered her legs all these years. It paid. Parts modeling had the cachet of a showgirl, but it saved her legs from the varicose veins waitressing was sure to have tipped her with.

Growing up alone with Charlene and her sister, Dawn, was bleaker than living in a factory town with no factory. From the age of ten, life was scant; generic label groceries from the Alpha Beta where Charlene worked in Accounts Payable. For sports, a county funded soccer league. All the extras—vacations, soccer camps, and even the coveted secondhand car to drive into the asphalt-covered parking lot of Livermore Valley High, were out of the question.

Four-fifteen. The receptionist doesn't offer any intelligence on Arthur McKnight's whereabouts. By four-twenty, Hope steps out into the warm afternoon, electric doors whooshing shut behind her. "I'm stuck," she reports into Carla. Another lie. Make that three, just today. She'll have to start a spreadsheet. It will be her Database of Deceits. That way she can double check who she's told what.

By 4:23 she's pacing. Ten minutes late is expected. Twenty says McKnight's running a power trip. She swipes onto her personal e-mail.

From: Dawn Subject: "WTF?"

"Could Charlene be any more inappropriate? After you left, I opened her present. It was a school backpack! Did she blank out the years before we could make our own breakfasts?"

Yesterday, at Dawn's baby shower, Charlene had cornered her while Dawn's lady friends sipped vodka punch cocktails. "Hope Ellson! We haven't done anything fun in ages! Let's plan a trip! I'll find out when the planets align. We'll meet our soulmates!" Charlene railed in vodka-infused enthusiasm. "The best thing about a cruise is being stuck with all these people, don't you think?" Her mother raised her eyebrows suggestively.

Hope had pitched her pink and blue polka dotted paper plate of deviled eggs and carrot sticks into the nearest trash bin. A trip? With her mother? "I already have a mate, mom. Remember James?" Hope assumed a defensive stance, even if she herself wasn't convinced.

What had started out as a sexy romance had quietly shifted these past months. Last month James had broached the topic of cohabitation. It wasn't that Hope was against living together, she just wasn't ready. Moving in with James meant getting closer. Getting closer meant getting involved with his life. Close with his parents and sister, James had initiated several cozy gatherings: dinner with his parents, a hike in Edgewood Park with his sister, a visit to the Legion of Honor for the whole crew. The easy way his family moved had a deleterious effect on Hope—it agitated her. 'Easy' was unfamiliar, the last thing she associated with family. Pleasant was not in her lexicon. Moving in with James would be like domesticating a feral cat, a job that posed a challenge to both parties. The cat was happy outside while the good-hearted rescuer was convinced it would be a better life snuggled up in a warm house. It was a tug of war she wasn't sure she could manage with grace.

And kids? She didn't know the first thing about raising them. There were no bedtime stories in Charlene's small house, no cozy snuggles and no comforting, glowing angel nightlights. Hope fell asleep to the drone of the 580 freeway, planes coming in from the east for landings in Oakland, and Charlene's television.

The long hand of the wall clock slips past the six. 4:30. Hope walks out of sight of the lobby doors. Should she tell the receptionist that she's got another meeting? Press her for McKnight's ETA? These things can be tricky. Sometimes, waiting for the CEO is a test. Is she cool? Laid back? Patient? A company could tell a lot about a prospective employee from how they managed their first challenge. Five more minutes. Thirty minutes late without at least inquiring would make her look like a pushover.

"Hope? Arthur's ready."

* * *

"Hope Ellson," Arthur waves her toward a guest chair angled perfectly in front of his desk. Arthur is tall, taller than she expected. Six-three at least. He's got the requisite cropped blond-grey hair of the Ivy League CEO, but his mouth curls up to the edges in a way that says trouble, and his strong, athletic looks make it clear that he is a man rarely far from a playing field. Tennis, rugby, beach volleyball, squash, and racquetball—he plays them all. Framed pictures on the glass shelves prove it.

Old-boy gravitas oozes from his body like the peaty scent of scotch from wood paneled rooms. Still, there's enough of a bad boy glint in his eyes to know that he would shoot you the finger across the board-room table if he objected to your business plan.

Smart, athletic. Great. But Arthur's resume is still fresh in her mind.

Corporate raiding. Initial Public Offerings. Mergers and acquisitions. He's done it all. His personal scoreboard is legendary for the short but prestigious slate of large and small companies that have made huge hits since he landed in the valley. VoxRead in 2010, Duotri, 2012, Glo, 2014. Not that he wins every time. There was the debacle with Cronos and two other failed companies. But the losses haven't registered on his face; his eyes are a clear, icy blue.

"Thanks for coming in. How are you for time?" Arthur's deep voice reverberates off the tall windowpanes and thick glass shelves lined with silver framed photographs and wood framed diplomas from USC and Harvard. Furnished the office on his own dime, Hope thinks. No self-respecting CEO takes hand-me-downs.

"I have time," Hope's voice flies out fractured, the song of a broken bird. Damn, she cringes. She might be lightning quick and clever in a marketing meeting, but her small self always rears its ugly head in job interviews. That small self was the child, led quickly away from the festive window displays at Neiman Marcus or Macy's—mannequins dolled up in chic black dresses for a gala or Saturday night out —by Charlene, to the shoe store where she would buy Hope her one new pair of shoes for the year. That small self was the teenager recoiling at her mother's histrionics: *And what are you going to do up there at UC with all those rich kids?* That small self is the worm in the apple, the ghost pain from an accident. Arthur doesn't notice.

"Good," he says, walking across the room. "Sorry I was late. My 3:30 ran over. Thanks for waiting." His lips are upturned now in the perpetually optimistic way of game show hosts, TV preachers, anchormen, and gurus. Arthur is the kind of guy who delivers bad news with a smile—the kind of guy that makes you feel like a putz for having trouble seeing things his way, or having trouble at all, ever.

Contrite. Check. Score one for the boss, Hope notes.

"Drink?" Arthur opens a small mini fridge.

"Diet Dr. Pepper?" Hope asks. She takes the cold can, waves away Arthur's offer of a glass.

"Mind if I dive in?" Arthur twists open a bottle of Voss.

"Go."

"Here's where we are. I discovered Jeff Price and Julie Tang down at *Plug and Play* in Sunnyvale. You know it?"

"Yes."

"I'm in their mentorship program. I've advised some of Fred and Randall's portfolio companies," Arthur explains.

Like a driver's test to renew your license, Arthur is starting easy, asking semi-rhetorical questions he's sure she can answer. Fred and Randall are old friends, early investors in Seven Arts where she had her first tech job. If he had studied her resume as he should have, he knew that she knew them well.

"Good guys. Lots of vision. So, Jeff and Julie are at *Plug and Play*, building an app for skaters. They got attention when they started sending out challenges on Twitter and all of these Twitch streamers started popping up, covering FearToShred video highlights and outcomes of challenges. The VCs loved it. 'We're all about tricks,' Julie told me the first time I took them to lunch. 'Unique tricks, quirky.' I liked her. The first challenge was 'shred it—under a full moon.' Skaters recorded themselves executing 360s, pop-shove-its and ollies under a full moon —near a beach, in the snow and then surfing. Once the videos were uploaded, registered users voted. Julie and Jeff were surprised that people were actually hopping on board."

"So to speak."

Arthur continues, oblivious to the double entendre. Seriously?

"Pretty soon, the X *Games* crowd hopped on. FearToShred grew from a random mobile web app to a fun game of dares and interpretation. Everyone was pumped, competing with each other, showing off their videos of half-pipes and bike tricks. Every player got their own Profile Page. The community could easily track their competitor's progress and stats. I came along just at the time that it occurred to Jeff and Julie that they had built something more than a fun app. I told them I'd look for money if they thought they could pull off building out the full user experience. They had the biggest challenge licked: tons of fans. I wasn't convinced that they had the tech chops, but I figured I would deal with that later."

Hope flips opens her iPad. "How many monthly unique users?"

"One million, or thereabouts."

"Good start," Hope says.

"We branched out from the skateboarders, went for the BMX crowd and snowboarders."

"You mean the Go-Pro gang?"

"No. We wanted something different, not just videos of athletes who'd strapped the camera on and hit 'record.' We organized the game so that all players respond to a posted challenge. They can't play if they don't create. Players upload a short movie, a creative interpretation of the day's challenge, A *double 360 under a full moon*."

Hope's fingers race across the keypad. What she really wants is to take a picture of Arthur's whiteboard; there's a boatload of intelligence scribbled there that she would love to decipher, but this is her first interview. Better to follow his lead for now. "Tell me more."

Arthur hits "Decline" on his ringing cell phone. "The challenge is tweeted with the #FTS hashtag. That's when the twenty-four-hour countdown starts. Fans are notified via text. The players add the quirks and also compete for votes from viewers or to be the first to upload a completed challenge to boost their chances of winning. Players and their crews plan out a scenario—a three-minute movie to enter into the competition. For example: catch air, wearing a blue shirt with Green Day playing. Quirk: With a rainbow."

Arthur opens the FTS app and rapidly scrolls through video entries ranging from the least complex challenges to X Pogo. Hope catches glimpses. Many videos didn't make the cut as players attempted half-baked tricks. There's one woman on a skateboard, getting drenched in a fountain. Above her is drone clumsily catching her moves. Another video plays a droning voice, interpreting "drone" quirk as the low, monotonous sound loop of a Gregorian chant.

"Check this out," Arthur says. "One for the FTS Hall of Fame. It scored high for both form and for the skillful way the crew captured the video, using a state-of-the-art, 12-megapixel flying camera drone." Arthur loads up the video and exclaims, "Look at this kid."

Hope watches a crew manually control the camera drone. It follows the surfer speeding along the massive wall of waves performing challenging skate tricks on a surfboard.

"Fancy drones with hi-res capabilities aside, this kid is the reason behind the success of this most spectacular feat in the short history of FTS," Arthur says. "The most spectacular that is, until *Free Solo*," Arthur says reverently.

"I was curious about that," Hope says. Knowing that whatever intelligence is offered up now is classified.

"Right," Arthur says, lips lightly pursed as if a zipper had been pulled across them. "All I can say is, bringing Alex on board was one of the reasons The Action Network came calling. That amped up the company stakes at least a hundred-fold."

Hope takes it all in—this crazy kid soaring along a massive wave, spinning three hundred and sixty degrees in the air. He lands facing away from the shore and spins again another one hundred and eighty degrees to face towards the shore again. At once, he is a surfer, a skater and a snowboarder.

"Viewers went wild for the video," Arthur reports. "They gave it more likes than any other entry in the competition. And, it raised the bar for other players. It inspired even more outrageous challenges," Arthur adds. "We need more of this kind of thing to really scale our audience and get more players. Obviously, sponsors flock to our star players."

"I get it. Not Go-Pro. But why would boarders and their friends take the time to record themselves?"

Arthur brightens, dimples deepening. "For one thing, we've got big stars. We've got Tony Hawk, Shaun White, Danny Way, Dallas Friday, and now, Alex Honnold to rate the videos. They get excited about getting their challenges rated by star players. Think eSports but the world is our playing field. Think about it. You're a talented fifteen-year-old boarder who hasn't qualified for the X Games yet. FearToShred could be your chance to do just that and could be your chance for big prize money. Who knows, maybe FTS will be its own sport one day and universities will offer scholarships to players like they do for League of Legends eSports players."

"Interesting idea."

Arthur steps out from behind his desk, starts pacing, his gesticulations growing increasingly animated.

"To keep fans hooked, players do crazy things like attach body sensors to themselves so that the final video uses their own heartbeat as part of the musical soundtrack. Or, they'll have their Fitbit data overlaid on the final upload."

Hope nods. As Arthur walks past her again, she catches the faint scent of aftershave—or is it soap? Whatever it is, it's designer—212 or Marc, slight scent of musk, coriander.

"Just last month The Action Network got wind of what we're doing, including how up close and personal we get with the players. They've proposed a FearToShred reality show. The idea of being on the show is the ultimate leveling up in the game for players. That is, if a player wins a lot of rounds—I did mention that other players vote before the judges, didn't I?"

"Yes. I like that."

"Right. So, TAN's idea is that when a player wins a few rounds, they get invited onto the show."

"Great," Hope says, sipping the cool soda and wishing she had asked for water. The faux sweetness is leaving a metallic taste in her mouth. She'd asked for the soda out of habit, hoping the caffeine would perk her up, but Arthur's doing that in spades. She grips the chair arms, careful not to leave scratch marks. Daring. Balls-out risks. Hope had been drawn to boarding and surfing the way people are obsessed with Second Life or Minecraft. When she was in school, it was all she could do to buy a one-day pass for the X Games or even steal a few hours to watch them on TV. But Arthur is talking about a reality show! Her dream job—squared.

Arthur points at a flat screen behind his desk: "Each episode of the TV show will feature the winning video. We'll share the backstory— how the video evolved once the Challenge was announced via the app and social networks, what sparked the core idea. That way, the audience will get to know these players and what makes them tick." A video of a snowboarder skirting an icy lake fills the flat screen.

"So, beside a vicarious thrill, the TV show is a way to engage viewers," Hope says.

"Right. TAN's show gets viewers behind the scenes. You know, the flubs, the falls, and the near misses. People love that stuff. And, they can watch as the votes clock in."

"Great."

"When I saw that Jeff and Julie had massive numbers of Twitter and YouTube followers, my first thought was, how can we go even bigger? Things are moving fast. My problem is that it's clear that neither Jeff nor Julie has the chops to scale the site, especially the back-end infrastructure. We need a solid VP of Engineering. Problem is, there aren't enough to go around. The good ones are snapped up by Google or Slack or they're doing their own start-up."

"I think there are still a few around," Hope offers. "I know one for sure. He's the best scale-up guy I know." The words tumble out before she has time to reconsider. Doug would be perfect. "We built an awesome team at Topia. Doug ran Engineering; I ran everything else. Product, press, marketing. Topia was the first company where I started running meetups. We gave away free stuff to our subscribers when they tried our products. We had everything from geeky kitchen appliances to motorized bikes. We didn't know what we were doing but it worked." There it was. The small self.

"I want Doug here—yesterday. Catch me the big fish, Hope. Next Tuesday, OK?" Arthur checks his calendar. "You can meet the team."

3

THICK GLASS doors sigh a soft exhale. Doug is definitely the right guy to fix FearToShred's tech problems; her problem is working with him again.

Hope fumbles for her keys, her heart still racing. If Arthur wants her to run interference with the founders and he wants to take FearToShred from Silicon Valley to Hollywood, she's in. TAN wants to launch the show by February. That means she would be working like a dog. No summer vacation, not even a slim chance of a cruise. That might give her mother time to figure out who her soulmate was and leave Hope alone.

Hope turns, scans the second floor. Would Arthur be watching her? He might be, but the windows are mirrored. Even if he could see out, she couldn't see in.

Pulling the car out of the FTS parking lot, she conducts a mental run through of her next stops. Gym. Home to catch up on the work she had missed this afternoon. Take-out. Maybe the run in with Doug was meant to be. Would she have thought to recommend Doug if she hadn't seen him in CVS?

"Great bumping into you today. I wanted to let you know that Arthur McKnight, the CEO over at FearToShred might be giving you call. . . I just had an interview with him. I'm not sure if you're in the market, but it could be a great fit. . ." Doug's voicemail clicks off. Hope won't call back. Knowing Doug, he'll check his log. She'll wait.

Speeding now toward the freeway, Hope checks her missed calls: Chuck: "Got your message about the late report. I hope everything went alright at the doctor."

Carlos, her trainer: "Puppy crisis. I have to reschedule!" Carlos and that French poodle—he's nuts!

Dawn: "Foursome dinner Saturday?"

James: "Hi Doll. How was your day?"

Charlene: "Are we still on for dinner?"

Edging into traffic, the effervescent bubble that had her in its hold fizzles. "No, mom," Hope instructs Siri to send a text to Charlene. "I'm sorry. James took your spot. I'll call you tomorrow."

Carlos's poodle crisis notwithstanding, she'll go work out. That should calm her down.

4

A HALF-MILE NORTH, Hope is caught at a dead stop between a Serv-Mor truck spewing exhaust and a ruddy-faced middle-aged guy sucking on a lollipop behind the wheel of a red Miata.

It's Tuesday. James catches a pickup basketball game at the Y between work and dinner. Tuesday is her dinner with Charlene night, but that hasn't worked for the past three weeks. *Why do I do this to myself?* Hope mumbles. Since her sister had pushed out baby number one and gotten pregnant with number two, Hope had been saddled with Charlene duty. Someone had to. Charlene works in Accounts Payable at the Alpha Beta, but her dependence on her daughters was their job. Hope wished she could say no, but it wasn't worth the guilt. Tonight, she'd canceled again, but she'd make it up to her next week. She'll spring for a nice dinner at Enrico's. She scans the radio. Talk radio. No. Classical. No.

A fresh-from-the-factory red Tesla cuts her off, sneaking into the carpool lane across a double yellow line. Hope slams on the brakes. Rude driving has migrated north from Los Angeles and west from the East like the Africanized bees that were working their way up from South America. What happened to mellow? What happened to "Let's chill?" What happened to "No worries," and "Whatever?" Damn.

More tunes. Oldies, eclectic, and three Hispanic stations deliver a jumbled cacophony. To the east, sun glints off glass-fronted houses nestled in the oak studded hills. Suddenly, Hope is homesick for open space, for the smell of oaks and bay, for country music, for a beer — and for her old self. Could she really work with Doug again? And what to say to Chuck, whose generosity saved her from unemployment two years ago? Did she really have the oomph for another startup? Oh, and on top of work, she was due to become an auntie to Dawn's second baby. What does that even mean? Would she be expected to babysit? Show up for endless birthday parties, park dates, and Gymboree expeditions? At 84 East, she turns off, heading over the Dumbarton Bridge. She'll catch up with Chuck later.

> *Oh, the wayward wind is a restless wind*
> *A restless wind that yearns to wander.*
> *And I was born the next of kin.*
> *The next of kin to the wayward wind . . .*

Hope clicks "answer" on the dashboard touchscreen.

"Doll?"

"Oui."

"Want to break free?"

"What did you have in mind?" Hope asks.

"Dinner and a movie?"

"Nah. Hey, isn't tonight basketball? And what about John from New York?"

"Missed my window at the Y. My four-thirty ran late, and John rescheduled," James reports.

"Aww. I'm sorry." Hope musters the sincerity from a reserve tranche. James loves b-ball nights. "Carlos ditched our training. Meet me up at the Circle Back. I'm heading there now."

"Forty-five minutes? I'm just leaving."

"Later." Hope blows James a quick cell kiss.

As her small car hugs Highway 84's twists and turns, Hope considers the interview again. From Arthur's last words "Catch me a big fish, Hope," it appears the job is hers for the taking.

She's breaking her own rules, but isn't that what rules are for? In high school, she would come up to the Circle Back on Saturday nights to line dance herself into a sweaty frenzy. Up here, she could forget

Charlene. She could forget the endless fights about college and money. Up here, she was freed from the small room she shared with Dawn and the blare of television. Up here, she had space to be herself.

Sometimes she regretted it when she woke on Sunday to piles of homework, but only sometimes. Besides, catch a high school kid at home on Saturday night and pretty soon they were being called out as a nerd, or worse, loser.

"For old times' sake," she whispers devilishly to the wind, steps hard on the gas. "Take me!"

* * *

Hope rounds the last twenty-miles-per-hour curve with the speedometer edging toward forty. *Here* is the beauty of living in the Bay Area: crowded as the freeway had been, she still knows places to hide. The lacy umbrellas of acacia trees shade the road. Alamitos Creek is bone dry. Eucalyptus shiver as she passes, their menthol perfume soothing her the way dry hay does; the scents are etched onto her homing DNA.

Was FearToShred really on to something? Was Arthur on the right track with The Adventure Network? Would Doug really come out of retirement, or was she just showboating with Arthur?

Wind. Air. Bay and acacia, eucalyptus and sun. Past and present roll up into a moment. Time. There it is again. Up here, time expands. The farther she climbs up the canyon, the farther from the valley, time slows. She might be giving up the gym, but once in a while, she has to break rank. Besides, she can wake up early and write a blog post. Tonight, she needs to think.

She pulls the Porsche into the gravel dusty parking lot with aplomb. The Circle Back lot is full, jocular sounds from the open door piercing the silence of the woods. Mirrored beer company logos and neon signs cover the length of the dark wall. Blue Moon, PYRAMID/IPA, and Sierra Nevada Pale Ale on draft.

A line of workingmen perches comfortably at the bar. She knows this crowd: contractors, tradespeople, union members, and journeymen electricians, plumbers, and framers who wake to five A.M. alarms, arrive at work by seven, quit at four, their reward a drink with pals on the way home. Their wives, if they have them, don't get a say about what time they pull in. After a day dry walling, plumbing, banging two by fours and setting tile, a little down time is non-negotiable. Besides, who could listen to gut-wrenching love songs on pop radio all day and not want to drown their sorrows — at least a little?

Two forty-ish women perch at a high-top table. Tight jeans, tight shirts, and come-fuck-me pumps. Heavy makeup, well-coiffed tinted hair, and bright lipsticked mouths. Was that Ruby Woo? Hope walks past them to the bar. She pulls off the blazer, rolls up her sleeves. She's way overdressed for the Circle Back.

"What'll it be, sweetheart?" the young, hard-bodied bartender with the silver stud in his ear leans over the bar. She hasn't been here in over five years, but beside the bartender not a thing has changed.

"Vodka tonic."

Hope turns to watch the Giants beat the Dodgers on the wide screen TV. The Giants had been on another losing streak, but if history repeats itself, they'll turn it around. She loves Posey, can't get enough of watching him squat, shooting out secret signals to the pitcher from behind home plate.

"Get your boots, grab a hat and come on down! Free instruction, half-price beer." A handwritten, poster board sign announces Monday night country dancing.

"It's on him," the bartender pushes a cold glass toward Hope, pointing to a hunky, square-jawed stranger at the far end of the bar. The guy nods, nonchalant. He's not her type, but he exudes *sexy* in a country way. Hope sips the drink, noticing his slicked-back hair, big-lidded eyes, and clean hands. Not a working guy, no. Maybe a contractor, or a boss.

Hope nods in his direction. Sipping the drink, she turns her attention back to the game, proud of herself for remembering the Circle Back, happy to be here in this dark place, where she knows no one. In two weeks, she could be at FearToShred. She'll have to think up a good story for Chuck.

The drink relaxes the knot in her stomach, her back, her neck. Hope is texting Dawn when contractor guy settles onto the empty stool next to her.

"Thanks for the drink."

"Uno mas?"

Hope nods. "Why not? I was good today—very good."

"Well, now you can be bad, very bad," mystery guy says, extending a cool, firm palm. "Dwayne."

"Lisa," Hope lies, trying to not stare at his lean forearms peeking out from under his freshly laundered flannel shirt.

The bartender slides over a bowl of mixed nuts, a plate of chips and salsa.

"It's Happy Hour, folks. Something to eat?"

"Make us up a quesadilla?" Dwayne shoots back.

Halfway into her second vodka tonic, Hope frets. James is late. She checks her screen: "On the way." She'll have to lose Dwayne. Fast.

"So, problem is . . . I've got to make a graceful exit." She recounts the interview and Manuserve. "Speaking of exits, my boyfriend's on his way."

"Check."

"Chuck's like a father to me," Hope rambles. "He hired me after my last startup imploded. And now I leave him?"

"Everyone leaves," Dwayne says.

"I know. I just feel guilty." Hope is talking to Dwayne like someone she's met on an airplane, spilling her guts to a stranger. She checks the door anxiously.

"The new gig sounds like a cool opportunity," Dwayne says. "Fun. Action. Young. You know, more you."

Dwayne's listening in a way that no guy from the valley ever listens. He listens like he's rooting for her, not one-upping.

"Yeah, but I might have to jump off of a building or something . . ."

"No!"

"Yes. This new company is into danger, big time."

"You look pretty smart, Miss Lisa. Just don't go BASE jumping."

"Why not?"

"Because not everyone lives to tell the tale?"

"But exciting, right?" Hope asks seductively.

"Not my thing. But the company sounds fun," Dwayne says.

"I know, right?" Hope winks, loose from the drinks.

"So, what's a nice girl like you doing in a place like this?"

"Walking down memory lane."

"You from around here?"

"Nearby."

"Me too."

For a few minutes, they watch the game together like old friends. Dwayne reaches for her hand under the bar. The touch of his warm, strong fingers shoots a heated message up Hope's arm. Dwayne holds her hand, making love to her fingers with the lightest touch. He slips a twenty onto the bar, leaving his business card on top. When he gets up to walk out the back door, Hope's eyes follow him. As she slips the card into her briefcase, James surprises her, kissing her neck.

"Hey you!" James settles onto Dwayne's still warm stool. "Why were you running late all day?" Hope leans over, gives James a peck on his forehead.

"I had a job interview," Hope's face goes hot. "I didn't want to tell you. But this one might be onto something." Hope shakes her head in the negative at the bartender.

"You're leaving?" James sips from a sweating beer bottle, looks at her with dark brows knitted.

"Considering, yes."

"After you just got that raise? And a promotion?"

"James," Hope says, exasperated. "Listen. The valley is hot. I don't owe Chuck my first born because he gave me a promotion. C'mon."

"And stock. And a raise."

"James!"

"Hope?"

Hope scowls. "I'm excited, James. Be happy! FeartoShred has an upside—and a future. I've got at least one more startup in me."

"You know what, Hope? I do believe you are losing your memory." James turns away to watch the game.

"Pyramid," he orders another beer when the bartender passes by.

Losing her memory? Really? On the big screen, the Dodgers hit a home run. James turns, his voice that of a TV journalist who's snagged the latest scoop. "Remember you promised you would wait it out at Manuserve—at least till you could cash in stock for a down payment?" James shakes his head. "Did we not agree?"

There it was again. We. Things have been moving too fast with James for the past few months. First, he was showing her real estate ads for apartments big enough for three or four; the next thing he was talking about down payments.

She isn't ready to shut him down, but she also isn't ready to take the next step. James is great. He's loyal and stable, but she isn't sure if loyal and stable is what she wants right now. Does she really want to marry a guy who has their whole lives planned out? What about chance?

"What about us?" Hope glowers. "James—what about me? I'm ready for a move. Something young. Fun. More me."

James grimaces. He turns to watch the game, nibbling on a handful of peanuts the bartender has slid across the bar.

"I'll be leaving," Hope announces, "whether it's this company or another."

5

DOUG LOVES the uphill best. And he loves training alone, not tagging along behind his best friend and self-appointed trainer, Aaron. He shifts his new Klein into seventh gear, takes a deep suck of air and steels himself for the steep incline.

He had left Topia two years ago, exactly a year to the day after the company was gobbled up like so much krill. As soon as his stock vested, he took his eight million and was out faster than you can say Garage-Band. His mind was teeming with guitar riffs and song lyrics. He called bassists, drummers, and Jake Lampert, the rhythm guitar player who was tearing it up in Santa Cruz. The Topia win was his fuck you money, funds that gave him time to figure out what he really wanted.

"One more chance," he vowed to Katie, his wife of three years.

One more year to see if he could breathe life back into a music career that had "shown promise." In 2010, the rock journalist Joe Selwich had written a laudatory review in *Hype Machine* about Doug and his first band, Covert Mission. "With Doug Wiser at the helm, Covert Mission nails tune after tune. The band braids together a combination of angry rock, alt, and folk rock. It works." A warm, southwesterly breeze cools his back. Doug pedals higher up 84 toward Skylonda. The crest, and Skyline are still five miles up the hill. He takes a deep breath, steels his core against the incline. "You deserve another chance," Katie told him. And so he had tried again. He formed a new band, Dystopia. He wrote lyrics. He snagged coveted gigs at

Great American Music Hall and they even played once as the warmup act for the GooGoo Dolls at the Fillmore.

Leaving Woodside behind, Doug turns onto Skyline, slows, letting the Klein cruise under a canopy of towering redwoods. Riding dangerously close to the shoulder, he's careful of the dusty piles of slick pine and redwood needles, focusing on the road ahead and praying that racing cars, trucks, and the motorcycles that are famous for whizzing around the corners of the twisty road slow down.

Training for a triathlon was biting off a lot, especially for an out-of-work engineer, but a year after leaving Topia, he'd crashed. For months, he'd sequestered himself practicing, composing, and sending out demo tapes for *Dystopia*. He was possessed. He'd work all day, barely getting out to walk Daisy, his English sheepdog. At night he practiced with the band. He was trying like hell to keep them jazzed while booking enough gigs to at least pretend that they were on their way. Mario and Darlene had a new baby. It was a hard sell, getting the guys to stay out late practicing, then play gigs on weekends for just a share of the door.

When Carlos, the band's drummer, quit to move back to Ohio, the band fell apart. Everyone said otherwise, but Doug knew that things weren't moving fast enough.

Training for the Run for Your Life triathlon, the reason he's just pedaled up the La Honda grade, is Plan B. If nothing else, the training would give him time to think; it would give him time to figure out his post band life.

Doug passes the ten-mile mark, buoyed by the plateau of the ride, the six-mile flat stretch that gives his legs a chance to recover. After that, he'll sail home. Home to return Hope's call that came in yesterday—she probably needed tech support.

Six months after Hope left Topia without a goodbye, Doug met Katie on a massage table. He never was quite sure if Hope had left because of the job or him. What ever happened to *you're the only one who understands me?* and *I think this could work?* Even though he expected her to leave the entire time they were together—he knew Hope was out of his league!—getting dumped without a warning threw him for a loop. They were in touch for a short time after she went to Seven

Arts, but after a while, he asked her to stop calling; her calls felt like a secret and he didn't like having secrets from Katie. But she had called yesterday. Her message had gotten cut off.

Rounding the last bend, dried redwood needles scrape the top of his helmet like the fingernails of angels—sharp but gentle. Ahead, bay trees shake their long, thin limbs in a shiver of wind, sending out a minty, herbal scent. Sun filters through the redwood branches, casting circles of light cut like a Russian Constructivist canvas. Doug cycles on through the alternating shadow and light, keeping his eyes trained ahead, watching for oncoming traffic, listening for engine sounds coming up behind. Another cyclist passes, waves a leather-gloved hand.

The only thing that matters now is the race. Not what comes after, or what came before. Bike, swim, run. Bike, swim, run.

A car engine screeches around the bend, breaking his reverie. Doug repositions his bike on the right side of the road; breathes the morning fresh air, wishing he hadn't been so adamant about training alone, wishing now that he was tagging along with Aaron. Aaron would be yakking away about his newest client, or the one he lost, or some girl he was chasing. Anything that kept his mind off of Hope and Katie, kept him from thinking about his lost bands. With *Dystopia*, after a while, he felt like he was trying to make love to an old girlfriend, and not in a good way.

Plan B. The race was a good start. Doug pedals on, pumping out frustration—frustration he didn't know he had until he'd mounted his bike. Last night was so weird. He took Daisy out for a walk, throwing sticks mindlessly, when a message from Hope Ellson popped up. He wasn't in the mood. Was she calling to apologize for rushing out of CVS? She didn't have to. Chance run-ins were weird. Of course Hope was on her way somewhere. She always was.

The road opens up. Through the trees the Bay is laid out like a steely blue curtain. The salt flats bake, white rectangles in the morning sun and the San Mateo Bridge is a white belt cinched on a model's waist. He's cruising now, dying to change out of his wet shirt. He keeps his eyes peeled for an easy pullout.

Up ahead about twenty yards, a beat-up truck is st[o]
side of the road. A young-looking woman, her face cover[ed]
of long blond hair, sits in a canvas camp chair in the dirt
ing a baby. As Doug speeds by he notices a bearded, m[an]
dude attending to some business under the truck's hood, [a]
opened on the soft ground next to him.

Doug waves as he cycles by, noticing the faded paint, the cracked
windshield. "Need some help?"

"Nah. . . . Timing belt," he answers gruffly. "We're fine." Passing
the old Skylonda lodge, Doug checks his stopwatch.

Twelve miles in thirty-five minutes. He'd lost a little speed during
the long climb, but he'll make it up now. From here it's an easy flat
cruise to the four corners, the intersection of Highway 92 and Skyline
Boulevard. If he stops, he could call Hope back.

The race is in twelve weeks. He's already lost ten pounds. And,
he's back on a schedule, sleeping at night. A cool breeze blows through
the tall redwoods. A cloud of morning fog covers the sun and drifts
through the bay and eucalyptus trees like smoke from a cigarette
left idle.

The road ahead curves sharply. Partially darkened by shade, the
blacktop is a confusing mosaic of sun, leaves, and dark patches. Doug
slows, carefully navigating the twisting road.

He veers the bike to the right, nearly dumping after the Klein's
front tire skids on a pile of dried redwood needles. A siren wails up
from the town below.

From behind, the buzzing of a hefty motorcycle. He rounds the
last corner before the intersection, slowing a bit, hugging the bike
closer to the narrow shoulder. From the thrum of the engine he knows
it's a four-stroke—a Harley or BMW. He rides as close to the edge of
the road as he can, trying to stay far from the center divider. Underneath his front wheel, the ground is slippery with dried redwood needles and loose dirt. The bike wobbles. He's steadying the handlebars
when a large rock blocks the front tire. Tire hits rock; like a surfer thrown
off a wave, Doug careens onto the road's shoulder.

"Shit!" He spits out a mouthful of dirt, brushes his hands off.

Closer now, the cycle bites the last turn out of this snake of a road—the sharp hairpin that had just snagged him. Doug pushes the bike frame away from his left leg. His right pant leg is torn, the skin chewed up with road rash. A shard of glass has cut through his bike glove. He drags the twisted bike off the road just before a motorcycle swoops past.

Breathing hard, he pulls off his gloves and sets his helmet down, rummages through his pack for the first aid kit. Easing out the glass from his bloodied palm, Doug douses the cut with a quick squirt of iodine, then covers it with a Band-Aid.

The Klein lies on its side, a wounded horse. The left wheel is askew, bent slightly, but not enough to keep him from riding. He'll fix the tire and ride home. Hopefully. With a quick pull, he loosens the bike pump to retrieve the patch kit. Just then, the rumble of another motorcycle, loud.

"Got some trouble?"

Astride a big chopper-style bike a stocky guy sits, looking like the elephant seals you see at Ano Nuevo. The kind of guy you wouldn't want to meet in an alley, dark or light. His face is deeply pocked, and his black hair is tucked up under his large helmet. Hard brown eyes focus in on Doug's freshly bandaged hand. The engine rumbles. Stocky guy offers a meager smile, but there is nothing funny about the look on his face. The smile is small, tight, more for him than for Doug. "Trouble?"

Doug's knees hurt from landing on the hard- packed dirt, and his head aches. "Yeah, a little," Doug points at the bike. "Nothing a patch can't fix. At least I'll get back down the hill," Doug says coolly, tugging a spare t-shirt from his pack and padding it on the hard ground next to the bike as a cushion for his scraped knees. Beyond the small patch of dirt is a rustic house, a plume of smoke rising from the chimney, a lazy "z" curling through the tall trees. With a tire lever, Doug separates the spent rubber from its metal frame. Two spokes are bent. The bike will be two days in the shop at least. The biker sits back, watching.

Doug twists the spokes, cursing the rock. He knew those redwood needles were trouble, slippery. He patches the tire.

The biker kills his engine, sits back in the leather seat against the hard metal backrest. Doug keeps half on eye on the biker, half on the business at hand, roughing up the inner tube for the patch. He knows bikers hang around up here. They hang around at Alice's, drinking beer and carousing. Harmless. They drive up here to get some fun out of the road, to get out of the car-clogged valley. Bikers and cyclists co-exist. No, they'd never done any harm up here. So why is he nervous about this guy? Doug's head is damp. He checks him again, just a few feet away.

"You wouldn't want to get stuck up here, would you?"

"I don't think it would be a tragedy," Doug answers, trying for nonchalance. He gets off his knees. He'd heard it was good to make yourself as big as possible if you ran into a mountain lion—he figured what the heck? Biker? Mountain lion? You never know. Doug slips the tire back around the rim of the patched inner tube, grateful for Aaron's lesson in bike maintenance. "If you're going up to Skyline on your own, there are a few things you have to know," Aaron had advised one Saturday afternoon. Doug had tried to delay the lesson, but now he's glad he let Aaron lead.

Did he say anything about cyclist/biker clashes? There had been a rash of home invasions in Mountain View recently. Was crime up or down? He couldn't remember the statistic. He pulls a pump from his backpack and stands up to give it pressure. Eyes focused on the task in front of him, his heart pounds. Was this guy friendly or just messing with him?

Tire pumped, Doug gathers the repair kit. He stuffs everything back into the pack, checks his freshly scratched watch face. 11:30. He wanted to call Hope at lunchtime.

"You make a killing down there?"

"What?" Doug stands next to his bike, anxious to be gone. The two share a thin strip of dirt, the small space between the road's shoulder and the fence around the house behind them.

"Money, what else? Who else would be up here middle of the day, middle of the week?"

"Why do you say that?" Doug braces himself, his muscles tense. He tests the heft of the pump in his hand. "Everyone likes a nice day."

The biker is chewing on a toothpick, his brows knitted close. Doug fusses with his pack, rights his bike, makes a move to get on, keeping the biker in view. Biker dude slips his wide frame off of the bike's long, padded seat, struts over to feel the bicycle's newly pumped front tire. "Feels a little light there."

Doug double-checks. Flat as a pancake.

"So, did ya make a killing?"

"Nah, I'm unemployed."

Doug pulls a spare inner tube out of his pack, pumps it up and rights the bike. Except for the bent spokes, it's rideable. Not raceable, but rideable. Aaron had warned him about cars and other cyclists, redwood needles not so much.

"I could use a small killing," the biker laughs, reaching for something in his back pocket.

A cool sweat breaks out on Doug's forehead. He grabs the bike frame.

"Well, looks like you got things under control there." The biker climbs back onto his motorcycle. Doug catches sight of the guy pulling a fresh toothpick from a package in his back pocket. He pops it in his mouth. "When I saw you down, I thought you might need a ride."

"Thanks, I'm fine, I think. Just fine."

The biker shoots Doug a little wink, or was it a twitch? The biker cranks his engine, throwing Doug a friendly wave as he heads off down the road.

Doug punches in a few details about the ride on Strava, his mobile training app—heart rate, how many ounces he drank from the CamelBak—and decides then that he will call Jared, the recruiter that e-mailed last week. Scared straight, scared crooked, who knows? It was time for a change.

He'll head home. Jared, and then Hope. If he's going to go back to work, if he's going to give up his dream of being a rock star, he needs to find out where lightning is going to strike next.

6

"Let me make sure I've got this straight. Jeff and Julie post a challenge on Twitter—360 under a full moon. But it could be BMX, or a surfing challenge, right?" Hope asks, catching sight of Arthur's strong back, wide shoulders. His gait is measured, even. He's got her beat with the Harvard MBA, but her Valley cred has opened many doors. Waiting for Arthur's explanation, her gaze catches on a shimmering, small body of water just below the plate glass window.

"Lake Chagrin," Arthur points. "It's our meeting point for private talks, broods, and head-clearing. And, you're right. Challenges are posted, players vote."

"And they use the app to edit and upload their video?" Hope asks. Lake Chagrin, eh? Distress? Humiliation? Well, if she worked here, she would change that moniker. More like Secret Lake, Whisper Lake or even Hidden Lake. Anything but Embarrassment Lake. She'd been there at Topia, and it wasn't her favorite.

"Yes," Arthur's basso profundo brings her back into the room. "But believe me, their efforts are not altruistic. Not by a long stretch. By players—the athletes—sending their videos in, they're building their reputations and growing a fan base. The show, if we can pull it off, is where things get interesting. The most popular players will be invited on. With TAN, FeartoShred will have a bigger stage. And, TAN sweetened the pot. Now players stand to win tons of cash on top of any brand ambassador endorsements." Arthur raises his eyebrows seductively.

Hope nods. It's coming together. App to show.

Arthur clicks "Play" on his desktop. "Here's this kid doing a 360 trick under a full moon up at Whistler. Look at these eerie moon shadows. The number near that eyeball icon shows the total number of viewers to date: three hundred and seventy-five thousand and counting."

Hope looks at arrows piercing the pristine snow, shadows of evergreens, pines, and firs. The boarder's white helmet, reflecting moonlight, is its own full moon. The whole mountain is illuminated.

Yesterday, Arthur called while she was in a meeting with Preston, Manuserve's new marketing chief. She hit "Decline," but called back the minute Preston let her loose.

"Do you have a minute?"

"Sure," Hope had said, stepping into a private phone booth. The room was large enough for a quick call to her mother, sister, or doctor but talking to Arthur, it felt small and tight.

And so, she had come by FearToShred at 3:55 this afternoon, slipping out of Manuserve, complaining of a migraine. This time, she had her Mac DIVA lip-gloss packed.

"How'd you get these rock star judges to sign on? I heard Shaun White is crazy busy building his own brand."

"True. But Jeff and Julie have almost a million followers. They're the top of the skating world. And, they're geeks." Arthur twists in his chair, gazes out at the office complex fountain. "For the judges, the association with Jeff and Julie is a good thing."

"How'd they get a million followers?"

"Jeff got famous when a YouTube clip of his eighteen-foot jump between two flat roofs went viral and Julie won gold at the X Games a couple of years back for a combination of back heel flips and two 720 turns in a row. The crowd went nuts."

"Yeah, I remember a skateboarder flying between buildings. That was Jeff?"

"Yup."

"Are they still touring?"

"Not officially. But once we get the site running smoothly, we'll get them back out on the circuit. Julie got injured, tore the ACL on her left knee, and broke her leg, so she only goes out as a judge. Jeff is still in the game. Their agents are salivating. They love the site and they're stoked about TAN."

Hope's read that Jeff and Julie were revered, but this is new news. "Fans and trophies are all good, but how's their coding?"

"Julie's very good. Learned at her dad's feet. Wayne Tang was the team leader for System 7 team that designed the guts of the Mac. Julie was home-schooled. She skipped college and went to Hack Reactor at sixteen, top of her class. She's a natural. Jeff was in Computer Science at San Jose State. Salt of the earth guy. Hard worker, but snarky. Acts like he's got one foot out the door."

"He's young." Hope makes a mental note to ask Jeff about Professor King at San Jose State. King founded Seven Arts in the early 2000s. "Scaling is really our only problem. TAN is asking for ten times our number of users," Arthur faces Hope squarely but she doesn't flinch. Tech was a problem. What else is new? Arthur paces. It's the end of the day and the guy looks as fresh and raring to go as she did at eight A.M.

"What're your numbers now?" she asks, flipping open the iPad.

"We're up from the last time we met—closing in on 1.5 million."

Hope scowls. "And TAN is asking for twenty million for the show?" A bead of sweat breaks above her upper lip.

"We're all about challenges," Arthur jibes.

"Can I tell you a secret?" Hope whispers as if the walls had ears.

"Tell."

"L.A. doesn't get Silicon Valley."

"Yeah. They think HBO nailed it." Arthur winks conspiratorially. "We'll get back to TAN in a sec. What about you? Manuserve is B2B, right? Whole other world over there."

"Manuserve made me an offer I couldn't refuse. Their marketing department was in trouble. They build great products. Sadly, no one knew. They wire up factories and warehouses, last in first out stuff. I got their customers yakking about how much they love Manuserve."

Arthur scribbles a note on a legal pad. "By the way, Ethan Farrell —over at Keener, Farrell, and Duvall—gave me your name." Arthur's boyish dimples appear, sun peeking out on a rainy day.

"Oh, yeah, Ethan was an early investor at Topia. He came out smelling very sweet."

Arthur sips the last of an espresso. "Good exits make good resumes, right?" Arthur utters the simple, upbeat statement with bravado, but Hope hears fraught words underneath. He was famous for his bad exit at Cronos.

Arthur lowers his voice an octave, utters gravely, "Your background is a great fit. But this job is not just managing the engineers; you'll need to do a graceful sashay between us and TAN." Arthur strolls across the room to the window, twisting his hips in cute, exaggerated steps. "We have nine months to build out a new platform. We need them to keep the faith."

Hope's stomach clutches—he could be wrapping up the meeting or about to divulge a confidence—like why he rejected the forty mil from Google for Cronos. "Tight timeline," Hope notes. "It's a stretch. Aren't you doubtful that you can you deliver ten times the viewers?" Hope sets a Voss on a glass table, joins Arthur at the window.

"Oh, by the way, did you watch the Baumgartner jump?" Arthur drops the non sequitur.

"I did. Guy's insane. But what about TAN?"

"Oh, sorry. Too big of a jump." Arthur chuckles.

Ahh, she thinks, he does get double entendre. Hope drains the water, sits back to collect herself. Arthur was offering her an invitation, holding out a carrot and here she was dissing TAN's expectations. She could backtrack but that would make her look indecisive.

"Can you believe that?" Arthur presses. "The guy gets flown into the stratosphere. Does a fucking free fall in a pressure suit and parachutes to earth."

"And broke the sound barrier on his way down!" Hope adds. "Broke the record for a human free fall—39,000 feet!"

Hope shakes her head. The day of the jump, over ten million people were riveted to their televisions.

"Guy's insane."

"FearToShred's raison d'etre, no?" Hope realizes now that Arthur has been quizzing her.

"The more insane the better."

Hope taps "Check out TAN clips on YouTube" onto her iPad. Taking copious notes in meetings is not a recommended interview technique, but Hope doesn't care. The notes are her ammunition for a kick-ass follow-up email.

"What's Jeff's problem with TAN?" Hope risks. She wants Arthur's take but needs to stay neutral. She's fact collecting, not gossiping. She closes the iPad. Whatever Arthur has to say won't be recorded.

"FearToShred's users on TV? TAN?" Arthur asks. "That just rocked Jeff's world."

"How so?"

"He's suspicious. Television equals commercial. Commercial equals evil. On the other hand, Julie is naturally curious. That's where you come in."

"Right. First, we make friends with every man, woman, and child in the X Games, extreme sports. Then we hit up the eSports crowd. We move beyond Jeff and Julie's networks."

Arthur nods.

"Then we organize meetups and develop curators."

Five ten. It's getting late, but Hope's got more questions. If she can keep Arthur in the room for another few minutes, she might snag the job.

Arthur checks his watch. Outside, shadows cast by a lazily descending spring sun look like long arms embracing. "Who's on the board?"

"Jim Cohen, he's our lead investor. Ravi Maddala was one of our angels. And myself, of course."

"What about Jeff and Julie?"

"Investors decided not to give them board seats. Not enough entrepreneurial experience. They have their founder stock, but they're not voting members. That was part of the deal when we raised our first round."

A team of aggressive winners, if you don't count Arthur's Cronos misstep. A pair of famous skaters. L.A. TV. Can do. Definitely can do. "What's up with the pins?" Hope asks, pointing to the wall map.

"The pins designate the countries where we've got fans."

"Uganda?"

"Big skater scene."

"Who knew?"

"We do. Skating is growing like crazy throughout eastern Africa, with skate parks built—or planned—in Kenya and Tanzania," Arthur reports. "It's a cheap leisure activity. Go figure."

"Yeah. They're forward thinking on skateboarding and brutal on sex?" Hope blurts.

"Right. But we don't play politics."

The leaves on the gingko tree clap like tiny baseball mitts. Good that they're building the team. Bad that Jeff is snarky. TAN is pushy. Hope's thoughts spin like a revolving door that she can't step out of. Doug. Doug could do this.

Arthur reappears, a look of consternation clouding his previously clear face. "Before you go," he says. "there's the job. You're a good fit. But I also need a bad guy—you know—to keep the engineers on track."

Hope takes a breath to balance herself between blurting 'Yes!' and playing it so cool that she'll have an offer in her in box in the morning. Deep breath, Hope.

"Interested?"

"Possibly. It's intriguing."

"Good," Arthur extends a firm hand. "Oh, one more question. Why did you leave a company that was on the way up?"

Topia. Hope swallows, her skull hot under her brow. Arthur wouldn't cotton to the fact that Manuserve had given her "an offer I couldn't refuse." Hope searches the photographs on his shelf searching for divine guidance, but there's only Arthur with his arm around a thin blonde on a beach. I left because I was finally falling in love with someone—mind, body, and soul? I left because I'm a jerk who can't keep her work and her private life separate? I left because that's what I always do. I leave.

"It only looked like they were on the way up. I saw the writing on the wall. I figured they'd gone as far as they could go . . ."

"But to Manuserve?"

"I needed a break."

"Got it."

Is this Arthur's version of a challenge? But she likes him; he's smart. Focus, Hope. "Can I have access to the site?"

"Soon."

Hope slips the iPad into her bag, wondering if he's interviewed ten other CPO's. Was she the first? The last?

Hope's hand rests on the metal door handle. She hates being dismissed. "What happened to your last CPO?" she asks, knowing how companies chewed up and spit out product people. One minute, they were the best thing since sliced bread, the next, off with their heads. It was a risky position in the company, especially in a startup where the product was invented, re-invented, and morphed at the founder's, CEO's, or lead engineer's whim.

Arthur: "There wasn't one."

Good. Hope extends her hand again, forgetting that they had already shaken.

A volt of electricity passes from Arthur's hand to hers. Shit. "Oh, and about that lead technologist? Wiser?" Arthur asks.

"Left him a voicemail." She takes out her phone, shares Doug's contact with Arthur.

"Great. Oh, one more thing?" he says.

Hope closes the door. She stands at the threshold, briefcase in hand.

"What do you do in your spare time?"

What is it with this guy? Hope flinches, feeling less like she's been interviewed and more like she's been whiplashed. The spare time question was code for questions you were, by law, not allowed to ask: Did she read books to sick kids? Find housing for the homeless? Support underprivileged women to build careers? Did she have a demanding husband? Two kids under age five? An aging mother? Bad investments? But Hope had never put down stakes, either in the home or the do-good camp. Where she came from, at the end of the workweek a person deserved a cold beer and some down time.

"What spare time?"

7

"WHILE YOU'RE busy living out your second childhood," Katie complains, "my biological clock is about to expire."

Katie's sweet, heart-shaped face is screwed up tight, revealing wrinkles in her forehead that Doug has never noticed. She's come home sweaty from a workout with Liz with that look on her face. Doug knows that look—the *I've been out with my girlfriend and decided I'm sick of waiting for you to grow up* look.

Liz, her doctor friend, is Katie's Tuesday workout date. Liz has been trying for a baby for over a year, working at it like a newly minted college grad on a job hunt, thorough and relentless. Through Katie, Doug has been privy to every gory detail. The late periods, the husband on a business trip just when she is ovulating, the miscarriage. TMI.

Doug is eating Chinese takeout on a little TV tray in the living room. The trays are Doug's least favorite furniture. They are unstable, shaky.

Doug lays down the chopsticks, two pencils on a blank page. "But wait, I thought the triathlon was your idea."

"Well, mine, and Aaron's. But Doug, the race will be over soon. I'm thirty-six! Or did you miss that?"

Doug winces. Has he forgotten a birthday?

"You want me to end up one of those frustrated forty-year-olds spending all of my vacation money in fertility clinics?" Katie gulps a long swig of water.

"OK." Doug says, his strength draining out of him like the last drops of a turned off spigot.

"Do you want to see me spread-eagled in an antiseptic-smelling office getting impregnated by an aftershave-stinking doc with bristly hair in his ears?" Katie throws herself against the pale-yellow couch pillows. "What's going to change?"

Doug's neck goes stiff. He knows his wife means business, but he is paralyzed, incapable of coming up with a smart retort or loving behavior that Katie so desperately needs. He restrains himself from cuddling or reassuring her.

"What's going to change?" he asks rhetorically.

Arguing with his wife in these states is futile. In his calculation, there are at least four years between thirty-six and forty, but he can see that Katie isn't much in the mood for math.

"I don't know. I'd have another startup under my belt. I'd get another band together. Lots of things could change."

Katie walks to the kitchen, grabs a cold Sierra Nevada out of the fridge. "You're right, Doug. The training was my idea—but now I'm sorry!" Katie's voice shakes. "I mean whoever thought a little training would leave you too tired to have sex! Doug Wiser—too tired for sex? Call the press!"

"You have a point," Doug says. At night, instead of reaching for her like he has in the past, he falls asleep the minute his head hits the pillow.

"Think about it, Doug. We'll have a family. I'm not going to stop you from doing anything . . ."

Doug walks across the room to the coat closet where Daisy's leash hangs. Standing in the open doorway of their Craftsman bungalow, he is suddenly hungry for air and space. Katie insists that she won't stop him from doing anything, but he knows the baby story. Guy friends who dropped like flies once a baby was in the house. Nine o'clock bedtimes, endless birthday parties, weekend park excursions.

No sex.

Some of them still hadn't gotten it back together with their wives after a year. Austin, Paul, Philip. When they did manage to meet for the rare guy time, the occasional beer, Doug saw it in their eyes: disappointment. They wouldn't say it, but their faces did: trapped.

"What about music?" He's standing on the porch, Katie hovering in the doorway.

"Hello? With a baby, I won't even have time to think about making music again for, say, what? Ten years?"

Katie slams the door, hard. It isn't the first fight on the baby topic, but it cuts him the worst.

Doug walks two blocks toward University Avenue. He'll sit at Illy Cafe and pull himself together. Then he remembers Hope's call. Two days after she'd left a message, she called back. Hope called every few months just to show him how well she was doing. She didn't have to. He knew she was good. Hope was always good.

"Hey," he says, watching Daisy sniff a neighbor's prized iris bed. "You called?"

"I did. I need a little advice. I'm thinking of leaving Manuserve."

"Aha! Ditching B2B! I wondered how long—or should I say, short—that would last."

"No teasing."

"Fine."

"Really? Just like that?" Hope's voice cracks.

"What can I say? You caught me at a good time."

"Can you meet me tomorrow at Central Park Grill in Burlingame? Noon?"

"I'll be there."

He's not sure what Hope has in mind, but he had been advising her on career moves for what? Ten years? He liked it. He liked watching her grow, become the uber product guru.

By the time Doug rounds the corner back to the house, his mind is dead set. He would find some way to buy another six months, a year if Katie was feeling generous. Is it a crime to ask for more time? Who has a baby when they don't know what they're doing with their life? But Katie is on edge; all her pals are either pregnant or raising babies. He was the last holdout. He knew he wouldn't get away with being absent half the time; babies were all consuming. He wanted it; he really did. Just not right now.

Up the walk to the porch, he is buoyed by a rush of affection for Katie. He loves her! They could work this out! They could get help, or she could cut her hours. He just may have relented earlier, if she'd been less angry. He would have made love to her with abandon! So what if he doesn't know what he is going to do with his life? Who does?

8

"FUCK!" JULIE jerks awake to a screaming riff from The Edge—Jeff's text on her phone.

"Wassup?" she texts, wiggling out of Angie's arms. Tenderly, she covers her with the feather duvet, closes the door and tiptoes into the kitchen.

"Our last tweet went south."

"What happened?"

"Guy got arrested!"

"Shit. Could be good, could be bad. I'll call you." Julie boils water for coffee.

By the time she went to bed at two A.M., she was seasick with ocean, pool, and bay videos that flooded in after Jeff put out the tweet "Quit the craft when the cradle becomes a cage." Videos of jet skiers jumping the crest of a wave, boarders jumping off of ski lifts. The one that got the most votes was a kite boarder taking flight off the deck of a yacht into a choppy bay. Julie grabs her phone to speed dial Jeff's number.

"Dude. What happened?" Julie asks, grabbing a terrycloth robe from the back of the bathroom door. "Did you see the kite boarder?"

"Totally! The guy that got arrested checked in a video of himself pulling the fire alarm on a college campus. His friend filmed him being taken away in a manacle."

"I like it," Julie says. She pours herself a cup of black coffee and settles onto the leather sofa in the living room. "What time is it anyway?"

"Seven," Jeff says, breathless. "Julie, listen . . . that isn't the main problem."

"OK."

"The problem is, MySQL Bieber-ed the site again," Jeff says frantically. "Write rates were way too high, and all the page loads were timing out. We got tons of tweets complaining that players couldn't load their stuff. We eventually had to ditch for an hour till the database cooled off."

A while back, after Justin Bieber publicly wiped out on his skateboard, he'd become FearToShred's failure mascot, their iconic Fail Whale. The engineers had created a page with an animated GIF that loaded whenever the site was down.

Outside the living room windows, the sky striates pink and blue. Back in the old days, users rolled with the punches when the site failed. But lately Arthur had been all over them about stability. Yet another reason Jeff hated TAN. They watched FearToShred's every move.

"Hon?" Angie calls softly from the bedroom.

For a microsecond, Julie is torn between climbing back into bed with her girlfriend and calming down her co-founder.

"Hang on a sec," she puts Jeff on mute and pads into the bedroom. "Hey, hon?" Julie proffers a soft kiss on Angie's temple. "We have a situation."

Angie turns over, exposing her yoga-strong back. "I'm sorry!"

"What time do you leave for work?"

"I'm off today," Angie whispers.

"Check."

Julie refills her coffee cup, unmutes Jeff. "OK. First order of biz: fix the site," she says, her voice raised and edgy. Every time a video went viral, they had problems with the database, which in turn overloaded the server. Julie knew they had to get rid of MySQL; they'd talked about it repeatedly.

But TAN kept asking for more features, and the DevOps team was busy fighting fires. There was never enough time to tear it down to rebuild.

"Listen, we both agreed to do a quick build. We hacked this site together with MySQL. We both decided not to shard. And, we didn't do any caching, if you recall," Jeff says.

Julie does recall. She had suspected that the shortcut might come back to bite them.

They were growing so fast when Arthur came up with the money that they just ran with the risk of lousy architecture.

"We need a real data store, too." Julie paces, her right leg dragging imperceptibly.

The engineers had been talking about storage for weeks.

"Here's the problem." Julie walks out to the living room deck, slides the door closed behind her. She'd been quietly obsessing about a fix, anticipating this moment for the past month since their traffic had exponentially increased. "Every single vote we get results in a database transaction. Every page view and mobile view needs to query the database."

"I'm listening."

"As the write rates on the database increase, the database gets so bogged down that the queries are slowed."

"So the database locks up," Jeff says, "and the slaves get behind the master, so when we crash, the slaves need too much time to catch up."

"Exactly. And we can't live with stale results."

"We'll have to," Jeff insists.

"No. Stale results are lame. Today we go to Arthur and we lay out a plan. It's gonna be rocky, but we have to rebuild. Now." Julie's tone is terse, frustrated. She's tired. Up late, up early, and the coffee's not performing its magic. "Arthur thinks we can fix the site, but we are going to have to lay it on the line and tell him we need to build a new one— from scratch. Tran and Ryan are going to have to rally. We may have to bring in a contractor or two. We can do it."

"Fuck."

"Fuck is right. But we promised Arthur we would show up bright-eyed . . ."

Today was the day Arthur was set to announce the deal with TAN.

"Fuck Arthur! Fuck TAN. This shit is moving way too fast," Jeff yells now, his voice hitting a middle C.

"Too fast? Too fast?" Julie harrumphs. "You're the one who says, *Too fast never is.* Julie's knee is shaking and her head pounds.

"Listen, I wasn't up till two A.M. just to watch videos last night. I was messing with the code," Jeff says.

"Why didn't you ping me?"

"I figured I'd let you sleep so you could wake up and fix it," Jeff teases.

"Thanks."

"My ass is going to be grass with these TV guys, Julie. Besides, *FearToShred: The Reality Show* isn't going to be about skaters; it's going to be about some middle class . . ." Jeff grunts sardonically.

"Jeff. Hang on." Julie slides open the deck door, limps across the living room, to twist the blinds closed against a harsh slant of morning sunlight. "You think Arthur doesn't know that we're in over our heads? The expansion, the back end, growing this thing—it's his problem. We built the prototype. We got the users."

Jeff moans audibly.

"Remember what he said? *You're our street cred,*" Julie winces, repeating Arthur's words, "He sold FearToShred on us. Our fans. We're doing the best we can, right?"

"No, not right. Arthur did not sell FearToShred. He raised a few bucks on a gamble. His VC pals were willing to throw down some change on a bet that we could pull off something cool and global."

"Are you implying that we ditch a rebuild?" Julie asks, her anxiety level pumping. She knows that they could patch the site, keep on with their tweets, and keep getting new users. But that is not a solution. Eventually, they'll crash.

"Why not? Once the show airs, we're fucking out of here."

"You know what Jeff?" Julie whispers. "I think Arthur's dreaming. There won't be a show. TAN doesn't have the patience for us. But just in case he's right? The site has to be tight. It's our reputation."

Jeff moans. The rebuild is out of his league and everyone knows it.

"GTG," Julie says, clicking off the call and hopping into the shower.

"What about our morning?" Angie shouts from the bedroom. "You said you were sleeping in."

"I'm screwed," Julie yells from the shower.

Her right leg hurts like hell. There's nothing more she would love than to get a rubdown from Angie. The metal pin in her leg has been acting up. Her leg had gotten crushed on an Olympic qualifying round in New Zealand three years ago. The fuckers had changed the course. When she hit a fast turn, her trick failed, and her leg flew out from under her.

9

JEFF GRABS his white fuzzy hat. He's locking the door to his apartment, when a text pings: "Remember who we R! FTS! We tear it UP!"

"Yeah, & U just miss YR sponsorships—that's why U want 2 DO TAN!" Jeff texts back.

Since Julie's accident, she'd thrown herself into FearToShred 110 percent. For himself, he was half in, half out. He didn't really care about the money. He could always go back to skating. His prize money was growing, well invested. "Diversify," his financial advisor recommended. And so, he had a portfolio consisting of stock, cryptocurrencies, and bonds.

If Jeff's old man had worked for Apple all those years, like Julie's dad, he'd be kicked back dreaming about all that stock. But Julie was the breadwinner in her family. Still. Fucking TAN? He was excited in the beginning. Being a founder sounded like fun. But now it was getting a little too real. Too much pressure. Investors, Arthurs, TAN. He wasn't sure it was all worth it.

But Julie is headstrong. Jeff isn't sure what makes her so cocky, but he wishes he had some. His personal stock has been slipping fast. Duh? A girlfriend! Julie has a girlfriend. He could sure use one of those.

Jeff scoots across town on his blue Vespa. Early morning. The skater park is quiet. Eight A.M. Plenty of time. Bright morning light creates a crescent moon shadow against the concrete ramp. Skinny birch trees quake in a morning breeze coming up over the hills. Jeff tears off his jacket, queues up "The Offspring" and "Dogwood" on his iPhone, sets the camera to record and throws down his old skateboard. He jumps on, spinning a few go-rounds to get up speed and loosen up his quads. He practices his ollies first, circling the crescent on two wheels, the board scraping the side of the concrete bowl. Sparks fly off the back wheels like the Fourth of July.

Maybe things are going too fast. First, he had agreed to put out challenges. Then Arthur raised money so they could hire more engineers. At that point, he wasn't sure his code could withstand the increased traffic. Who knew they were going to six times their users in thirty days? "I checked it out with my dad. We have to shard if we want the site to stay stable," Julie had insisted just last week. But they had been distracted and hadn't gotten to it.

Rounding wheels, the satisfying sound of the scrape, the sparks. Early in the morning, he can focus in a way he can't when other people are crowding the lanes. Taking a sharp turn, he realizes that since they got their funding, he's been working more and skating less. If he loses his edge, he loses, period. Now someone's gotten arrested for playing our game. Is that what we wanted? Is that our fault?

A light breeze caresses his face like a silk-gloved hand. Jeff is ranting loudly to himself.

A couple of turns into his routine he decides today is the day. His pop shove-its are stale, shaky. If he's going to compete in Santa Cruz next week, he's got to get this trick perfect. His adrenaline pumps at just the right flow. He moves his right foot back, the board lifting off. Quickly, he moves his left foot into position, heading for the steps. Up! Jeff flips up his board—shouts to the empty park: Ta-da! The rest of the skate is a variation of ollies and pop shove-its defined with a high-hat trick thrown in for good measure.

When they first started FTS, it was a lark. He was a local hero.

But when he moved down to the Valley with VC money, the other skaters, and even his friends, started treating him with thinly veiled distrust. He's lost a few local fans, but he's gained thousands around the country and, lately, the world. But it's not the same.

He misses his homies. And, he often feels out of sync with Julie and Arthur.

Julie seems to have a special bond with Arthur. Maybe it's the lacrosse shit. Lacrosse was the collegiate sport Julie's brainiac dad had gotten her into during her early home-schooling years. When things got down to team sports, Jeff always felt left out. "Not my thing," he told his high school running coach, who pressed him to go out for varsity track. The truth was, nothing mattered but skating. No boss, no coach. The only authority he had to answer to was himself. Barely a day passed in high school when he wasn't dressed down by a teacher for disobeying. "Trouble with authority" his school counselor told his mom. Duh.

One last pop shove it. Jeff leans his back leg on the lip of his skateboard; he flips the board up at the perfect 45 degree angle. He jumps up to let the board spin and reverse direction. He lands just as a ray of sun blinds him. Losing sight of the ramp, he misses a turn. All at once, his ankle gives way, his right foot crumples.

"FUCK!"

Jeff's shoulder rips, the sound like masking tape pulled from the molding in a freshly painted room.

10

TEN MINUTES early to meet Doug for lunch, Hope angles into a space between a black BMW SUV and a grey Tesla. Throwing her phone into her briefcase, Hope is alerted to a new e-mail. "From Richard Ellson." Richard Ellson? Her father? Her heart skips one beat and then two. Today? After twenty years?

She'll read it later.

Now, she's got to convince Doug that they can work together again, even if she has her fears. We'll make a great team. No. It's a great opportunity. Nah. He probably hears that daily. It's fun. That's it. She'll play the fun card. So much more fun than shopping bots, right?

But between the parking lot and the gravel walkway to the restaurant entrance, the idea of playing the fun card hits her as ludicrous. Recruiting Doug to FearToShred isn't about whether he'll like the job, the people or the company; it's whether they can be in the same building without sneaking off to fuck in the utility closet.

✳ ✳ ✳

Pulling open the heavy wooden door to the Central Park Bistro, Hope is greeted by the din of a pumped-up lunch crowd. Iced teas are ferried on trays like the martinis of yesteryear. Waiting in the vestibule, Doug's wearing skinny jeans and a button down. When Hope calls out, "Hey," Doug's eyes light up. He hugs her, but it's not the I'm your old boyfriend hug. It is the CVS *didn't count—this is the real thing* hug. Doug hugs. Women, men, dogs, babies. The feel of his lean body against hers and the imperceptible scent of peppermint soap brings her back to his apartment in downtown Palo Alto, the one where they fell madly, excruciatingly in love. Hope examines her ex sideways. "Looking good, Wiser. Very good," she says. *Be cool, Hope, cool.*

The officious hostess, clutching menus like a nurse with medical charts, leads Doug and Hope to a booth. Hope thinks, I'll tell him. He deserves to know. He can handle it. Besides, he's a married man now! It won't mean much, right? I just want to set the record straight. I wasn't being flaky; I was scared. But when? Before I tell him about the job? No, after is better, right? After.

"Are you really leaving Manuserve? After that big fat promotion?" Doug plunges right in, over a grilled burger with onions and cheese, no bun. "Don't tell," he whispers. "Katie's got me on the meatless Blue Apron plan. If I eat one more veggie burger I'm going to keel over."

Like she was going to call Katie to report on Doug's menu choices. "Guilty as charged. Yes, I am leaving after that big fat promotion. But you know me, Doug," Hope chuckles a sinister laugh. "In my house, guilt is a low-grade fever—two Advil, and I'm over it."

Doug cracks a half-smile. He knows the blithe Hope.

Hope spanks herself for being flip, but Doug's got her amped up; he asked about Manuserve the way he would ask an ex- colleague, not an ex-lover. Not like the Doug who advised her on every career move, every strategic e-mail. This is married Doug.

He doesn't really care that she would leave Manuserve. He's warming up. She's got an opportunity and he just might want in.

"How bad is it?" Doug asks, meeting her eyes for the first time.

"At Manuserve? It's alright." Hope glimpses the old Doug, the Doug who actually cares about her career. Hope's throat tightens.

"I'm doing my job. It's fine. I just don't find yakking about the latest in warehouse services exactly inspirational." Hope draws air quotes around "inspirational." "I mean, c'mon, Doug, enterprise software?" Hope's eyebrows arch.

"Not our speed."

"Exactamente."

"Yeah, what's the point of a good workday without those gut-wrenching nights?" Doug smirks.

"Totally! Boring!" Hope laughs conspiratorially. She leans in. "And all that shit from the fucking gadget bloggers? What about that article when we launched? 'Topia: Sharper Image for Geeks?'"

"Yeah, Carlson Wain really banged us around on *Boing Boing*. Fun."

"I miss those days," Hope says. "Besides, FearToShred worked some magic because the offer was everything I wanted. Salary increase, VP title, and a stock package that, if things go as Arthur claims, will be worth two million or more."

"I'm listening."

While Doug returns to his close encounter with the carnivorous, Hope sits across the table from the man she's thought about, grappled with, left without saying why, and taken on an imaginary roller coaster ride of her shape-shifting emotions for the past three years. She's not sure working with him is a good idea.

Seeing him every day could fan that low burning flame into something much bigger. Now, she's not even sure why she arranged this meeting.

"So what's the new gig?" Doug asks.

Hope stabs a lettuce leaf. She's stuck. How can she, Hope Ellson, ex-girlfriend who ditched without so much as a Dear John note, convince Mr. Life of Leisure to give up his band, or at least the dream of a band, forgive and forget their past and jump with both feet back into a startup? Never mind that he's training for his first triathlon. She might be good, but she's pretty sure she's not that good.

Fuck words. She'll just sit across from him and stare him down. She'll convince him telepathically! She has to. It's not only that Doug could stabilize the site, manage Jeff and Julie, and keep Arthur under control in his unique Ninja-Doug way, it's that she really wants him at FearToShred.

She wants him at FearToShred and not just because they are an inspired team. She wants him because working together might clear things up, give her a chance to create a new history, write a new story. It could be dangerous, but wasn't that life? Anything worthwhile is risky.

"FeartoShred is up your alley," Hope says, after telepathy fails. He looks at her expectantly. She rests the heavy salad fork squarely on the side of her plate. "Especially now—with your interest in extreme sports."

"Ha! Because of the triathlon? Because I'm running and biking?" Doug laughs for real. "It's so not extreme! However, the swim is another story." His eyes cloud over, the etched lines between his eyes get deeper. "The swim might be extreme. A mile in the shark infested bay. . . . yeah. . . ."

"Pffft! You'll be fine," Hope assures him. "But then again, for you, yes, you're right. It might be extreme."

The two catch one another's eyes. No need to recount Doug's scary childhood watery near-death encounter.

"They have sag boats, and besides, the sharks don't want you—not enough to chew on," Hope razzes. "You can film it."

"What's the problem?" Doug asks.

"Problem?"

All of a sudden, time takes a spin and there she is at the clinic, and then there she is coming out, and after, sobbing in the taxi. Is he asking about a problem with her? With them?

"There's always a problem," Doug asserts. "With the site. The architecture. Tell."

"Right. Yes, the problem," Hope sighs, remembering they are here to talk about FearToShred. "Here's what I know. The site won't scale. Not unusual except that The Action Network is hot to turn their web game into a show. The code's shaky." Hope talks about the code, resisting the urge to tell Doug how good it is to see him again.

Doug cuts off a piece of burger, places it on the edge of Hope's plate. Hope nibbles the small bite. She stops herself short of rushing him for an answer.

"Shaky code. What else is new? More importantly, what do you think they're on to?" Doug pushes his plate aside, leans in dangerously close. "You never know who's in the next booth," he whispers.

Hope's mind goes blank. All she can think is how beautiful his hand looks caressing the saltshaker, how his long, thin fingers knew the landscape of her body.

"They're onto something," Hope says, lowering her voice. "First, there's the game. They've got the X-Games crowd. People create quirky videos and then users vote." Hope musters her enthusiasm from the first interview with Arthur, the one she left so giddy she had to go to the Circle Back. If there is a hole in the FTS plan, Doug will find it.

"What's the hook? How do they get people juiced to make a video challenge?"

"Prizes. Money. Fame." Hope starts. "Listen. FearToShred could be epic, or it could implode. My boyfriend sure doesn't like the idea of me leaving Manuserve. But I . . ."

Doug pauses in his attack of the last of his burger. He knew Hope well, very well. She did not skip out on a job for no reason.

"I think we could do something great together," she says. There it is.

Doug gives her the recognition nod. They both knew how they had torn it up at Topia. Hope's eyes sparkle. "I think there's a 'there' there."

She doesn't say it, but Doug knows; the taste of money and the prospect of an epic win have already worked their way under her skin. It's the startup drug, that siren's call: *We're going to change the world.* It's the wish of every new company. The right chemistry to go the distance wins the startup triathlon because it is always a race. It's the drug you need to push further than you ever thought your mind, or body, capable. She doesn't say it directly, but Doug gets it.

"He's in," she thinks. She can tell by the way he nods, a mischievous smile that lights up his eyes.

"Here's the million-dollar question. When we worked together . . ."
"Yes?"
"You were brilliant; we all knew that . . ."
"Hope . . ."
Hope rolls her eyes. "Brilliance aside, there were projects when you wouldn't stop iterating. FTS is on a fast track. And, the code might not be as elegant as you . . ."

Doug cuts her off. "I'm finished obsessing."

"That's what you say now. But this is your work. We both know how you get. At Topia, it wasn't just that you snuck off to get stoned at five o'clock with your team. I never cared about that. It was that every time we hit a deadline, you seemed to come up with a new rationale to delay shipping, a reason to not deploy. You insisted it could be better. That drove me mad. You'd have to work with me on this. TAN's got deadlines."

Doug nods. "Got it."

"I think FearToShred could finally earn you your hero's badge, Doug."

"I'm not sure I still care about badges, Hopi." Doug sits back, the endearment slipping out as naturally as breath. Doug looks like a newly svelte Yoda taking in important, but manageable, data.

"Listen, it's not about badges. I like it. It's quirky. In a good way."

"Right? Fans, fun? Easy way to post videos. They could be great. Maybe we could allow fans to wager and even bet real money on challenges. Would that even be legal? Anyway, as I've said, Arthur wants to go big-time. That's another problem, but it's not your problem."

"Aha . . . the lure of TAN, a real network behind them."

"But the company is not going anywhere if they can't get the back-end up and scaled."

"I assume that's why we're here."

"You know I'm all business, Mr. Wiser."

Doug shoots her an impish grin. So far so good.

"Be right back," he says, his Apple watch flashing.

Wiser slides out of the booth, walks to the front door and out of the Central Park Bistro. Yeah, all business, Hope thinks. Me too. Was that the good news or the bad news? Business as usual, a perpetual list of problems to be solved, shelved, stored.

Hope's stomach tightens. The unexpected e-mail from her father mixes with the surprise of Doug looking awesome—a cocktail by turns thrilling, scary and enervating. Both men are linked in her heart like music or Grimm's Fairy Tales—familiar, discomforting, compelling. Both men have left her with long gaps in which to construct stories, fantasies, long gaps in which to ponder unresolved feelings.

As Doug walks back toward the table, Hope wonders: Was he expecting another job offer? An important message from his wife? Is she pregnant?

"Sorry about that. Had a roofer at the house."

"Got it. So—are you ready to talk to Arthur?"

"Yeah, I think I am," he says, pulling a credit card out of his wallet.

"I've got it," she says, grabbing the leather folio.

"No," he wrangles the check away.

"Hello? I am shamelessly recruiting you."

"Recruiting me? No way. You're doing me a favor."

Hope rolls her eyes. "You can make FearToShred work, Dougy."

"Maybe."

Hope sits across from her ex and frets. If she doesn't tell him now why she left, how does she know she can work with him? If their welcome hug had been any measure, she would have to admit she's stepping into hot water. All morning, before arriving here, she'd had the jitters. The white lies aren't feeling so white; they're feeling dirty. Telling Chuck she was ill. Not telling James about seeing Doug. And now, lying to herself about not wanting to see her dad. Why not tell Doug everything? Is there going to be a better time?

"Where were we?" Doug asks.

"Madame?" a serious waiter appears offering her a dessert menu.

Hope waves him away. "Where were we? Last time we talked, you said you were practicing, starting a new band."

"Not happening," Doug dismisses the subject. His face clouds over, the spark extinguished. He rearranges the salt and pepper shakers.

"You're not giving up?" Hope asks returning the salt and pepper shakers back to their original position.

Doug's answer is in the slow way his hands move across the white tablecloth as if rubbing a magic lamp for answers. She notices the new wrinkles running like railroad tracks across his forehead.

"Some plans don't work out," Hope says, her own voice catching. "Even if you are the best fucking lead guitarist around." Doug's eyes narrow, his forehead crinkled to a "V." She knows that look. He's weighing whether to open up to her. And she knows if he opens himself up about his music, he's opening a door to her sympathy. Not that she wouldn't give it to him, but if she does, he will have something of her, a piece of her.

In that moment, she wants to give him that piece, but he doesn't open the door. Hope sips the watery iced tea with a sinking feeling that Doug is having second thoughts about the job.

Dangerous. It could be dangerous. A glimpse of sadness, hidden just behind his eyes, melts a hard place inside of her. Working with Doug could be dangerous on so many levels. It was a long shot that she would come out of another work stint with him unscathed. All she wants to do now is to ask those questions they have artfully avoided: How is his life? Katie? Daisy? He picks up and fingers her car keys absentmindedly.

"What about the other stuff?" Doug asks as Hope turns to go.

"What other stuff? The last I checked, you were married." Hope waves goodbye. One full body hug with Doug was about enough for today.

* * *

In the parking lot, Hope checks her e-mail before gunning it back to the office.

From: Richard Ellson.

Hope's heart thumps. The last she had heard, the year before her Aunt, Richards' sister, died, was that her father had relocated to Washington, D.C. The farther away the better.

Hope speed dials her sister.

"Dawn?"

"Huh?

"Fuck. I woke you up." Hope checks the dashboard clock—1:55. "Go back to sleep!"

"Hope? I'm sorry I was up all night."

"No worries. I'll call you tomorrow."

Hope clicks off before her sister can protest and scans the parking lot for Doug's Leaf. Fuck. Fuck. Fuck. Richard Ellson?! What could her father want? Hope's heart thumps fast and irregularly as she calculates her father's age. Fifty-eight. Not exactly old, but old enough to be caught in all kinds of trouble. Money problems, health problems, love problems. Problems. She gulps from her traveling water bottle, choking on the cold liquid. Dabbing her chin, she smudges her lipstick. Bravely, she clicks: Subject: "FearToShred."

Huh. Richard Ellson writing to her about FearToShred? OK. She won't delete it, but she will ignore it. Backing out of the parking spot, she mutters aloud: *Don't think about him.* How can she? Seeing Doug for the first time in three years was more than enough drama for one day. The CVS doesn't count! They didn't even talk! Now, her estranged father is back?

Hands shaking on the wheel, Hope pulls into an empty spot at the far end of the lot. James. She could send him the e-mail and he could read it. That would soften the blow. Hope resists. She can't call James. She's never told James much about Richard Ellson. Why would she? But she could talk to Doug. *Not appropriate*, scolds her inner critic. She scribbles a challenge for FearToShred,

"Touch anywhere to begin."

11

BIG, CRAZY bouquets of red, yellow, orange, and purple balloons are as bright as ranunculus in the spring—abundant and festive but they block Hope's way into the Sequoia conference room. The largest of the small company's three conference rooms, it was too small for today's meeting. Stella, FearToShred's front desk receptionist, accounts payable, and all-around admin had set up for ten engineers, two production people, two admins, two founders, Hope and Arthur—sixteen in all—in a room built for ten, max. A reproduction of Ansel Adams' "Half Dome," a granite wall shining silver under a full moon, illuminates the far end of the room. Stella's taken out the large, bulky conference chairs, replaced them with small folding ones. And, she had the conference table moved up to the front of the room, turned horizontally. Julie is up on the makeshift dais, alone. Staring at her cell phone, her small, oval face framed by a short tuft of black hair. Only the vertical lines etched between her eyebrows give her age away.

Arthur sidles to the front of the room, twisting this way and that, smiling widely.

"Doug Wiser is coming in to talk this afternoon," he whispers in her ear, even though whispering in team meetings is frowned upon. "But I haven't told anyone. I got his VP of Engineering hire pre-approved by the board."

Hope listens, poker-faced.

The din, loud even by FearToShred's standards, is no doubt inspired by the prospect of money and the presence of a large chocolate cake.

"You good?" Arthur asks Julie.

"All good."

Arthur does a double take. "Where's Jeff?" Arthur asks, two decibels too loudly.

"Skating accident," Julie reports. "He sent a clip."

"Jesus fucking Christ," Arthur moans.

Hope watches Arthur bat away a colored balloon. Her ears are tuned like a dog's, catching the cacophonous high pitches of nervous-sounding small talk. With all the chatter in the small room, the acoustics are skewed; she can only make out a word or two.

Platform. Ruby. Mongo. Python.

On Julie's side of the table, Caitlin and Liselle, two thin, industrious-looking early twenty-something women—rectangular specs, black slacks with smart, pima cotton button-down shirts—lean in close. Stella taps a bronze meditation bowl with a small pestle and waits for the room to quiet. Hope pictures herself inside of a double helix, all the intelligent matter circling around her. Showtime. Snapping her iPad shut, she checks an impulse to fold her arms across her chest. The buzz quiets when Julie stands to speak.

"We've just signed our first deal. The Adventure Network is going to create a reality TV show from FearToShred." Julie's voice is loud, enthusiastic, but a hint of sullenness shows in her eyes.

"Wahoo!"

"Way to go!"

Loud whoops and hollers fill the room. The troops are buying it. Cheering even. In the corner, Tran, Jeff's bestie, is visibly unmoved, but that doesn't mean he's not enthused. He never shows his feelings.

"Our partnership is going to turn FearToShred into a household name," Julie finishes. "Now let's give it up for Arthur!"

Big round of applause.

"I'm sorry Jeff isn't here," Arthur starts. "Julie just told me that he had a skating accident this morning. Well, at least our founder doesn't suffer a fear to shred!"

Boos and guffaws.

"I knew FearToShred was a winner when I came on board six months ago," Arthur starts. "You've all worked hard. You've won two million users, loyal fans. And you've added more fun to the world."

Arthur flips open his iPad, projects his slide onto a screen behind him. Two words, white letters against a blue sky: "Nine Months."

"We have nine months to increase our numbers, get the site stable, and get our winning players prepped to be filmed for the show. You think we can we do it?"

"Yeah!"

"Sure!"

"Totally."

12

"I WOULD rather skip it," Doug groans, sotto voce.

"I know, but a launch is PR, and FearToShred is show business. If we don't host a party after announcing the deal with The Adventure Network, the valley's tongue starts wagging," Hope counters.

"Be cool. And keep the unresolved shit to ourselves," Doug says.

"Exactly," Hope mimes.

The lobby of Bimbo's 365 Club is a rococo nightmare. Gold-flecked mirrors mutate passersby into diseased aliens. Two skinny, androgynous beings—one with platinum hair with intentional black roots and blue fringes, the other with a pink rinse—slink through the crowded lobby. "Cigar, cigarettes, roses?" Doug hands over his beat-up North Face jacket to the waifish-looking coat check woman.

Doug steers Hope across the black-carpeted foyer into a large room where the FearToShred launch party is in full swing. He watches his ex sashay her way through the crowd toward the bar. A loud din, partially absorbed by burgundy-velvet-flocked wallpaper, fills the fifties-style hall. Doug doesn't like the idea of a party celebrating a contract. From where he sits, getting cocky before the prototype is solid could jinx success. But that's the way things go: engineers off in a corner, stressing, while everyone else gets buzzed.

Hope sips carefully from a dangerously sloshing Cosmopolitan. "Can I talk to you for a minute?" Doug asks, chugging from a lime-flavored Perrier.

"Talk."

"In private," Doug whispers in Hope's ear.

"Lobby in five minutes."

Seven-thirty. Most of FearToShred's people and their guests have arrived and are circling the buffet like pelicans swooping in for the kill.

"What's up?" Hope perches on a padded stool at the lobby bar.

Doug stands. "Arthur sincerely believes the company exit is going to be epic." Doug starts, shaking his head. He's trying to stifle excitement, but he's never been good at hiding his feelings; he's too transparent.

"Back up. What happened?"

"Well, Arthur told me the state of the code. Jeff and Julie's prototype needs an overhaul. Everyone's happy until you put the load on, right? They've increased their number of users 100% since they built it. Now, with TAN, once it has to really perform, all the bugs are going to come out like termites in a rainstorm."

"OK."

"I told him I have a great Java guy. Arthur knows the back-end is shaky, but he's agreed to ten times our current base for TAN."

"Right."

"And, I told him I'm a hard-ass for performance testing. It's going to be a culture shift, but the company is young. They'll adjust."

"Except for the founders," Hope frowns. "Speaking of . . . Hey Jeff."

Jeff, arm in a cast, waves with his good hand and walks by.

"Did you find Arthur subterranean?" Hope asks.

"In a way, yeah. He acts all buddy-buddy, especially with that Harvard-Amherst thing he started. He was intimate and remote—at the same time—if that's what you mean."

"I think he's charming. You know, in a bad-boyish sort of way." Hope blushes ever so slightly, raises an eyebrow, and sips the pink liquid sloshing over the side of the martini glass. "That guy could charm a terrorist out of an Afghani cave." Hope's eyes dart toward the door. "Still I'm not quite sure if he's really a team player."

"Well he charmed a few million out of Kleiner, Perkins back in the day," Doug jibes, swigging fizzy water like there's no tomorrow.

Doug follows Hope's eyes darting around the room. "Expecting someone?"

Hope shakes her head. "Nope. Everyone I know is here," she winks.

Only Hope could wink at an ex-lover and not mean a thing by it. Weren't her easy ways exactly what had enticed him into Hope's sphere? Her warmth toward the team was a plus at Topia. That, and the fact that she always had her eye on the prize, never played the maternal card. She was one of the guys, but one with high emotional intelligence. She was smooth in a way he could never pull off, especially when greeting an ex, or even a friend from whom he'd grown apart. He was awkward and shy. But Hope was hardwired to pull off weird social engagements. When Hope winked at you, suddenly it was it's cool and no thang.

Doug had left his interview wondering what Arthur really wanted. Not just from the company and his founders but from him. Did he want a fix-it guy, a yes man, or a high-level architect who could scale FearToShred to billions? Having answered all of Arthur's questions, Doug was left unsettled. Who was this guy, really? "He charmed you out of Manuserve."

"Nah. I was ready." Hope touches a slim, long finger to her lips.

"Listen, Hope. These guys are never team players. Not really. They're out for maximum profit, and shareholder value. We might be working for a game company, but it's serious business."

"Duh." Hope moans. "One more thing," Hope's eyes scan the room. "Was Arthur late for your interview?"

"No, why?"

"Just curious."

Doug notes a pearl and diamond band on her right-hand ring finger. It would be just like Hope not to mention that she and James were getting hitched.

"And he's charming you out of retirement," Hope jabs him gently in his ribs.

"Listen," Doug whispers. "Arthur sweetened the pot. He threw another 500,000 stock options at me."

"Ooh, lucky you! But now, this is a party, right? We'll talk shop on Monday. Now, we're chillaxing." Hope does a little wave-like move with her chest and waist, indicating a marked downgrade in her usual vigilance level. It won't last long. Hope likes to think of herself as a work hard/play hard girl, but her defenses don't go down easy. She's sort of a human train crossing—the warning lights go on, the train passes, but she's always on alert watching for more trouble coming down the track.

"Catch you later," Doug takes off for the buffet. Hope's got his number. At work, Doug thinks about training, at a party, he wants to talk about work. At home, he wants to talk about anything other than the baby topic. Focus, Wiser. He takes his plate over to a small table in front of the stage, trying to remember if Hope had that same ring on when they had lunch, or if it's a party ring, a bauble, a meaningless, albeit expensive, accessory, bought perhaps by Hope herself.

The band finishes the warmup. In the past five minutes, scattered riffs have run between salsa, hip-hop and jazz funk—a rhythmic cacophony bordering on the insane. Now, three women shimmy across the stage in matching, skintight, shiny silver dresses, their gyrations generating enough energy to power the lights of a small town. Behind the singers, the band wails: a white, forty-something long-haired sax player and an African American, dreadlocked twenty-something hard-driving drummer pounding away behind an athletic, pretty-boy lead guitarist struggling to stay on the beat. The lead singer, a slim, queenly African-American, struts in front of the bass player and the lead guitarist belting out "Rolling! Rolling! Rolling on the River!" The musicians are in their zone now, oblivious to her thin waist, strong shoulders and the languid way she moves.

"Too loud," Hope shouts over the drums and rhythm guitar solo.

They walk away from the stage back through the hall of mirrors. In no mood to see his reflection morphed into an alien, Doug averts his eyes.

"What did Arthur say?"

"About what?" Hope yells.

"About me!"

"You're here aren't you?"

At the hosted bar, Doug flips open his wallet for tip money. He notices Hope's gaze land on a photograph of Katie with Daisy, on the beach. A deep blue sky fades into orange at the horizon. Katie, serene with old-moneyed ease. Hope turns away.

"I'll look for you later." Hope heads toward a scrum of people munching on cold shrimp and sushi.

Doug watches her back muscles ripple ever so slightly through her gauzy shirt. *That woman should have yellow caution tape wrapped around her.*

Hope sidles up to Julie. Doug stares impolitely, enjoying the study in contrasts. There's Hope, flawlessly dressed, Julie, at least six inches shorter, decked out in a button down and tomboy black jeans. Suddenly Jeff sneaks up behind him, throwing his good arm around Doug's shoulder.

"Hey, Wiser."

Just as Doug turns to notice the angry red scratch on Jeff's right cheek, a lithe, tall blonde joins Julie and Hope's tête-à-tête.

On stage, the lead singer croons a particularly raucous cover of *"Heard it Through the Grapevine."* Soul music isn't Doug's thing, but this version turns him on.

"Hey, Jeff. Listen—this song is cool." Doug closes his eyes. There it is. The drummer's added a backbeat that Tammy and Marvin Gaye never dreamed of. "Be right back."

"Have fun."

Doug sneaks up onto the stage, whispers into the rhythm guitar player's ear. The desire to play had been working its way into his blood since he had walked in. When the urge strikes, it's chemical, like a fever. His fingers vibrate.

Doug picks up the guy's Telecaster. Up here on stage is like walking into his front door after a hard bike ride, or after walking Daisy in the rain. It's like being in his living room, in his garage. It's home.

Guitar in hand, he quietly picks out a few notes to find the key. He needs breathing room. Steering Hope around the room like he owned her made him feel dangerously close to being out on a date with his ex. Not good.

Doug noodles along, finding his way. The band is hot onto the rocking backbeat, when the African queen lead singer turns and nods in his direction. For a minute, his heart jumps. A solo? He hasn't soloed—besides playing on his own in his garage. Doug nods back, no idea what the fuck he's going to play.

He starts slowly, a trick he learned when he was just getting started. He finds the notes of the chord, mixes them up, but doesn't let go of the beat. "You can hide a lot if you're on the beat," Doug's first guitar teacher taught. The lead singer joins in and Doug finds a combination that wouldn't have occurred to him in a million years. He's not following her voice exactly, he's off to the side, but his chords are complementing her minor E. Doug nods at the beefy bassist. He nods back. Pretty soon, the room gets quiet. They're watching the lead singer—she's so freaking hot! He closes his eyes. He takes his new-found combination a few steps further. He moves his fingers up an octave, and over with an F and then a D sharp. And then something clicks. The riff he played in the Knitting Factory two years ago is back at his fingertips. It sounds great with the D sharp key the band is jamming in, so he keeps going. And just like that, he's playing that lost solo, or at least a respectable rendition of what blew Joe Selwich away in New York. For the life of him, he could not have found that combination yesterday.

Doug steps off the stage, careful not to trip on the taped down coils of electrical cords. Back in the crush of his new coworkers, Doug hears a lone applause. The singular clapping gathers steam, until the whole gang is whooping:

"Wiser! Wiser!"

Doug shakes his head in a vehement NO. "No, really," he digs his chin into his chest, pointing at the band and clapping in their direction, but the truth is, he knows he's done something worth clapping for. He hit that place, that elusive space in a solo—inspiration.

Hope is there, about three rows from the front where a small crowd of people are circling the stage. Doug can't remember ever seeing her smile that widely. Maybe once, when they were first together.

"Dude!" Jeff is patting him on the back and Julie is giving him a warm hug.

"Where'd that come from?" Julie asks.

"Beats me," Doug arranges his face into a question. But he knows.

"Can I talk to you for a second?" Hope whispers. Her hand touches his back, sending familiar surge through his damp shirt.

"What's up?" Doug asks, pulling himself back from the stage and into Hope's orbit. She hands him a cold water as his mind races. He pats his pocket for paper. "Hang on. I need to write down that riff."

Doug scribbles. Hope stands sentry next to him, gesturing to well-wishers to get in line. "Done. Shoot!"

"Beside the fact that you were just beyond awesome . . . did you see that bitch?"

"Who?" Doug spins around.

"Don't look!" Hope grabs his shirtsleeve.

"At what?"

"That blonde. Kelly. The Adventure Network Producer."

"The one who butted into your talk with Julie?"

"Yes. I can't believe Arthur invited her!"

"Hope. Hope. What's going on?"

Doug steps back, wondering how many pink cocktails she's had.

"She's marking her territory. Yakking it up with Julie, acting buddy-buddy."

Doug nods.

"Second, her face is polished to a sheen. And spike heels? When you're 5'8"?"

Pot calling the kettle black, Doug thinks. He draws his finger across his lips. It was a private joke between them whenever two women at work were at odds, Doug stopped it short. "Hey, Hope. Relax. Arthur's crazy about you."

Hope is perilously near tears. "I don't know how, but she dragged me into a conversation about how we have to go viral. I told her I'm writing the blog, and setting up meet-ups, and she starts poo-pooing it like I'm some idiot."

"Oh?"

"Yeah. All haughty. 'That is so yesterday. We're not waiting for some Magical Mystery Moment,'—she even put air quotes around my words —'we've got research, science. Leave the viral part to me.'"

"Too cool, eh?"

"I think so."

"Not to worry. It's the L.A./S.F. thing. We've got her outnumbered."

Hope pouts.

Doug whispers: "You're working, Hopi. It's a party. We're chillaxing."

"Did I say chillaxing? We're never chillaxing. You know that." Hope shakes her head. Hope is not one to denigrate female colleagues, but there's always a first time. Besides, this is a new playing field. Kelly's knocked Hope down a peg, but Doug has her back.

"I'll make you and the whole damned team golden in no time," Doug says, orders her a drink, and slaps down a five. Before he knows it, Arthur's there, roping her into a conversation with Frank, FearToShred's Business Development guy. Doug heads off toward the coat check, forgetting to ask Hope if she needs a ride.

"That's it!" he nods to the waifish coat check girl. Suddenly, his jacket embarrasses him—he should have made an effort, grabbed a sport coat out of the back of the closet. He doubles back to check if Hope needs a ride. But she, the consummate party girl, is on a roll. Doug knows that roll. Two Cosmos into the evening when she's just the right amount of buzzed, and she's everyone's best friend. She's right there with you. Gorgeous, bright, and totally funny. Doug waves, but she's back with Julie now, bubbly as can be.

Doug turns to leave as sober as when he arrived. He had promised Aaron "no drinking until after the race."

While the valet pulls the Subaru around, he worries, how will Hope get home? He doubles back to check on her. She's talking to Arthur. "Need a ride?" he mouths. Hope shakes her head no. Hope always finds her way home.

Riding up together was ostensibly fine, except that since their lunch, Doug had found himself thinking about Hope in ways he hadn't for a long time.

Doug tips the valet, slips behind the wheel and is pulling away when he notices a note under his wiper blade. He rolls down the window, and retrieves it with his long, left arm.

"The lyric, by its habit is always looking for the exit the minute it enters the room. Should I tweet this?—Jeff"

Doug grabs his phone, texts: " :)"

Daisy is waiting in the front window when Doug pulls into the driveway. The orangey porch light is on. Flinging his jacket on the sofa, he picks up his guitar. He turns his amp to the lowest volume and pulls out the note he scribbled at the club.

Wiser, Wiser echoes in his head as he plucks away, notating the solo combination.

The oversized kitchen clock reads eleven P.M. Doug's buzzed. *Fantastic*, and *awesome* skip across his brain like happy dancers, cheering up the part of his grey matter that's been in a funk for six months. He grabs a bowl of cereal and tiptoes into his office, closing the door behind him. Tentatively, Doug picks out the combination, but it doesn't sound quite the same without the bass and the drums. The riff fades minute by minute, like a magnificent tropical sunset—pink then orange, and finally fire red, but by the time you find the camera, the color is all gone—it's black. He takes the guitar and amp out to the garage, settles in by his workbench, plugs in the amp, and twists the knob to the right. Finally, there it is—the riff—the sweetness and the angst, the longing and the despair, all there. He fires up GarageBand to transcribe the notes. Crazy how stuff like that happens. Two years thinking about a riff. Three years since sleeping with Hope, and a year and a half since reporting in for a job. Four months training. The Knitting Factory feels like yesterday. And tonight, Hope seemed like just yesterday, too. Time was collapsing.

Doug kicks back, picks up the Strat again and picks out notes beyond the riff. He's playing and transcribing the notes, humming the singer's jazzy accompaniment. Mid-strum, his skin breaks out in goose bumps. "YES!" he yells at the garage wall.

When Carlos quit and the other guys mutinied, Doug figured it was a sign. Dystopia's timing was off. Now he wonders if their leaving just kicked the ball of self-doubt rolling. And once the ball of self-doubt started rolling, it picked up steam like lead running downhill. The band was no good; he was no good. Nothing was good.

One A.M. Doug is bone-tired but too buzzed for sleep. He locks the garage, wanders back into his office and logs on to FearToShred's backstage, testing the code. The code doesn't look so bad, but when he digs deeper into the design, he can see that they haven't cached. No caching means this site won't scale. No scalability means no growth.

Got it. Hope warned him and Arthur told him also, but he had to see the problem for himself. The code is a mess.

Contemplating a solution, Doug falls asleep on his ratty old office couch. The last image in his mind is that of Hope and Arthur laughing. Hope has a way of getting things going. At Topia when everyone was down Hope thought up competitions to jazz them up: prizes for the best UI, announcements in *TechCrunch* for the best design, dinner for anyone checking in code on weekends. According to an article in *Gonzo*, she had even turned Topia from "Bleak to Baaad." It was as if she saw defeat as just another challenge.

If Hope is making Arthur happy, that can only be good. There is already enough angst brewing over at FearToShred to slow them down. If there is one thing you need to be great, it's energy and excitement; nothing fabulous ever comes from pouting. For a great startup, mojo is Ingredient One! If Hope is the spark that gets this engine started, so be it.

13

"Wassup?"

Hope stops short. Wassup? Their meeting had been on Julie's iCalendar for the past week. Julie's face is office lighting wan. A black elastic support wrapped around her wrist is an eye-catching accessory, butch in a self-care kind of way.

"I wanted to see you in your native habitat," Hope says, settling onto a white bean-bag chair.

"If you want native habitat, you'll have to watch me getting crushed by a wave. This here is my pretend home," Julie frowns.

"I'll do that," Hope nods. "Today, I'm on a mission."

"Shoot." Julie focuses her attention on Hope, a sweep of color pinking her cheeks.

Had she caught Julie at a bad moment? Whatev. Now's not the time to second-guess whether Julie is or is not in the mood for a chat. She needs Julie's support.

"Game Founder Strikes Gold." A large photograph of Julie catching five feet of air on the cover of *Thrasher* dominates the wall of FearToShred's co-founder's windowless office. The idea of starring in a FTS video sounded like such a good idea but now, here with Julie, a world champion, Hope withers. There's no way she could pull off a stunt like water skiing and singing or snowboard tricks in the dead of night.

"TAN's proposal is predicated on getting our numbers up, right?"

Julie rolls her eyes.

"I know, I know. L.A., T.V., blah blah. But you're on board, right?" Hope asks.

"Kind of . . . It's Jeff—"

"We'll get to Jeff later. For now, it's my job to get our numbers up." Hope flips open her iPad. "Mind if I take a few notes?"

"Note on," Julie quips. "But seriously?" Julie says, her voice the voice of defeat. "Ten X more users? After we finally hit two million?!"

"Yes, Arthur and I have discussed. Twenty million is over the top. I told Arthur to push back. He actually tried. It's TAN that won't budge. L.A. doesn't get the fact that five times our current base is respectable for a launch. But T.V. numbers are different than web numbers."

Julie shakes her head skeptically. "Not only are 20 million users total pie-in-the-sky, it is so beyond the site's capacity."

"Yup," Hope says, thinking that Doug will fix it, but not wanting to over-promise. "Can I switch gears? I have an idea I want to pass by you."

"Hmmm. . . ." Shaking her head, she walks from her desk to gaze out at the fake lake, the key feature of the business park. Hope doesn't know her very well, but she's impressed by her silence. It signals her ability to listen, to absorb new information without a knee-jerk reaction.

"Yeah, let's switch gears. Can I show you some new clips?" Julie brightens. "Then we'll circle back to your idea."

"Promise?" Hope asks. If history is any lesson, Julie has a proclivity toward distraction.

"Scout's honor. Here's one that came in last night from Australia," Julie flips her screen so Hope can see. "Leave a trail of tears . . . with a ukulele . . ." Julie flips through videos of a roller skater with a watering can balanced on the top her head, a trail of water in her path as she strums "I wanna go back to my little grass shack in Kealakekua, Hawaii . . . where the honohononumukamuka go swimming by . . ."

The next clip is a water skier leaving a blistering wake of lake water that splashes up into the camera lens—a plastic ukulele strapped to his back. "This one got 1,203 votes—it's the leader."

Hope is bewildered. Whoever Jeff and Julie's two million users are, they're quirky. Part artist, part athletes? Park voyeur, part performance artists? She'd have to get to know the community better if she was going to build it.

"Check this out." Julie flips to another series. "Leave no trace. With a straw broom."

Videos of carpet sweepers, street sweepers, baseball diamond sweepers, golf course sweepers, and witches on broomsticks flip by in quick succession. "Photo-shopped videos were checked in, but they were voted down by the purists," Julie explains. "It's too easy, right? Remember we want our people to take risks."

"Which brings me to my proposal," Hope interjects. "Be honest, OK? Just tell me if I'm out of bounds with this. I don't want to step on any toes."

"We're all about stepping on toes, remember?" Julie laughs, the corners of her eyes wrinkling.

"Oops." Hope sees James' number on her screen. She declines the call. "I want to do a challenge," she blurts.

Julie jumps up from behind her desk, dragging her right foot ever so slightly. "Let's do it! But what was I supposed to be honest about?"

"Duh! Julie! You're the queen! I snowboarded in college. I mean I could pull something off . . . but I'm no Shauna White."

The two women chuckle at the thought of Hope with red, curly hair, flying down the side of a mountain.

"What's the trick?" Julie asks. She limps over to the white board, scribbles: 'Hope's Challenge.' We'll create a special tweet just for you . . ."

"Really? But what if no one votes for me?"

"That's not the point! You want to see how players do their thing, make their videos, right? We don't care if no one votes for you! You have a job, remember?"

The two women shoot each other a high-five.

"I'm taking one for the team!"

"How about snowboarding down a bunny slope singing "I Will Survive?" Julie poses.

"Nah, anyone can do that. Let's ratchet it up."

What Hope really wants is to parachute while singing "I Will Survive" or BASE jump in a bikini, but she won't confess. Not now anyway.

"I've got it!"

"Got what?"

"The tweet that's going to put us over the top – I mean beside your trick which will of course get a million hits."

Hope shakes her head. "Spill."

Julie jumps up from behind her desk. "It's crazy. I'm not sure anyone can pull it off but it will get us some free PR."

"I'm all about free PR."

"Ok—so the Tweet is: "Your best ally-oop. Quirk: On a wave.""

Hope's brow creases in confusion. "Alley-oop on a wave?"

"Right. It's crazy. If someone can do it, we'll be golden for TAN."

"I'm game," Hope agrees. "Go for it."

Outside Julie's office, Hope's phone blinks with a call from Charlene and another e-mail from her father. Back at her desk, she checks Richard's note: "Lunch next week?"

10:45. She's got a blog to write, two meetups to organize, and a one-on-one with Arthur at three. Her iCalendar says she's having lunch with the engineers and a call with TAN at two. Charlene can wait. Before settling in to watch the clips that have come in since last night, Hope dashes off a line to Richard Ellson: "Not a good time."

The truth was, Hope had ignored his e-mail all week. With everything going on at work, she still couldn't bring herself to look at it. She would. Just not today.

14

"Ready?" James peeks into the bathroom.

"Give me two," Hope says, deftly applying a last stroke of eyeliner. "I'm conflicted," she complains, settling on James' chilly new leather couch.

"What's up?"

"I promised Arthur a blog post about the last community meet-up in Austin," she says, withholding the part of her day that she wants to spend setting up her ice rink challenge with Julie. "I also promised to post an interview with the winner of "The Ultimate Descent. Quirk: Wear an Aviator Cap" challenge.

"You'll have all afternoon and night to work, babe. C'mon, we haven't seen my parents in what? Two months?"

Hope knits her brow. She'd gone shopping with Dawn yesterday, thinking she would have today to play catch up. It wasn't until they were having tea at four P.M. that she remembered the brunch.

"You look fabulous. It's a beautiful day! Remember fun?"

"But it's always a beautiful day," Hope says. "Fun? I think I re-member . . ." Hope's phone buzzes. "Hi Mom, hang on," she mouths to James. "Charlene . . . Really, James. I should stay."

James eyes narrow. "You see? I told you things would go south if you took this job."

"Who says things are going south?"

"Hope, not taking a morning off on a weekend . . ."

"OK, OK . . ." Hope acquiesces.

She settles into James' midnight blue Audi. On 280 south, the Santa Cruz Mountains are steep pale yellow slopes covered with wisps of fog, meringue on a key lime tart. A hike. That's what she really wants to do today. Fresh air, bay, redwood. Hope tunes in Sirius Jazz. Bill Evans. Yeah. James is a jazz freak with an encyclopedic knowledge. With him, she's learned to love the form. He knows who played with Miles Davis in 1952. How Dave Brubeck's "Take Five" and Terry Riley's "In C" changed jazz. Hope only balks when James plays experimental composers, categorically refusing Hiromi and John Zorn.

"I love this cut. It's a classic from the late 50's. It's Scott LaFaro and Modian. Listen to that bebop piano riff—Evans was famous for that."

"So cool," Hope agrees. The music's melancholy beauty matches her mood.

No, there would be no hike today unless they abbreviate brunch. On the radio, the jazz band's repetition of a heartbreaking chord change, the notes slide from major to minor, from optimistic and playful to aching need, slither and slide into a secret place in her heart. There are the challenges to set up, blog posts to write, and Charlene to call back. And then, there's her dad. Should she have refused him a visit? What if he is sick? But after twenty years? The canyon of missing him had turned from days into weeks, and then years. After the bitter overheard fights with Charlene, Hope never dared to ask, "Is he coming back?"

Hope turns back to the landscape. Not hiking is the least of her problems. James' parents make her nervous. The first time they met Hope, they staged a thinly veiled interrogation about her upbringing. What were normal questions about schooling and family were landmines for her. She's learned to skate the surface, go minimal, but the lies are still there. *Yes, yes, grew up in the Valley.*

Yes, public school. Cal. She breaks into a sweat worrying about their judgments about her dating their prep school son. Today they could very well graduate to Advanced Hope, asking about work, Charlene, her sister. No easy answers there either.

"Did I tell you what Kelly did this week?" Hope asks, if for no other reason than to pull herself out of the darkening vortex of worries.

"No."

"In our product meeting, she said she thought the first show with TAN should be filmed somewhere exotic. We were brainstorming. I said Hawaii. She said Hawaii was old hat. Uganda, she insisted. She knows there's a big skating scene over there and that we have a lot of followers. 'Count me out,' I said. 'I'm not flying from SFO to Africa.' She flipped."

"What happened?"

"She made it into a tease, but she was really surprised that I wasn't gung-ho about filming in Africa."

"Well, that's the perk of having a rich company to partner with— lots of cash for crazy shit."

"You think she'll try to home in on my job? I mean, I'm all about taking one for the team, but if I go to Africa, it will take me weeks to adjust, and besides, I hate long flights . . ."

"She's a go-getter, Hope. You can handle her." Hope takes James' assessment in, but it's no comfort. "And when I told Julie . . ."

"Hang on," James points at the radio. "You mind?"

"Nope." Hope gazes out the window, her body aching to be out on a trail, breathing bay and pennyroyal, and not in an air-conditioned car barreling down 280 toward James' parents' house. The brown hills of Stanford land and SLAC pass by on the left, blighted oak-studded hills on the right.

"Before we get there, I just want to check. Is it alright if I tell my parents that we're thinking of moving in together?"

Hope's stomach clutches. "Now?"

"Why not?"

"Because we haven't made any decisions?"

"I thought we had."

"Really?"

"Yes. Really."

Hope reconstructs the last conversation they had on the topic. It was after a particularly joyful lovemaking session, about three weeks ago. "What are we waiting for?" James had asked, stroking her hair. It was midnight on a Saturday night. They had been out with Leslie and Carl, friends of James' from Williams. Hope had waited a long minute. What was she waiting for? She didn't know! A sign, a lightning bolt, a moment when she would feel like she didn't want to be anywhere else but with James? And, when she could see them together for the long haul? That moment hadn't arrived. "We're not waiting," Hope had answered. We're having fun.

Fun, sure. But time, she is passing. James had kissed her then, an irresistible, delicious, gut clenching kiss.

"We'll talk about it in the morning," she'd said. But the next morning and the next, time was short, and they hadn't.

"Can we wait?"

"Absolutely." James flips the radio back on. A lively bebop fills the car's space.

James turns into the circular driveway. Hope cringes at the sight of two Greek columns. The way James had described his family's home is 1950s ranch. The first time she saw it, she almost turned around.

James opens the front door with a gallant sweep. A quick scan of the foyer is blinding: a large mirror over the mantle shoots out light caught from the entryway.

"Come on in," Cathy greets them. "I'm in the kitchen," James' mom sings. "I'm just finishing the pastry cream." Cathy is a well-preserved late fifties, early sixties. Size four or six, she's fit, not skinny like some of the wives on the Peninsula. She's got sensible, chin length natural grey hair with strands of deep brown. Her face is regal; large eyes and a sharp nose could be French, or English. Hope has never asked. She didn't want to go down the ancestry path with James or Cathy. Not because it wouldn't be interesting, but because she had no idea of her own genealogy except that Charlene's people were pioneers who came to California from Ohio in 1810. Hope was a fifth generation Californian. That was ancestry enough for her.

"Game's on," Paul, James' dad, shouts from the den.

Golf on TV? She'd rather watch paint dry.

On a large granite topped island, a marble rolling pin, circular flour board, and a freshly baked pie crust are evidence of Cathy's industrious morning.

"The crust is baked?" Hope asks, settling onto a stool.

"Pre-baked. Then I pour in the cream and top it with sliced peaches. It chills for an hour or so. Don't tell me you never made a fruit tart!" Cathy exclaims.

Hope shakes her head in the negative.

"James tells me you have a new job."

"Oh, you know, a startup. It's a game based on challenges the founders . . ."

"Cath? Can you get the door? I think Lauren just pulled up." Paul shouts from the living room.

At the perfectly set table (a centerpiece of stargazer lilies, Villeroy and Boch tableware—white with a gold rim), Paul proffers a fatherly buss on the top of Lauren's head. "Our newly minted Stanford grad." Paul has the booming voice of a man in charge and the body to match. He's six feet-two, just slightly paunchy, but that's recent; he retired a year ago, and he's been taking it easy. At least that's what James reports. Hope doesn't really believe that James' folks ever really take it easy.

Lauren smiles demurely. A petite, fresh faced young woman with long chestnut colored hair and deep brown eyes, Lauren is a softer version of her brother. She's got her father's narrow eyes, and James' full lips, an intelligent face.

"So, Hope, how is your mom?" Cathy asks, delivering perfect eggs fresh from the poacher, and warm brioche, tucked in a checked cloth in a gay wicker basket.

"Charlene?" A small place in Hope's chest clenches. She wants to crawl down a rabbit hole, alone, all the way back to when Richard helped her with her homework, all the way back to the Formica kitchen table where he would end their homework sessions with rifling her hair. All at once, Hope is sick with loneliness.

Can she tell them that she's canceled the last three dates with her mother? And not because she's too busy—the excuse that she gave Charlene—but because her mother would bust if she found out that Hope had left Manuserve for FearToShred? Charlene wasn't a risk taker.

The poached eggs on her plate go cold and Cathy touches her hand lightly. "Are you OK?"

Hope startles at the tender gesture. "Yes, yes," Hope digs in enthusiastically to the toast and eggs.

Across the table, James teases his sister about her new job at Google. "Selling out, heh?"

"Making any big changes yourself, heh?" his sister razzes.

"Now, now," Paul chastises. "To each her own."

In the hubbub of eating, passing and razzing, Charlene is forgotten. Just as well. Hope is lost in this family, a square peg in a round hole. She should have stayed home, insisted on working. No one would miss her, would they? Instead, she guzzles the champagne that Paul refills without asking.

"Did you hear about Nathan's back surgery?" Cathy asks. "And Isabel? She had her baby!"

Family conversation turns to aunts and uncles she's never met, a dull background noise of gossip. Sunday mornings in the Ellson house consisted of cold cereal because Charlene was working her second job selling handmade soaps with her friend Daria at the Farmer's Market. The small booth gave Charlene a chance to flirt with farmers and their hunky sons. Charlene gone on Sunday mornings gave Hope and Dawn a few hours of peace to watch TV and finish their homework. A month after their father left, Charlene had this great idea to take the girls to church. That lasted three Sundays until Daria offered her the soap-selling job. But it didn't stop the church from trying to recruit Hope and Dawn for Sunday school. For a minute, Hope was tempted. Church formality and the stories that were her first myths, her first fairy tales, the kids and the hot lunch afterward were attractive. It was the talk of a punishing God and a suffering Jesus that sent her running home.

"Any summer plans?" Paul booms in James' direction. "We were thinking of renting a house on Maui in July. You guys game?"

"Not sure yet, dad. With Hope's new job and all," James raises his eyebrows in his dad's direction, but throws Hope the hairy eyeball when Paul gets up to help Cathy clear the table.

Pie eaten, dishes washed and the PGA over, Hope silently signals, *leaving*, in James' direction. He's on the couch with his sister, reminiscing about his Williams days. He does this to rile up his little sister; he knew going to an Eastern school had upped his game.

"Now?" he mouths over Lauren's head.

"Now."

Heading north afterward is like gaining on home territory after an afternoon dodging bullets and restraining herself from imploding. James stays her hand when she reaches for the radio. "So, now that you're at FearToShred," James starts, "can I ask you something?"

"Sure." Hope's been dreading this conversation for two weeks.

"Did you think about discussing it with me before you accepted your offer?" James stares straight at the road ahead. "Did you think I'd have nothing to say about you starting another job that's going to have you running in circles? Oh, and not let you have a summer vacation, I assume."

Hope swallows hard, the champagne's effervescence playing havoc with the eggs. "Yes, I didn't raise the subject on purpose. I knew you would have an opinion," Hope protests. "But I knew what it was."

"And what's that?"

"Don't do it."

"And what about your promise?"

"I thought I had a better shot at FearToShred for an upside than waiting three years to vest at Manuserve. End of story."

Sometimes I can be such a bitch, Hope frowns. No wonder she was fretting this morning. She could smell a fight on James like a baby smells milk on its mother. He knew she needed a day to catch up. But did he not know how hard it was for her to relax in the bosom of his nuclear, cozy, everyone loves everyone family? His mother was sweet; that wasn't the issue. It was that she couldn't be herself. In James' family, there were no demeaning asides, blatant putdowns or even loud voices; no hiding in the bedroom while parents railed at one another. In James' family there was plenty of love to go around.

Hope turns the radio to public radio. The sound of Tony Kushner's voice discussing playwriting and the new movie he's working on for Steven Spielberg takes them out of Silicon Valley, out of James' anxieties, out of their future. "The screenplay is based on a work of history," Kushner says. *"The Kidnapping of Edgardo Mortara* is about the kidnapping of a Jewish child by the Vatican in 1858." Hope's thoughts jump from Spielberg to Kelly and TAN. But James wouldn't want to talk about TAN now, or the heli skiing in Canada challenge she's cooking up with Julie or her meetups. The sight of her street coming into view relaxes the roiling in her stomach, eases the flow of bile.

"Later?" Hope kisses James on the mouth. "Thanks for brunch. I'll call you."

James waves half-heartedly and drives up the street and out of view.

In the apartment, Hope slips off the pearl necklace, the Blahniks, and changes into her running clothes. A run will clear her head. That and a coffee on the way home. Down the steps, and up the hill she considers the morning. It isn't that James' parents aren't warm, or caring, or friendly. The problem was that, in a million years, they would never be her people. She could never imagine another Sunday afternoon in Los Altos, making pies with his mom while James watched PGA with his dad. And it isn't that she doesn't like the idea; it's that the thought makes her throat close and her skin itch. It isn't her.

Tomorrow Julie was going to publish her challenge on the "alley-oop: on a wave." Hope would have liked to talk about it today with James, but her anxiety about the site was gnawing at her. No wonder she couldn't eat her eggs.

They had decided at the last minute to use the tweet for the load test they would run this week. If someone pulls the trick off and they break the site again it's going to be hell.

Pushing up the hill toward Skyline, Hope hears Terri's admonishment. "Maybe if you let him in a little bit, you'd see how great James is."

She had been out on a girl's night with Terri, a friend from Seven Arts, a couple of months ago. "I'd grab a guy like that. He's steady. Loves you. Wants to move things forward. He's a catch."

"I know," Hope sighed.

"Is it the "C" word?"

"Ha-ha," Hope laughed, but Terri was on to something. Commitment was an issue to be sure. Or, it had been in Hope's younger days. Now, her concern is more that James would want her pushing out babies sooner rather than later—her clock was ticking—and, after growing up with a working mother, she wasn't convinced that she wanted to raise kids, at least not while she was working. Besides, how would they agree on things, big things like daycare and school, nannies and food choices when they couldn't even agree on Hope's work choices?

Maybe Terri is right, James is a great boyfriend, even if he is a bit conservative. The real question was would he be a good husband? Because she wasn't giving up work. Up the hill, Hope puffs.

Maybe Terri was right. Let him in a little bit. She'll tell him about her dad. If he could handle the fact that her long-lost father had shown up, and that she was actually open to seeing him, that might help. As she hits Skyline, a cramp hits her in her right side. Maybe not such a good idea to run after champagne and eggs. Walking it out, she heads down the hill toward home. What was she waiting for? Was it really true that she couldn't make a commitment? Getting married didn't mean she had to make pies did it?

Home again, she texts James. "Come over tonight?"

"Sure. What time?"

"An hour?"

"See you then."

Later, under a hot shower, water drips off the crown of her head and onto her face, until salty tears flow, a stream of past and present, safe and scared. Damn! Why open up this box? Didn't she have enough on her plate? Would seeing Richard Ellson make her life better, or worse?

Hope towels off. She reaches into the fridge for a cold water and shakes some fresh kibble into Skimpy's bowl. The calico rubs her body affectionately against Hope's calf. Curling up with her laptop and water Hope is musing over analytics when James calls.

"Getting things done, sugarplum?"

Hope can hear his post basketball endorphins electrifying the airwaves. David Allen's book, *Getting Things Done*, was an inside joke, although Hope didn't agree with the book's premise that productivity is directly proportional to our ability to relax; she thrives on stress. "And when do we chill?" James had challenged, clearly worried that a life with Hope would be a merry-go-round ride of work, social engagements, and workouts.

"Went for a run. I'm catching up now," Hope answers dutifully. "Did you slam them at basketball?"

"Nah, but I had a good workout. See you in a half hour? I'm running a little late."

"Sure."

"Oh, one thing. Can you do Thursday?"

"What's Thursday?"

"Sent you an e-mail today. Marcus, our VP is out from Washington. I was hoping you'd join us."

"Darn! I have training."

"Hope! Really? Just this one time? We could drive up together."

"OK, I'll see if Carlos can change . . ."

"Uh, you're the client, right?"

"I know, it's just that we've missed a few sessions lately." As soon as the words escape, Hope wishes that she could suck them back in. She'd told James she was in training the night she canceled on him to have dinner with Chuck. She hadn't wanted to tell her boss that she was quitting during work hours.

"Oh, really? It sounded to me like you've been on your regular schedule . . ."

"Right, right. OK, sure. Thursday."

Hope clicks off, cursing. She wasn't planning on telling James about meeting Doug for lunch the other day, either.

James arrives two hours later bearing a bag of Thai takeout. Before they'd hung up, they agreed to watch a movie, but Hope knew better; James was still holding out for a little nookie before Monday.

"There's something I have to tell you," Hope starts. "But you need to promise to just listen."

"Is it about today?"

"What about today?"

"Well you went all dark. I thought you were going to cry when my mother passed the eggs."

"That's kind of what I want to tell you."

"The eggs?"

"No!" In the kitchen, Hope fetches a beer and a bowl of nuts. "Brew?"

"Sure."

"James."

His face drops, his mouth curling down into a sad arc. "This about us, right? About me pushing the moving in issue?"

"No."

No wonder she never tells anyone anything.

Hope sits on the edge of the soft couch, leans in. "I got an e-mail from my dad."

"Huh?" James crosses the room, sitting next to her to throw a strong arm around her shoulder. "You never talk about your dad."

"Not much to say. He hasn't been around for twenty years."

James ponders the new information. "Did you answer him?"

Hope swigs from the long neck of the beer. "Finally. I told him I was busy."

"Hope. You can't see him. Not now."

"Why?" Hope is dumbstruck by James' pronouncement. Even if she knows where he's coming from: her emotional plate is overflowing with work issues, her mother's criticism and the growing pains of readjusting to startup life. She knows James' protective side; but still, she needs to find the words to tell him that seeing Richard now might be a good thing. Maybe now more than ever. James is such a family guy; it's hard to tell if he's really thinking about what's right for her or standing on some moral high ground. Richard left the family, he hurt Hope, he's *persona non grata*, but Hope still holds a candle for him.

"Well, you would have to tell Charlene about it, right? No secrets?"

"I can't do that."

"Why?"

"Telling Charlene that I'm thinking of seeing my dad is throwing gasoline on a fire."

"Tell her."

"Really?"

"Really."

15

"READY?" HOPE scans the group, running a quick head count. Julie. Ryan. Doug. Brett. Jeff?

Twenty-eight minutes until show time. The offer of prizes, cash and fame has brought new users to the site. But it was a surefire way to catch their users' attention. If they didn't have at least a thousand videos being checked in within the next hour, today's load test would be a waste. She texts Jeff: "R U nearby?"

He's late, but she has been advised by Arthur not to pressure him. "Keep it casual with Jeff." Egad. In her brief tenure, she has already learned to handle Jeff with kid gloves, Arthur with poise, and Julie with no bullshit. Thank God she has Doug. No pretending with Doug. And, his emotional intelligence has been a real asset.

Hope picks up a black sharpie, writes on the top of the white board. "Best alley-oop." Julie adds the quirk: "On a wave."

"We've got a decent load average now. We're at point one—a perfect starting place. Noah has been playing out load scenarios for the past few days," Brett reports. The kid is wearing a crisp butter-colored button-down with the tail tucked in. Preppy and unflappable, Doug's protegee is a winner. He can execute whatever Doug deals out, often improving on it to make the site faster, more reliable.

Across the room, Doug is trained on the logs like a cat stalking a mouse.

"What's our outside limit?" Hope asks.

Jeff texts back: "Nearby"

"We're starting," she types.

Doug gets up, empty coffee cup in hand.

Hope's text beeps.

Doug: "My office. Now."

Hope waits a few beats, and then reaches for her coffee cup. "Be right back." Checking her watch, she turns the corner to Doug's office.

"You're worried," Hope says sotto voice.

"A little. And where the fuck is Jeff? Take some ownership dude! Face the music!"

They hurry, stopping at the café for a hit of espresso. Walk with too much purpose and their co-workers would get nervous.

"Agreed. What else?"

"The crappy coding, that's what else," Doug frowns.

Hope's eyes dart around the hallway anxiously. Be cool, girl. She spies Jeff wearing his arm sling and a baseball cap and FearToShred t-shirt. A pimple or an inflamed cyst has surfaced on the side of his cheek; it's hot and red.

"The crappy coding is why we're doing this test, right?" Hope whispers, edging into Doug's office.

"I just don't know if I'm cut out for this anymore. I was up all night," Hope confides, rubbing her eyes.

"You're right. We're testing to flush out the bugs." Doug closes his eyes, as if praying for divine guidance.

"We'll fix it. Remember, this is just a test." Hope says the words like a prayer, clearly wishing to convince herself that today will be OK, no matter how the test goes. She walks briskly back to the conference room, a wave of guilt threatening to shake her already fragile equilibrium. Doug! What did she get him into? She takes her place next to Meg. Meg's sipping water and looking all perky. Bet she didn't go to the movies last night, Hope muses. Nor did she stay up till three A.M. pounding Twitter to cajole every last one of their users to post today.

"Everyone listen up. We only have a few minutes," Hope takes the lead.

Arthur slips in. Who invited him? Hope stiffens, her back as straight as a soldier. Was he on the invite list? She can't remember now.

"Here's the deal. I've got agreements from over a thousand users. They will be checking in videos this morning. I've also got a big group of watchers—people who are going to be commenting and voting. They're the folks that have come on board since the meet-ups in Brooklyn and L.A."

"You go, girl!"

"Woohoo!"

Hope smiles wanly. "We just want to do a dry run. Doug and Brett are testing to see how we hold up while people upload, comment, and vote. It's probably going to push the servers to their limit." Hope checks the wall clock. Two minutes. "Noah is going to monitor load averages. He's running 'Top' on his monitor if any of you want to follow along. Before we start, I just want to thank you all of your help. You got your pals on board, came up with great tweets."

Fist bumps, elbow bumps and high-fives. Even Arthur cracks a smile behind his laptop screen. Is he trying to disappear into an alternate universe or is this how he looks when he's really focused? No time to dwell.

"Let's roll!" Brett watches the clock turn to 10:59.

"Oh, and let's thank Arthur, who helped get us over the hump when he put $1,000 on the table for the winning team."

"Go, Arthur!"

"Shred it!"

Hope touches her index finger to her lips as the digital wall clock flips to 11:00.

Doug starts a scoreboard on the whiteboard—scribbling notes on videos and parsing out the technology.

"MySQ," he writes on one side of the board. He draws a thick black vertical line—"Consider for Prize."

By 11:10, videos are being checked in at a feverish pace. Doug scribbles: "Load average: 5"

Hope turns back to the monitors.

"What we have here is our users uploading videos at a fast rate— so we partition. It's a technique for splitting up a database into manageable-sized chunks; load average is a measure of how busy a server is," Doug says.

Jeff sits back, his arm in the now stained canvas sling. According to Meg, he'd cooperated with Doug on the test prep.

Hope takes up residence behind him.

"Ouch!" Jeff yells at the sight of a kid at a skate park in Japan crashing an alley-oop.

"This is great!" Hope whoops.

"What about running 'It's all a test' next?'" Jeff asks.

"Good one. I'll file for later," Hope shushes the antsy founder, watching videos check in from Argentina, Connecticut, Japan, and Brazil.

"Oh my god!" Jeff gasps. Huddled around the large display monitor, the team watches as a shaky video of a surfer at Venice Beach appears. As a giant wave begins to curl, the surfer flips his board to execute a perfect alley-oop.

"He did it!" Julie yelps.

Other videos roll in quickly. Doug is scribbling numbers from the servers.

The site is holding up. Good. Why shouldn't the site hold up? A thousand simultaneous uploads are not that many.

Across the room, Noah is tailing the server log scrolling by madly. "Load average: 10." He's shaking his head. "The write rate is too high." The write rate climbing too high is the first indication of a fail. The videos check in faster than Hope had anticipated. Doug has stopped taking notes on 'Consider for Prize.'

"Load average: 28."

"These won't load."

By 11:30 Hope searches Doug's face for answers, but Doug is behind Noah, watching his screen. Hope feels her face go hot as Arthur stares at her over the rim of his coffee cup.

"Site's down. #fail." Julie posts the hashtag.

Jeff sits upright, a worried dad.

"Shut it down," Noah says. "We're getting #epicfail tweets and users are dropping."

The air in the room shifts as all the happy, excited, optimistic molecules are sucked out and all of the "We're fucked" molecules multiply like so much stinking algae cluttering the bay.

Noah posts "Site Down. We're shredding" on the site.

Hope sits back, letting the change in atmosphere sink in. I left Manuserve for this?

But wait, there's Doug. "This, all of this? The #epicfail? The Load numbers? It's a test. It's not the end of the world. It's WHY we do the tests. They can be a drag, but they're informative."

Arthur looks up from his screen, listening to his "fix- it" guy. Hope perks up.

"We hit the wall with MySQL writes. Things were working fine at first, but that alley-oop got a ton of comments! It's good—no it's great! We're going to have to go back in and re-architect this puppy."

"Do you mean scratch everything we've built?" Julie interjects.

"Whoa! What happened to patching?" Arthur adds, irritation quickly undermining his recent compliment.

"It's classic—too many writes, too many queries, too big a dataset. It's the devil's triangle," Doug asserts.

16

"WE FUCKED UP."

Julie is walking the path out at Paradise Point with her dad, Wayne Tang. Barefoot, blonde, androgynous pre-teens ride by with kid-sized surfboards mounted on metal racks soldered to their bike frames. The big boys are catching waves out beyond the break. When the winds die down and the water is calm, the ocean lays down flat and the bay just below Santa Cruz becomes a practice area, a mellow hang-out spot where the small breakers can make beginners feel like real surfers. Julie learned here, before skating consumed all her free time. The water was her first love, but skating won her heart.

"We don't 'fuck up.' We iterate." Wayne corrects his daughter. "Didn't I teach you anything?" he kisses the top of his daughter's head.

Julie watches the sun angle down, remembering the endless lectures about how great failure is, and how every experiment that ends badly only brings you closer to the answer. She hated the talks but at least they trained her out of the tantrums she would fall into when a math problem didn't proof out. Her parents had designed her homeschooling curriculum to their strengths. Her mom focused on Geology, History, Japanese, and Chinese. Philosophy, English, Math, and Science were with her dad, who indoctrinated her: fail fast.

The Tangs firmly believed that no school could keep up with the pace of learning that they demanded. "Why should our kids be brainwashed by some harried teacher who is going to lose her job when the kids don't turn in high scores on standardized tests?" By the time Julie was twelve, she was devouring Dostoevsky and Pushkin, TuFu and Lin Pao in their native tongues.

"Can I at least tell you what happened?"

"Absolutely. Absolutely." Wayne pulls Julie close.

Julie leans over the wooden railing. Rust-colored cliffs turn golden in the setting sun. She gazes out to the lighthouse. Maybe she'll find her answer in the mirrored warning lights.

"I think we reached too high."

"Why?"

"Well, we ran our first test. It was a disaster! Epic fail! It was partly my fault. I got this idea."

Wayne chuckles. "You know what Steve said?"

"Ideas are the boobie prize," Julie moans. "But he was wrong! I mean look it got our name way out there! This guy flipped an alley-oop on his surfboard. No one ever did that! It changes the game."

"Well. So what's the problem?"

"It probably wasn't the right day to publish a tweet like that. Not during a test. But all that aside, the architecture is a mess."

"Wait. Back up. Why the epic fail?"

"Well, ultimately the servers failed. It was a problem with the code. Jeff and I patched it together with MySQL. We didn't shard. We didn't cache. We thought about it, but it was going to take us twice as long. We were in a hurry to get the site up."

"OK, so that was mistake one. . ."

"And two, and three!"

"Agreed. But that's what you guys were testing for, right? The weak spots. Besides, you know the deal. 'Your work is going to fill a large part of your life, and the only way to be. . .'"

". . . Truly satisfied is to do what you believe is great work."

"Don't settle. As with all matters of the heart, you'll know when you find it." Julie and her dad quote Steve Jobs' address to the Stanford graduating class by heart. The motto was posted on the wall of the home-schooling room.

"The bummer was, Jeff and I agreed to do a rewrite after we got the site stable. But we never got it stable. We got so busy, so fast. And with the test? I know we were testing load and that's all OK, but Arthur was there. It was embarrassing."

Julie stops, listening for something beyond the surf. Wayne motions for his daughter to walk on with him but she hangs back, her narrow waist leaning against the wooden railing. Below, out past the first line of breakers, seals bark madly at a long line of pelicans swooping to skim the crest of a wave in a graceful ballet. As the sun drops toward the horizon, the light against the rocks glows orange. Julie looks up, staring at the glow on the underbelly of a seagull sailing up high. Even the edges of clouds are painted a pinky-orange. She pulls her iPhone out of her back pocket, shoots a quick frame of her dad in profile, his skin glowing the softest peach color.

For a moment, everything is luminous, liquid; gold light is painted on the clapboard beach houses, the palms, the bushes, and aloes. It's on the kids on their bikes, and TV antennas; it's reflecting off of glass windows, windshields. Everything is glowing as if it's lit up from the inside. And just as quickly as it glowed, the moment the sun dips behind the marine layer, it's gone. Grey.

"Jules. Building a startup is like jumping off a cliff and building the plane on the way down. It's hard! You were lucky that so much went right early. You know I'm so proud of you! You can fix this."

"I know. I know it's hard. But there's hard, like work hard and hard like painful hard. It's hard not to own the test as a personal failure!"

"Most projects that are worthwhile break your heart, baby. It's OK. The heart mends."

Julie's eyes well up, remembering her shame as Noah posted "epic fail."

"Well, we've got Doug. And Brett. They're going to rebuild the backend. Jeff and I are going to wire the front end to the new backend. We'll be OK. I guess."

"Well, maybe I could help some."

"So you can get a vicarious thrill?" Julie pokes her dad in the ribs, smiling for the first time in days.

"We all have our own thrills, right?"

Julie shakes her head, limps quickly down a flight of steps to the beach.

"Remember what we did when the guys didn't let you join the skate team?"

"Yeah. So?" Julie remembers when she came home in tears. The guys down at the skate shop said she was too young to join the team, but she knew it was because she was a girl.

Wayne registered her for the competition, talked to the judges himself. In the end, they relaxed the rules on age and Julie stole the show. Came in first in a field of over a hundred of the top skaters.

"So? What did we learn?"

"Don't take no for an answer."

17

Hope leads Meg and Julie to her two-seater 911 Porsche.

"Rochambeau!" Meg shoots out an index finger.

"Founder gets the front seat." Julie laughs.

"There's a news flash." Meg frowns, scrunching her arms and folding her long legs to squeeze into the tiny back seat. "Have you considered a Leaf?"

"No Leaf's for founders! You'll be driving one of these in a hot minute," Hope counters.

"Nope," Julie counters. "No Porsches, Maseratis, Alfas, Jags, Teslas, Beemers, or Mercedes for this Santa Cruz girl."

"That's what she says now . . ." Meg chimes in.

Meg, an engineer, is a new hire—a friend of Brett's from MIT.

"That's what they all say," Hope laughs, spinning the red car out of the parking lot. Pedal to the metal she beats a fast path to the freeway.

"Shit! It's one fifty," Meg moans.

Hope's Apple Watch buzzes but she ignores it. They'll be back soon enough. The giant roller coaster at Great America takes a dive and the forty-foot spinner spins.

"Megan Smith is a badass. Obama's CTO teaching all those girls to code," Meg moans. Her short brown hair flies scattershot in the wind whistling through the open window. "As if that wasn't enough, she founded Shift 7, bringing tech opportunities to underrepresented groups."

"Girl's got game," Julie says.

"I wonder what it took to get Made to Code off the ground," Meg asks.

"Hey, she was working in Google X's Moonshot lab. She had major cred," Hope informs the fangirls. "'None of us created all this bias in the world,'" Hope quotes Smith's talk with deep reverence, "'but . . . we need to debug it.' I love that!"

"It's people like Megan who gave permission to Susan Fowler for her "Whistleblower" book," Hope interjects. "We all need to keep breaking ground."

"AMEN," sing Julie and Meg.

"Totally. I just hope the perception problems—you know, how girls think coding and computer science is boring—changes," Meg says wistfully.

"It will. The girls will see people like us, and they'll know it's cool." Julie high-fives Meg.

"I just saw the *General Magic* movie. Smith was a rock star back in the 90's." Hope tells her colleagues.

"Yeah,' Julie says excitedly. "My dad knew all those General Magic people from Apple. They were so close! My dad says they had the prototype for the iPhone but ran out of money."

"And faith in what they were doing," Hope explains.

"And don't forget, Smith founded Planet Out, one of the first LGBT sites," Julie adds.

"Visionaries are not a dime a dozen," Meg muses. "Even if it isn't always the easiest path to walk."

"Well, at least it's better than a few years ago. When that gender study was done, sixty to seventy percent of all employees at Google, Facebook, and LinkedIn were male. Now, there's us." Julie posits.

"But Smith got to make new rules at Google and look where she went! CTO in the White House!" Meg enthuses.

"Starstruck, dear?" Hope asks, extending a comforting hand over the back seat.

"Aren't you? I wanna run a Made with Code program—like now," Julie says.

"We're a little busy right now, n'est-ce pas?" Hope asks. She unwraps a pack of Juicy Fruit, hands it around. "Don't wanna be walking into the Dev Ops meeting with wine breath."

"I'll start a Girls Who Code group after we sell. But Smith is right! The problem of being behind the boys starts so early," Meg complains from her supine position behind the front seat.

"Maybe in ten years, you'll be our next guru," Julie exclaims. "What I can't believe is that we had an out lesbian mom in the White House! How cool is that?"

"I just wanna know how she got that messed up Obamacare site working," Meg says. "There's her FearToShred's hero badge, right there."

"Totally!" Julie yells.

Hope merges two lanes over to the right to exit, slows the car to sixty.

"How did you start?" Meg asks Hope.

"Just a sec," Hope maneuvers the car into the right lane, back up 101 toward the office. Which horror story should she tell? The legs and parts modeling to supplement her schooling, or her chagrin at Topia when they blew it with the expensive ad campaign? Or what about Seven Arts tanking with no warning? She would have to dial it down; she doesn't want to frighten the newbie.

"Like Julie said, I was lucky. I had a role model," Hope starts. She restrains herself from cursing out of the drivers ahead; getting stuck in traffic always brings out her inner sailor. "My Aunt Lucy would load me and Dawn into her shiny silver BMW and drive us up to San Francisco for fancy lunches at the Town & Country Club."

"Never heard of it," Meg says. She angles her body sideways, a reclining Buddha.

"Town and Country? It's members only. On Union Square. We ate like proper ladies, all dressed up in our city best. Patent leathers, stockings." Hope's mouth waters remembering the sundaes with peppermint ice cream and whipped crème. Those Saturdays, Hope gave up her afternoon at the movies, or, later, cashiering at the Alpha Beta. "Aunt Lucy was a Stanford alum. Graduated Cum Laude. Hewlett Packard recruited her in the seventies. Started as a Product Assistant, then moved up the ladder to Head of Product for printers. She worked at HP for thirty years!"

"Yeow!" Meg whoops.

"She loved that company. And, she insisted that I stick it out with math. Well, my dad did too, but that's complicated." Hope remembers sitting up late with her father pouring over her first algebra problem sets.

"But at least you knew that women could have tech careers," Julie says, dreamy eyed. "That was like my dad."

"At least you West coasters had role models. We were all tracked to the Ivy League. Law, medicine, or academics. Brett was my only friend who branched out!" Meg says wistfully.

"Brett! Brett!" Julie whoops.

"You guys have been hacking that site like Tweedle Dee and Tweedle Dum," Hope jibes, punching the gear shift into third.

"I do believe that you are a little sweet on him," Julie vamps. "Maybe just a little . . ."

"But we don't mix work and play, right?" Julie shakes her finger, going all schoolmarm.

"You mean don't mix pleasure with pain?" Meg laughs.

"Which one's the pleasure and which one's the pain?" Hope asks.

"Tell us, O great one!" Meg teases.

"There's the dirty little secret that no one wants to talk about," Hope starts but quickly wishes she hadn't.

"Secret?" Meg spins around to wink at Julie.

"When your work is your passion—like ours is—heat is generated. It's like a stick and a rock—rub long enough and sparks fly, right?" Hope explains.

"Oh really?" Julie asks.

"Not always. But when there's the thrill of working on a project that really comes from your heart," Hope points at her heart. "Sparks do fly."

"The fire in the belly," Julie says. "Or somewhere in that region." Julie says. "It's primal, right? Doing what you love taps into that place where pheromones and neurons mix it up. Add money to the mix, the possibility of making a pile of it and you've got a perfect storm of drive and thrill."

"Not a bad mix to get you to work in the morning and staying late at night, right?" Hope adds.

"OK, drive and thrill that's all great, but don't you think that's what this backlash against women has been about? The brogrammers not wanting women around—because it distracts them?" Meg poses.

"I'm not sure if it distracts them or restrains them," Hope muses. "Without women around, they're back in school, in the frat house."

"Arrrggghhh," Meg moans.

"Well, that be changing!" Julie nods. "But back to that heat thing? I hear you, Hope. Even if the heat we generate isn't sexual for me, it's still heat. I see it as a mental heat—the white-hot excitement of solving the gnarliest math problem. It doesn't have to be sexual. It's a creative heat. The satisfaction of tackling insurmountable challenges and solving them. I think that's the reason we need to put protections in place—to make sure the heat doesn't get misplaced."

Hope ponders her younger colleague's stance on excitement and sexual energy at work, remembering how having a secret with Doug at Topia made going to work that much more exciting.

18

"You're late," Doug reprimands.

Ryan, Tran, Jeff, Brett, and Arthur are spread out around the table, a veritable council of FearToShred's generals.

Doug stands at attention in front of the wall sized white board.

"Wouldn't you be late if you had a chance to meet Megan Smith?" Julie quips.

"Whatev. Let's get started."

Meg and Julie settle in, flip open laptops, dispense coffee into their personal cups. Julie smiles to herself, Doug's reprimand rolling off her like rain water down a spout. Since her alley-oop tweet broke the site, they'd been written up in the *New York Times*. Unique users were up by 600,000 in just a few days. They were on their way.

Doug starts. "There's good news and bad news."

"Shit," Jeff mutters, scowling. "Why does there always have to be bad news?"

"Way of the world, friend," Doug says. "The bad news is those problems we've been having with the site falling over. Your code is on the funeral pyre. Today." Out of the corner of his eye, Doug notices Jeff staring down Julie. If she does notice, she doesn't acknowledge it.

"Replacing it with . . .?" Jeff asks.

"Not to worry," Doug answers. "So who's ever heard of the CAP theorem?" He looks around, but no one raises their hand. "Google it," he tells them. "I've been sketching out new architecture for the past week. I finalized it this morning. Have a look." Doug plugs the HDMI cable into his laptop, and an architecture diagram appears on the screen. He walks over and points at the database icon on the diagram.

"Having the MySQL database in the middle of the system is the root cause of our pain. When a contest is in progress, the database gets pounded with updates for every single vote. Meanwhile, the website is polling the database for the current status of the contest. These queries take longer and longer as the updates pile up. Eventually the website times out, but then it retries, torturing the database even more. This whole approach has got to go." Doug waits a beat. "For persistence, we're replacing MySQL with a NoSQL data store like Dynamo DB or Cassandra. This is where we'll store the historical data on contests. These databases use a model called eventual consistency, as opposed to atomic transactions. This means that updates are guaranteed to make it into the database eventually but are not required to be visible from the moment they're written. This is much more appropriate for historical data than a relational database."

Brett, Tran, Meg and Ryan nod in agreement. Ryan scribbles notes on his tablet.

"Another way of describing this consistency model is 'optimistic replication.' That was the architectural change that Twitter made years ago. If you're following someone on Twitter, it's not required that you see their latest Tweet instantly. Eventually, you'll see it. Eventually, everything is revealed." Doug takes a breath to let the new information sink in. "Our apps will write the real-time data to a Kafka message queue. Workers will dequeue the data and feed it into a Storm topology. Storm will tabulate the votes in real time. The tabulated results will be stored in a Redis cache. The website and the mobile apps will subscribe to Redis pub/sub notifications to keep their displays current." Doug cuts to the chase, delivering the harsh news quickly.

Jeff sighs audibly. So audibly that Doug sees Julie shoot him the *we're screwed* look.

"I know this is a huge change. It's a total rewrite of the core of the system. But it's the only way to scale. The only way we can handle five, let alone ten times the number of users."

Silence.

"I've put together some assignments. Each of you will be responsible for an individual component or for some aspect of the system integration. Some of you will have to come up to speed quickly on a system you're not familiar with. That's why God created Stack Overflow."

Nervous laughter.

"Jeff, you're going to set up the Cassandra ring. Brett, you'll set up Kafka. Ryan, storm. Meg, Redis. Tran, you'll work on feeding all the real-time data into the system. Julie, you'll be responsible for overall system integration, and for refactoring the apps to use the new system." Doug looks Hope's way, but she's tapping away at something or other. "What do you all think?" he asks.

"It's tight," Brett says, nodding to the group.

"We'll push the deadline back," Doug answers.

"I'll talk to Kelly," Hope offers, looking up from answering e-mails and Slack.

"We can't," Arthur says. "And that's the last word on deadlines."

Hope blanches.

"Without a strong back-end, there's no site, and without the site, no show," Brett counters.

Good try, Doug thinks, making note of Brett's attempt at diffusing the tension. Doug looks over at Hope beseechingly. Calm Arthur down, his eyes beg, *man up*. But Hope won't acknowledge him. She's wearing a fuchsia and chartreuse button-down that accents her auburn hair and hazel eyes. It's like looking at a Joseph Albers color chart. Put red next to green and the eye sees pink. The clothes are bright, but they're a ruse; Hope's face is wan, dark circles ring her eyes. Black pants hide the shape of her legs but announce their length—cattails on a still pond.

Hope jots more notes on her iPad, sips a Diet Dr. Pepper from the can.

Doug draws a message bus, explaining to the group that they'll need one to propagate user updates.

"And we'll need to push notifications, instead of polling," Ryan adds.

"Check," Brett nods.

"And an orchestration layer," Doug adds.

Hope looks up from her iPad.

"Man, this kid kills it," Doug IMs Hope on their Slack channel.

"Can you bring me up to speed on Storm?" Hope asks.

Across the room, Jeff slams a can of Red Bull, shaking his knee at rocket speed. Doug knows Jeff is being one-upped by Brett but there's no room for ego trips, not now.

"Storm was invented at Twitter. It's used to power their Trending Topics feature. It's open source. It's a scalable, distributed real time event processing system—we'll use it to count votes."

"How long will the re-write take?" Julie asks.

"Four weeks? Five at most. If we need more time, we'll have to do a hacka."

"Noooooo . . . ," Meg and Jeff moan in unison.

"Whatever it takes," Tran adds. "I'm all in."

"It's tight but I think we can make it. If we can't scale—there's no deal with TAN." Brett says.

"Let's go," Ryan packs up his laptop and Coke. "Leave a trail of genius."

"Huh?" Jeff asks.

"That's what we're doing, right? Let's put it out as a challenge," Doug eyes Brett. He had noticed Jeff's furrowed brow during the Cassandra discussion. He's sure that Brett could teach him, but only if Jeff wants to learn. Since last week, Doug has noticed Jeff's firm remove edging him toward isolation. Could he bring him back into the fold? He makes a mental note to discuss.

"Quirk: With a light bulb?" Brett chimes in.

19

"Was I dreaming or was Jeff pouting?" Hope asks. "Is it hot in here?" She pushes up her sleeves.

"Well, duh," Julie says, limping over to twist the blinds shut against the late spring sun that's been beating against the window all afternoon.

"That's the last word on deadlines? Ug. Arthur! Why?" Hope shakes her head nervously. "I'm the Product Manager here, right? If we don't have a good product—Brett is right!—we can't even think about TAN."

"You do what you need to do, girl. I'm behind you. But I do have some bad news," Julie says.

"Why is there always bad news?" Hope whines, mimicking Jeff.

"Way of the world," Julie says lightly.

Lisette passes Julie's office, nods and looks away respectfully.

Privacy is a rare commodity.

Hope and Julie high-five. Noticing the pale scars criss-crossing Hope's forearm, Julie flinches.

"And the bad news?" Hope asks, pushing her sleeves down.

"No funding for your Canada trip."

For a split second, Hope fears that "no funding" means "won't fund." Were they short of cash? Julie might know but it's probably not worth asking. No is no.

"I'll do it low rent. Forget boarding in Canada. I'll ice skate." Hope had aced ice skating in junior high, motivated by the short skirts and the pompoms. Who cared that her jacket logo read: Tri-Valley Skate Sisters? "I'll choreograph a routine. We'll make it a challenge."

"You talkin' Olympic ice dancing?" Julie asks, slipping into Santa Cruz vernacular.

"Well kind of, but less hokey. I don't exactly want to be FearToShred's product ballerina." Hope ponders herself in a short skirt—maybe minus the pom poms.

"What about a skating Wonder Woman?" Julie offers.

"No Photoshopping! Remember? Disqualifies," Hope interjects. "How about yoga? Headstand on ice skates."

Julie leans forward, her brown eyes lighting up: "Quirk: With a Santa Cap . . ."

"Headstand on an ice pond with purple tights?"

"Lift 30-pound weights while executing twizzles and mohawks?"

"Lit by tiny electric bulbs!" Hope riffs. "What I really want is to BASE jump, but. . . ."

"What? You are so not BASE jumping," Julie shakes her head. "Hey, Hope, I didn't know you were Miss Adventure!" Julie's eyes light up and she strokes her chin in admiration of this newly revealed side of Hope.

Hope extends a graceful hand, "More like Ms. Misadventure!"

"Forget it. You don't even have to skate. We don't have to go down this road."

"I told you," Hope insists, "a good Product Manager uses the product. I need to know what people love and what they don't. We'll keep it low key . . . for now." Hope winks. "But I won't tell James," Hope says, immediately regretting bringing her boyfriend into a work conversation.

"And why's that?"

"He's convinced I'm suffering another bout of PTSS."

"What's that?"

"Post traumatic startup stress."

Julie rolls her eyes.

"Yeah, he thinks I'm choosing amnesia and blanking out how frazzled I got working at the other startups. He said my cat was dying and I wasn't on top of my life when I was at Seven Arts."

"AWPUWI.

"Huh?"

"Aww, Why Put Up With It? Don't you know? Of course you want to work in a startup, Hope. It's where the action is!"

"Or the fear."

"Speaking of boyfriends," Julie raises a dark brown eyebrow, leans close to Hope. "Are you a little sweet on Wiser?"

Hope blanches. "What is this? Truth or Dare?" she cuffs Julie.

"Yeah, I'm putting out the challenge, 'work with your ex-boyfriend and see if you survive.'"

"Ex-boyfriend?"

"Hope! Hope!" Julie rests her hand on Hope's forearm. "The Valley—she is small."

20

"ENOUGH WITH the balls out challenges," Kelly scolds.

"No. We have to push it," Hope shoots back. "FearToShred is X Games. X Games are not Little League, Kelly. They're dangerous."

"We've already got one arrest. Do you want another Strava on our hands?"

"No one dies," Arthur pronounces.

Kelly upbraiding her is bad enough; in front of Arthur adds insult to injury. The Strava debacle had burnt through the tech community like a wildfire. After a cyclist died competing with another player, the company had been summarily sued.

"Strava countersued. Claimed that they weren't responsible," Hope adds.

"Still. Lawsuits cost money—no matter who wins," Arthur says.

"Alright. I'll talk to Jeff and Julie about the challenges. Still, you have to understand. We can't control what our players do. If we put out an ambiguous challenge—like 'catch air with Green Day,'—it's not our fault if people sky dive, parachute, or bungee jump in the Grand Canyon listening to 'American Idiot'."

"Mainstream it."

Kelly's tone stung. And when Arthur chimed in, *No one dies*, Hope felt as ganged up on as a fourth grader. Leaving the door open behind her, she heard Kelly ask Arthur to come down to L.A.

". . . Got extra box tickets for the Dodgers. . . . Can you and Cindy come down next weekend?"

Arthur laughed, a clubby laugh. "I'll check with my social secretary."

Hope was pissed. Kelly had been gracious enough to send a congratulatory group e mail after the alley-oop trick was written up in the *Times*, but she hadn't relented about the deadline. Clearly, Arthur had her spooked about the #fail test and the crappy code. Besides, Hope had never flown anywhere to see a ball game or anywhere that wasn't business. Who had time? No, Hope's life was definitely not Kelly's. And those Blahniks? She only wore them for the interview and the launch party; Tod's were her work shoes. Nope. Hope's life would never consist of glitzy cocktail parties, celebrity fundraisers, and baseball junkets. She was working.

✳ ✳ ✳

"Thursday, right?" Hope squeezes the three syllables through clenched teeth. Sweat drips in thin rivulets down her scalp and neck to the small, cramped canyon of her cleavage. Carlos, her trainer, hands over a dry towel.

"Not so fast, Miss Speedy! That's only forty-seven. C'mon—three more!" Hope powers through the final three crunches.

Carlos pats her soaking back. "Good work."

A thin blue-green vein runs through Carlos's left bicep. Hope stares at her trainer's muscular arms and wide chest—a terrain that she's been fantasizing exploring.

"Remember last year?" Carlos leans up against the metal sled. "Twenty-five crunches and you were crying."

"Ah, my flabby past." Hope flexes her arm in a Popeye-esque bicep curl and bows. Hazelnut-skinned Carlos is stunningly multi-cultural —Japanese mom, Argentinean dad. Hope adores him. He's her kind-hearted taskmaster.

Peeling off her wet t-shirt and bra in the locker room, Hope pinches a last inch of tenacious belly fat. By next week she should be free of these last stubborn pounds. She heads for the shower, quickly drawing the curtain closed before making eye contact with Shari, Manuserve's Accounts Payable manager. Shari is famous for igniting the grapevine. A C-list blogger, she is a take-no-prisoners snoop, asking directly about Hope's prospects, or the increase in salary she had won by job-hopping. She prides herself on having the scoop. Hope can't abide her.

Hope rubs her aching, fifty ab crunches belly, wishing she could just soap the pounds away. All at once the jet lag from three back-to-back meetups in Brooklyn, Austin and LA hits her. Sleep. She needs to sleep.

In no mood for snoopy Shari, she slips behind the curtain of the private changing area to dry off. She'll skip dinner. That should move this diet along. No more regrets! Pulling a clean t-shirt over her head, a wave of sadness shoots up her center, a hot poker of pain.

Hope scours her mind like a beachcomber with a metal detector. Shouldn't she be happy? Isn't the first month on a new job the honeymoon? The power struggle with Kelly is wearing, but she is a pro; she knows it isn't personal. Stand your ground, Richard taught her when Charlene harassed her about spending more time with her books than with the boys.

Hope perches on the edge of a wooden stool, bending over to zip up her shorty boots. Something is breaking. FearToShred is playing havoc with her schedule. She can't remember the last week she had stuck by her weekly plan.

Behind the curtain, alone in the changing room, her throat tightens. James was acting proprietary and Arthur's been distant. Maybe that's why she was sad; the men in her life were either acting like they owned her or that she didn't exist? No, that's not it. It's not the meetups, the blog, not even Jeff's negativity.

Slouched against the changing room wall, Hope resists a chokehold of sadness until tears surface from a deep well. If only the tears were for work! But no. The tears stream for her past, and worse, for her future.

Will she ever fit in? Do her dark Livermore Valley roots show? Her made-up life takes so much effort! When coworkers talked about playing rugby, or going to raves, or theater or opera, she was on guard, ready to change the conversation.—"Love those Giants!"—No one would ever suspect that she had erased the pain of her childhood, the pressure of student loans, or never having a parent at Parents' Night.

And now, Richard Ellson reappears. Was it beyond cruel to put her father off? What if his appearance is a fluke and he's just passing through town on his way—to where? Australia? China? What if she's missing an opportunity to find out why he left?

Remembering Shari just beyond the privacy curtain, she picks up a damp towel, silencing racking sobs. Leaving. Staying. Did it really matter? Work went on without you. Life went on with or without you.

Hope zips up her size six pants—she's on track for a size four any day now!—and slips into the Armani leather jacket she splurged on the day Arthur sent over her offer.

Unanswered e-mails and unwritten reports blast through her funk like multi-colored confetti shooting out of a cannon. E-mails, reports, and rallying more groups to post videos for Doug's first load test. Kelly wants a response to her revised deadline ASAP. Arthur wants the latest blog post and analytics report.

She grabs an iced tea from the club café—black, no sugar. Just the right amount of caffeine to get her through the night's work, but not enough to keep her up all night.

But back out on the road, between Redwood Shores and B Street, her enthusiasm for work evaporates like steam from a whistling kettle. Ambition, her benevolent angel, an angel with a capital "A" that has been tracking over the crown of her head, has flown the coop. Work. Fights. Burned bridges. Nasty ex-colleagues. The test. E-mails. Arthur. Kelly. Get over your fucking self, Hope. She hears Carlos, quoting Ananda, his favorite yogi, "There is no life without discipline." *OK. I'll do everything. I'll go home, and I'll write that fucking status report for Kelly.*

Waiting for the light to change, Hope's nascent resolution turns into slippery-ice she can't skate on. She hears Charlene, home after a long day at work: *Girls! You are getting on my last nerve!* And James, insisting that she tell Charlene that her father had gotten in touch. *I will*, she promised. Shit. The light turns.

Gunning the car through the intersection, her eyes blur with tears. Freaking Charlene! Could it really be that no matter where or how hard she runs, her mother will always haunt her?

And, that no matter how far she gets from that acrid Livermore Valley, no matter how far she moves up the hierarchy, the ladder, the food chain, or how much she has in the bank, she can't trust that she won't have this sudden unannounced pull, back to her past, and the memory of Charlene's denigration: "Now tell me: how are you going to afford that, Hope Ellson?" The night the acceptance from Berkeley came in the mail, Charlene turned to wash the dinner dishes. Her mother railed, *You? Up at UC Berkeley? Four years for college?* And then, under her breath: *For what? To prove you're better than me?*

Driving past the marquee on the Alhambra Theater, a Faux-Spanish revival on El Camino, she sees black two-foot high letters spelling out *I Am Love*. The words call to her like chocolate cake calls to chocoholics. *Who* is Love? And which filmmaker would have the audacity to proclaim it? Who cares? It sounds like a secret she can't wait to hear. She jerks the steering wheel into the Alhambra's spacious parking lot.

Tossing her gym bag into the trunk, her cell rings. "Doll?"

"C'est moi," Hope answers as guiltily as if she were heading for a peep show and not a fine art movie.

"Quick question. I know it's your work at home night," James says.

"Ask." Hope stands in the cooling dusk.

"The boss just handed me two tickets for the Giants tomorrow. You free?"

Hope does a mental scan of her calendar. Her evening is free, but she's got the load test this week and is behind on getting their numbers up. And there will be the work from tonight that she is ditching.

"No can do. I'm sorry. Can you ask your dad?"

"Sure," James answers, disappointed.

"I'll see you this weekend. Just let me get through this test. Every-one is stressing. Not a good time to be out of pocket."

"Got it."

Hope locks the Porsche, remembers the thumbs up *I Am Love* had won on IMDb from a notoriously cantankerous reviewer. The blog post offered up a few salient details about the actress, Tilda Swinton: "Ethereal, perfectly cast." And: "Thought-provoking treatise on money, power, beauty, and passion. A short trip to Italy for foodies and Swinton lovers."

"One, please." Hope pays her money, treats herself to popcorn—no salt, no butter—and a Diet Coke. That's better than the ice cream rink she was sure to slip on after skipping dinner.

Hope finds a seat in her favorite section—twentieth row from the front, right side aisle. While coming attractions roll, she succumbs to a popcorn-induced carb coma. Movies were an indulgence that Charlene never condoned, but for Hope and Dawn, they filled in the gaps in their education. Movies gave them a look at the world, gave them insights into history never taught in school, not to mention a model of love and romance. The sisters developed a penchant for the revivals that played a town away. They sniffled into their tissues through *Two Women*, *Life is Beautiful*, Greta Garbo in *Queen Christina*, and Katherine Hepburn in *Philadelphia Story*.

Hope shakes off her day, the locker room tears, and her obedient Girl Scout to-do list. *We'll run the test and it will be fine, or it won't. We have time.* Hope closes her eyes in the darkened theater, letting go of the sadness that had hit her like a sudden storm. She'll watch the movie and work later; it's still early. Now she is going to Italy.

The movie opens with Swinton swishing to dinner in a couture gown. Not long after a formal family dinner celebrating her industrialist husband, Swinton embarks on an affair with her son's best friend.

The movie carries her on a magic carpet of stone villas, Italian countryside landscapes, and cuisine so sublime it inspires an illicit affair. Swinton, a rarified creature with translucent skin, delicate features and a lithe body, is two-timing her devoted husband. The story hits a little close for comfort.

Maybe she hadn't betrayed Doug, but she had run away from him, a man, who, in his own way was America's version of an Italian industrialist. For wasn't tech Silicon Valley's answer to Europe's mega riches? Hadn't she also sabotaged what could have been a fruitful partnership? Doug aside, wasn't she just about to do the same thing now, with James? Wasn't she poised to run? And, again, not because she didn't love him. It was more that she worried that James' position in line for old family money was a set-up for her feeling imprisoned, claustrophobic.

Unlike Swinton, she will *not* depend on men for status. She has her own destiny, even if the way was a little blurry.

Driving away from the theater, Hope is a dolphin caught in a net. Institutionalized love. Is she staying with James because a part of her relishes the idea of being James' wife? With his family's old California wealth? Joining his family would mean a catapult up several steps of the social chain. At work, she was part of a level playing field. Show up, be smart, all good. But in a family, she would be expected to fit in, to know the inside jokes, to understand golf, and tennis and even horse racing. A woman could fake it, but Hope wasn't the "sit on the couch looking pretty" type. She craved engagement. The truth was the time she spent with James' family often left her feeling the exact opposite of cozy; it was isolating and lonely.

The movie's take-away hits her hard. Money often translates to entrapment. Fancy, glam entrapment in Swinton's case, but entrapment, nonetheless.

Hope flips on the radio. The Pagan Babies belt out *"Ella Quiere Ser Alguien Mas."*

Turning onto her darkened block, elm leaves caught by streetlights cast creepy shadows on the sides of houses and car roofs. Taking the stairs up to her apartment, Hope sinks back into the pre-movie morass. Will her life ever fall into place? Or is she destined to ride this schizophrenic cycle, spinning between two worlds—money and power, flashing lights, expensive wine and fabulous clothes, and her sad, dark inner world, the dark, lonely world of never good enough and *can't afford that.*

Swinton can afford to be a sensualist, afford to let herself fall in love with her son's best friend, because she has the time—and a misguided fantasy that she won't get caught! Hope has never had the luxury of time, or that fantasy. Sex and movies are an escape, a seductive one that she fights against, but she isn't about to give her life up for either.

She flicks on lights, sets the kettle for tea. The only person she ever could imagine a life with is Doug Wiser. Even if Doug is no master chef and she is no Swinton.

"Oh, there you are!"

Skimpy pads in, claws clicking on the kitchen floor like Swinton's heels in Rome.

"Awww . . . maybe you're the Queen, yeah?" Hope snuggles the cat's neck. What if she cheated on James like Swinton on her industrialist husband? Truth was, she could cross the line with Carlos; she's thought about it enough. If one night, they found themselves alone in the gym? And what about Doug? Working late, out for drinks with the gang. She didn't like it, but she knew she would sleep with him again —if the opportunity presented itself.

She flips on the television to escape thoughts of dangerous women and seductive men.

Is she waiting for the excitement, the thrill, even the dread she knew with Doug to kick in with James? Or is she running now, right now, idealizing Doug just when things are rough with James?

Hope slips into PJ's, finishes the report about meetups in Brooklyn, L.A. and Austin. She pounds Facebook. They need the maximum number of play-testers for the trial run tomorrow to push the site to capacity. The bedside clock flickers three A.M. Hope falls into bed. Julie's "The Valley. She is small," echoes through her mind, just before the lights go out and everything turns black.

21

"Have a sec?" Hope texts Kelly.

After a long and restless night, Hope made the decision. It was a hard one that could potentially backfire, but if she is going to deliver a great product to TAN, she has to put herself on the line.

"Give me thirty."

Hope sets her iPhone timer for twenty-five minutes and starts on the blog post that was due last week. It was a hard one to write; she wanted to spin the tech failures in a positive light. Yes, they had gone down a few times. Yes, their response rate to votes had been too slow, but they were committed, and hey, the good news is that they are growing fast. Skaters, surfers, and snow boarders have signed up in the past month from New Zealand, Fiji, Mexico, and South Africa. Their user numbers were up—not exactly the number TAN wanted, but they still had two months to deliver.

Hope scans the archives, pulling videos that hadn't won rounds but were really cool. There was a paddle boarder in Australia flirting with a small gator; a skateboarder in Uganda doing double backflip ollies with a smoking pipe taped to his jaw; a surfer catching waves in Fiji wearing a French flag as a cape, and a team in Africa, hiking up the flank of Kilimanjaro lugging the four-man bobsled in which they promised to film themselves descending.

Hope sets the blog aside. For the life of her, she can't find the words. Iterate, she promises herself. Never ship too early.

The blog was good, but it might be missing something. She'd figure it out when she was less tired. Waiting for the timer, Hope leaves her screen with the blog post to sketch out her ice rink trick. "Tight skate pants and a pink skirt. With a Santa hat? Skate three rotations around the rink, landing in a perfect headstand. Alt: do splits while wearing a crown. She'd have to see how she felt when she got to the rink. She sketches out music: Bee Gees, Snarky Puppy, The Go Ahead? Ha Ha? She wasn't sure yet if she'll go with dubstep, jazz, or indie rock.

Hope's alarm rings.

"Is it a good time?" Hope practically purrs into her polyphone.

"Yup."

Hope hears Kelly closing her office door.

"What's up?"

"A couple of things I wanted to talk about but what I'm about to tell you isn't for public consumption."

"Meaning don't tell Arthur, right?"

"Yup."

"Shoot."

Hope waits a beat. Going behind Arthur's back was tantamount to treason; it was jumping the sacred hierarchy of the company org chart. But did it ease the punishment if she were doing it for an altruistic reason?

"Well, first the good news," Hope starts, wishing she hadn't set up a paradox so soon. Maybe Kelly wouldn't see her request as bad news at all. "I mean the private part."

"Hope! Tell me already!"

"I'm taking BASE jump lessons. I'm going to do a trick that should shoot our numbers up. Oh, I'm also going to do another trick—but that one isn't as risky."

"Hope Ellson! You are not going to BASE jump! I will not have you risking life and limb."

"How the hell else are we going to get you 10x?" Hope lets fly. Shit! She never even promised Kelly 10x—why was she bringing it up now?

"Hope—10x is our goal. You know as well as I do, we'll still go with you—even if you've got 5x. Ten million users to us is gold. We'll get our hands on it, ratchet up the reality show and we're at 10x in no time. You know the game."

Hope paces her office. "I get it. You think the BASE jump is too risky. Well, I want to do it for a ton of reasons, OK? We don't have to get into all of them now, but one reason is that I'm not seeing enough women on the site."

"I hear you. Listen, I gotta go . . ."

"Before you go? I need a favor! Badly. We need an extra thirty days. We ran into some trouble with the load test . . ."

"Hope—take whatever time you need! We're here."

"Hey thanks. I really . . ."

Kelly clicks off before Hope has a chance to thank her.

22

WHAT COULD Hope possibly say to Richard Ellson? Where have you been? Why did you leave me with Charlene? Worse, *what if he has something to say to her?* What if he asks her for a loan? What if he is dying? After refusing his invitations for two weeks, she has relented.

Hunky daredevils performing life-threatening tricks on FearToShred's site was a cakewalk compared to this challenge. Hope passes the restaurant, circles the block. How different life would have been if he had stayed! How much easier to have one parent who believed in her. Every step she took she took alone. Apply to college? Sure, she'd had a college counselor, but the applications and fees were taken out of her after school waitressing job. That was actually fine.If she paid for everything herself, she wouldn't owe Charlene. But worse than being alone was the persistent doubt. Doubt about her capabilities, her aptitude, her impact. Slowly, as she became successful in school, with boys, with professors, those doubts receded, but she always worried, that if something, say a health problem, or a lost scholarship had derailed college, she would not have gotten back on track.

Now, now her father is dying. Yes, that's it. He's terminal and he wants to see her one last time to ask for her forgiveness. The question is can she give it?

By the time Hope reaches the door to *Il Fornaio* for the second time, her stomach is as tight as a clamp on a sawhorse. Hand on the door handle, she moves aside when two smartly dressed, well-coiffed women exit. *What do I owe him?* she asks herself for the hundredth time. She turns, walks in the opposite direction. Muttering, she walks one more full turn around the block. *If he is dying, do I need to know?*

"Hope!"

Richard Ellson is there in the vestibule, hugging her tightly before she can even get a good look. The familiar scent of Old Spice and his strong arms around her incite a chain reaction. Hug to heart. Heart to throat. Tears. Silent, angry tears.

"I'm so sorry, Hopi. So sorry."

Hope pulls away. She swallows the lump in her throat, dabs her eyes with her sleeve, follows Richard across the crowded, noisy restaurant. She's a duck following its mother, mindless and automatic. Richard is wan, thinner, but under the wrinkles and creases, he's still movie-star handsome.

"You look awesome, Hope. Oh, God, I've missed you! And FearToShred! What a wild ride," Richard Ellson shakes his head as if shaking himself out a dream—or was it his personal nightmare—seeing Hope after twenty years?

"Was I right?" he asks rhetorically, eyes locked on hers.

"You said it in sixth grade. I was two grade levels above the class. But now? Now I'm just a run-of-the-mill Valley girl."

After a quick shared happy-sad guffaw at the prospect of Hope as a Valley Girl as in the San Fernando Valley, not Silicon Valley, Richard's face turns stern.

"No, you are most certainly not a run-of-the-mill Valley girl!" A white jacketed waiter appears to take their order.

"Are you OK?" he asks, tenderness oozing like water from a soaked sponge.

"I am," Hope asserts. She sips the iced water. Richard's features rearrange from stern to soft. "Why?" is all she can muster.

"Why what? Why did I write to you?"

"Yeah." Hope agrees to an answer for the least of her "whys."

"I couldn't contain myself. FearToShred is getting such great press. When I saw your name in *Tech Crunch*, I preened like a peacock! You did everything! Our plan! College. An awesome job!" Richard's eyes narrow. "Should I not have?"

122

"I don't know." Hope prays for language, prays for words to articulate the elusive thoughts and feelings that won't stay put. No, you shouldn't have called. Yes! I'm totally happy to see you! But, hey, why didn't you write to Dawn? Her head feels like there is too much air or water inside, her brain unsteady in her skull. And, she's overcome by Richard's enthusiasm. The enthusiasm that is slowly melting her knots, warming her like the sun warms a cold lizard on a hot rock.

"Why now?" she asks gamely. "I've been in the news before."

Richard shakes his head. "I've thought about finding you before —only at least a million times."

Hope tries to imagine if he had called five, or even ten years earlier. He could have called her when she was in college, or at Topia, when she was running around with Doug. No. None of those times would have been the right time. In a way, he's right—she's in a good place now. Maybe he knows that, the way a parent just knows.

"What have you heard?" Hope asks.

"I've read that Fear to Shred signed a deal with TAN. And TAN thinks the partnership is epic. They called FearToShred a unicorn."

"Ahhhh." Hope wonders when the bomb is going to drop. He looks well kempt, prosperous even.

"The Valley—she is small."

Did her father just utter Julie's very words? Has she missed a meme?

"Well, we don't know that the TAN deal is going to happen . . ."

The waiter sets down a basket of bread, along with her tomato soup. Hope utters the words, realizing too late that the failed test and their vulnerable status is top secret.

"I mean, we're not sure we really want to pursue the deal with TAN. There's some internal . . . how shall I say, strife?" Hope's heart races. She spoons steaming tea, blows to cool it down, a trick that her father's sister had taught her years ago. "Blowing on soup or tea is accepted table etiquette," she instructed. "And, when you spoon soup, you scoop the spoon away. By then it's cool enough to eat. But no slurping!" At that the girls would giggle, watching their aunt's fastidious demonstration. At home, eating was a quick affair. As often as not, she and Dawn ate microwaved popcorn or franks and beans out of a can.

With their aunt, they learned the wonders of finely-chopped salads, tangy dressings, *hollandaise* on artichokes and their favorite—popovers with soft butter and strawberry jam.

"You have to pursue the deal with TAN!" Richard falls back into his old habit of imploring Hope to do something that was just beyond her comfort zone. He hasn't forgotten how to keep her hooked. "TAN's the shit! TAN will make you rich."

Hope sips tea, listening to her father speak, watching his arms fly. There are his delicate hands. There the kind eyes. There the quick smile. He loves her. He loves her as no one else loves her. He loves her unconditionally. And, he's energized by her. All he wants is the best of the best for her. Why put him on the spot? But maybe, just maybe, there's something she doesn't know. Needless to say, Charlene was a bitch to live with. He had suffered after his first firing, a rite of passage which threatened to be a career setback. But still. Richard reaches his open palm across the table, a familiar gesture. "I'm behind you. You can do this."

As much as she wants to, as much as she wants to go back to being ten years old sitting at the kitchen table and laboring over math problems with her solid, loving father, her hand holds tight to her spoon. The other clutches the butter knife.

"I didn't mean to shake you up, Hopi. I just thought . . . well, it seemed like maybe enough water had flowed under the proverbial bridge . . ."

And then her words spill, torrents out of a broken water main. "I get it. I really do. Let's say we do reconcile. I can't do that without knowing why you left." Hope's stomach turns.

"Why do you think?" Richard's face rearranges itself again. This time, he's all business.

"Charlene's a bitch?"

"Partly."

"You lost your job? You couldn't deal?" Without warning, Hope's voice turns snarky, sharp words shredding.

"It was bigger than Charlene, Hope. Or the job." Richard sips his iced tea, contemplates but doesn't touch the food on his plate.

"I'm listening."

"Charlene and I were young," Richard looks at Hope squarely. "I needed more time. But Charlene wasn't about time. When I said I needed time, she took it personally." A sneer forms around her father's lips. He stares at the table for a long time as if watching an invisible movie. For a minute, across the table, the sun slanting in at just the right angle, Hope catches something distant and unfamiliar. It's as if he, the man who calls himself her father, the person whose leaving has tormented her life, has wizened, and withered some, too. He looks less whole, fractured. His enthusiasm for seeing her doesn't match the sadness in his eyes; his smile doesn't match the troubled visage. Even his slim body doesn't match the weariness around his neck, the wrinkles around his ears.

"We were caught in a fantasy, Hope. Smooth sailing. Sex, love, kids. We had it all. The minute it cracked, Charlene had a fit."

"That's not the way she tells it." Hope looks away. She stabs at a piece of tomato-soaked bread, grateful for the warmth and comfort of the herby soup.

She wishes now that he wouldn't tell her, but she can't seem to utter two simple words—"Forget it." Why would she want to know? Why now?

"Let's skip it," Hope says, the words coming out clipped and mean. "Let's eat, and say goodbye . . ."

"No. That's not what I want, Hope. But for now? Can we talk about you?" He pats her slender hand across the table.

Her father's touch shrinks her, back, back until she *is* that little girl, listening to her dad, doing as he tells her to do. What does he want? Gory details of her love life? A recounting of her Database of Deceit? Or maybe, simply, how she's coped with Charlene these twenty years?

"Can I tell you how proud I am of you?"

"You told me."

"OK. I'll say it twice. You did everything. You followed our plan."

Hope might have followed his plan—go to college, earn a hefty salary, but her real life had been unplanned, a mess. Where was he to help her out with the lost love, the failed companies? In no mood to divulge details of the furtive relationship with Doug Wiser, the tensions with James and every other man she's known, she soaks up her father's pride like so much honey. Why not enjoy her moment? It's not like Charlene is calling her up to take her to lunch. Across the table, Richard looks to be composing a masterpiece. While he eats, his eyes are blinking in that way that Hope remembers he did when he was figuring out the answer to insanely challenging problem sets.

"You want to know what happened?"

Hope nods weakly.

Richard balances his knife and fork on his plate. His voice is quiet. "I did get fired. And I needed some time. I could get another job, that wasn't the problem. The problem was, I fell in love," Richard says. "I know this is hard for you to understand. It wasn't about you girls. I just knew that I could never satisfy your mom, never meet Charlene's expectations. And even if I did, we would never be a good couple."

Hope swallows a soft piece of bread. Absorbing the news, she wants to laugh and cry at the same time.

"Could you say that again?"

"Once I asked for some time away—just for a while to sort things out, Charlene flipped. So, I left. I found another job. And that was when I met Ellie. Ellie loved me for who I was. Not who I was going to become. Not who she wanted me to be. She loved me in that very moment—four years out of college, clawing my way through business. That was something Charlene could never do. She could never love me for who I was! She also didn't have the patience for a long climb up the ladder." Richard shakes his head as if shaking out echoes or ghosts.

Hope processes this redrafting of Ellson family history. "Why did you write to me and not Dawn?" Hope asks, painfully aware that her sister's presence could have added a dose of levity to this reunion.

Dawn never took their dad as seriously. "Less fighting," she whispered to Hope from her twin bed. "Think about it. Charlene works late. It'll be just us." Dawn was sunny, perennially optimistic. She was the type of kid to whom life was an adventure—even her dad moving out was going to be an adventure. Some adventure! All Hope could see was the dark side—no one to help with homework, no one to run interference with Charlene.

"I just wanted to see you one time on your own."

"I understand." Hope pauses. "Can you see things from my side? You left your wife, but you left us with Charlene!" Hope whispers, trying to quell the vitriol.

Richard's eyes narrow. "Being separated from you girls was the heartbreak of my life!"

Hope listens to the words, a crazy collage of images cutting through her mind in fast succession: sitting on her bedroom floor at two A.M. slicing her forearms with a razor, crying herself to sleep. The razor wasn't meant to cut through vein, or artery; it was to draw blood, draw feeling. She was numb. She cut first one way, and then the next, anything to feel something, anything to mark herself as damaged.

"It's true. I left," Richard's voice catches. "But I knew where fighting Charlene for visitation would have gotten me—big, fat lawyer bills. I knew where I stood, *persona non grata*. I called after I left. I promised her child support. 'Keep your money. Just know this, you're never going to see the girls again,' she railed. I didn't believe her. No judge would keep me from seeing you. I sent checks. They went uncashed. What could I do? I thought about coming over to see you when she wasn't home, but knowing Charlene, she'd have me arrested!"

"Oh, Dad," Hope says, exasperated, "Don't you know? Charlene is harmless—all bark and no bite!"

"Oh no, dear. She bites!"

Hope finishes the last of the soup.

"I'll be right back," Richard says, pointing at his cell. "Quick call." Getting up from the table, he rifles the top of Hope's head the way he used to when he was saying goodbye or hello, goodnight, or good morning. Hope flashes a weak smile—her first.

Everything he's said makes sense—logical sense. Charlene, the perfectionist. Charlene, the impatient. Charlene, the mixed-up bitch who thinks she's still the Sunol Valley Beauty Queen. Charlene who still doesn't want her own daughter to have a better life. All that aside, Hope can't square how her father could have stayed away all these years. The archeology of pain, the years of pent-up anger argue with logic as she tries to figure out where to land. But why does she need to land at all? Nothing has to be resolved today.

Richard returns, finishes the last bites of chicken parmigiana. Hope watches the efficient marching back and forth of service personnel, the obsequious white-jacketed waiters and their grey-suited busboys. The restaurant, with its tiled floors and windows, has reached a pitch one notch below grating.

"OK—so Charlene was a tyrant, you couldn't be yourself, but I turned eighteen fourteen years ago. Why didn't you look for me then?" Hope is on a tear by the time Richard reappears.

"I figured you hated me!"

"So why now?"

"I think eighteen and thirty-two are two different life stages, Hopi. Aren't you different now?"

"Uh, yeah."

Pulling away from *Il Fornaio,* Hope heads down El Camino toward Palo Alto. A wave of nausea engulfs her. It's like smelling diesel gas fumes when she was pregnant those two months. She didn't know why she wanted to puke every time she got stuck in traffic. This time she knows she's not pregnant. She just had her period a week ago.

She's late for a product meeting at the office, but she can dial in. Turning around at the Seven Eleven, she hightails it back to her apartment.

The visit with Richard has whipped her body chemistry into a bizarre cocktail: *Who am I? Who was I? Who am I pretending to be? And, how can I not want to see my dad?*

Her father reappearing after twenty years is like a horror movie where the villain shows up, promising that he's rehabilitated. How does she know he won't pull her in only to disappear again?

Tonight, she's going to film the trick at the ice rink. But all she wants to do is go home and lie on the couch with an ice pack on her head and a hot water bottle on her stomach.

23

JULIE FLIPS a switch. The cold, empty Sunnyvale ice rink blinks to life.

"Music?" Angie asks from the DJ platform above the rink. Julie's crowned her production assistant and gifted Angie with a black beret for her new job.

Hope checks an impulse to request a wistful country tune. She doesn't dare embarrass Julie. She dances a few cursory spins around the rink to warm up.

"Looking good, Ellson!" Angie yelps from the stands. Her voice echoes through the empty arena.

"You know you don't have to go through with this," Julie shouts, their voices overlapping.

Hope nods. "Just get those mats tight there at the far end, OK?" The plan is for Angie to get the lighting just right. Hope will skate. Hope thought about a headstand, but has been fantasizing about something with a little more pizazz.Something like a series of twizzles and a solo Choctaw. She'd done it once, but it's been eons. In seventh grade, the skating school in Danville presented her with a scholarship. And so religiously, for two years, she had taken BART to Walnut Creek, and then the bus to her lessons. It was the most fun she'd had. The most, that is, until she discovered boys.

"Wait! Your Santa cap." Julie waves the red hat to Hope from the edge of the rink like a bullfighter waving down a bull.

Hope cuts the skates to a hard stop, pulls on the tight-fitting red cap. "Props, we gotta have props." Julie high-fives Hope as she takes off.

On her fourth spin around the rink, Hope executes a back flip, the move executed as easily as riding a bike. Julie and Angie applaud enthusiastically. Hope's heart pounds. She wants to blow this out.

Another spin around the rink. All that time in the gym is paying off; her legs are strong, and her arms feel relaxed. She thinks of Carlos, his strong forearms and hands pulling her up after her fifty crunches. Did he do that with all his clients? He wasn't flirting, exactly. A curve nearly topples her. Focus, Hope.

A leap and then Hope is in a split. She has forgotten how much she loves being on ice.

She circles to slow her heart rate. "Coming in for a landing!" Hope bends, her hands make contact with the ice. The idea is to pigeon-toe her skates to come to an abrupt stop to fold into an elegant, if slippery, yogic wheel. But her hands don't stop. In a split second, she's skimming the ice, her hands fast in front of her. She's trying to keep her face from making contact with the hard surface. With a rush of will power she wills her hands off the ice. If she can stand up straight, she can avoid slamming her face onto the rink. Her hands come off the ice, but once she's upright she wobbles like a Japanese maple in a strong wind. Angie and Julie are giggling uncontrollably as Hope tries to right herself, grasping the air like a mime pulling at a rope. Righting herself has never been so hard. Her legs are moving, threatening to collapse under her.

Finally, her legs are moving in synchronicity with her arms, she's standing up and skating toward Julie and Angie. The two are snuggling at the edge of the rink.

"Was that the trick?" Julie asks, wiping away a tear. "It was pretty good."

"Oh, you mean the big mistake trick?" Hope gulps water from the bottle Julie hands her and takes off.

"Keep an eye on her." Julie points at Angie's camera. "She's full of surprises."

Across the rink, Hope cuts a straight line like a baker slicing a cake in half.

"Another backflip?" Julie muses but Angie is silent, closely tracking Hope with the camera.

Hope slows, puts her hands on the ice as she's reaching the edge of the rink and throws her legs straight up. "Ta-da!"

"Handstand on an ice rink with a Santa cap!" Julie shouts.

Wild applause echoes through the empty arena.

Breathing heavily, Hope brushes her fingers across her chest. "I didn't know I still had it!" She chugs water, sweat dampening her forehead.

Julie pats her back as she bends to unlace her skates. "Hope! You shredded it!"

Driving home, Hope resolves to tell James about the BASE jump. If she is going to move forward with him, she has to start with a clean slate. Further down the road, happiness embraces her with a lightness that has eluded her these past weeks.

The trick went well. They'll post it and it will win hits. The deadline extended now, Arthur, and TAN will get off of her case. And, she resolves to tell Doug why she left. Why not? Everyone else's dirty laundry is airing out. Meg has the hots for Brett and Jeff is frustrated and recalcitrant. Her mother doesn't think much of James, her father's crawled out of the woodwork, James wants more from her than she can give, and Arthur—well. . . . What the hell was Arthur up to anyway? Since the test he'd been MIA. She'd have to pay more attention.

After the race, she'll have a tete-a-tete with Doug. It will be healing, cleansing. It will give them a clean slate. No more lying, no more secrets. She breathes a deep, fresh breath of salty bay air. God, she loves this place. She's been lucky. Her life has carried her along. She's won, she's lost, but she's not complaining. Now it's time to make decisions. What does she want? And how to get there? She's not exactly sure just yet, but she'll think about it. No more tears, Hope! She chastises herself. It's time to ground herself in her life, put things in perspective. "The past has to stay in the past. The present is a present," Tina said.

Dusk descends as she heads up 101. Summer, dusk. They'll fix the site and launch. Maybe this time, she'll win. That would be killer. She needs a change.

24

BACKYARD PARTIES were never Hope's scene. Mariachis and tequila, totally; *piñatas* and wood smoke, not so much. The street in front of Doug's house is packed with cars. Hope parks around the corner from his charming Craftsman bungalow on Waverly. Two nights of no sleep has left her nerves jangly. Her insides feel like empty cans, metallic and crusty.

For better or worse, the site's traffic had slowed. "Let's cut back the challenges," she advised after the test. "Give ourselves a week to get stable."

It was a risky, but important move. "Our fans won't jump ship," she reassured Arthur, even though no one really knew if their fans would ditch them for the next new thing. Developers were building apps to compete head on with FearToShred fast and furiously. They might be building, Hope mused, but they didn't have Jeff and Julie and other star judges! Those two attracted fans like hummingbirds to fuchsias, ready to risk life and limb to sip from the nectar of fame.

Lawnmowers and leaf blowers whine. The ice rink trick had provided a brief respite, but since then she's been stressing about how quickly they can get the site ready for TAN. Hope starts up the steppingstone walk. Is this really where Doug lives? In a charming neighborhood, with a charming wife and a charming dog charmingly resting on the charming wraparound front porch?

"Katie's Birthday," is pasted to the wooden gate. Hope's confidence unravels like a loose stitch you tug only to find no knot on the other end. Her head is a stagnant cloud, her nervous system is maxed, and her neurons won't fire. She is tired, very tired. She hasn't had a day off in a month.

At the squeak of the gate closing, heads turn. She's an hour late and the festivities have begun in earnest. Brett, Meg, and Tran wave her over.

"It's the Ice Queen." Jeff waves his good arm cheerfully. He's got a bat ready to fling at the tissue paper piñata. That poor donkey doesn't stand a chance.

Hope cringes. The video at the ice rink had been super silly, slapstick almost, but she'd posted it anyway, complete with the near faceplant and the headstand.

"It's hilarious," Julie pushed. "People totally relate to it!" So, she'd taken one for the team.

The air is redolent with redwood and gardenia. A thick blossomheavy Cecil Bruner rose bramble climbs up the side of the one-story, wood frame house.

Across the lawn, Katie smiles politely, but only just. They had met, once, at a gig of Doug's band. Katie looks as surprised to see her now as she had the first time.

Standing next to the picnic table where the gang is assembled, Brett drains a shot glass. Ryan clinks his beer bottle with Brett; his pregnant wife sips water. An image of Brett sleeping under his desk last week crosses her mind. Curled up in his sleeping bag, he looked like a high schooler after a bender. But now, here he is, fresh-faced. Ryan, Tran, and Doug haven't fared quite as well.

Doug mans the grill, an expensive-looking monster around which wafts the scent of roasted eggplant and seared something. Fatigue screams in the angle of his shoulders. Tran rests on a lawn chair, his feet slung onto a picnic bench. Yeah, the guys have taken the hit in the last couple of weeks. The circles around Tran's eyes have gotten darker.

Hope strolls as nonchalantly as a tall woman in heels walking across a soft lawn possibly can. A tall, blond-gray haired man stands talking to Doug. Arthur?

"Hey, Hope," Doug greets her, refraining from a hug. "You remember my pal Aaron?"

"You mean, 'my coach!'" Aaron offers a strong hand.

Hope blushes, shy suddenly in Aaron's robust presence. With his thick crop of stylish hair, strong square jaw, a large, regal nose, Aaron could be a Sports Basement poster boy. Shaking his firm hand, Hope forgets to let go. Aaron's warmth is a life raft, a safe harbor. Aaron puts his two hands up, curling all his fingers except his index and middle. He levels his hands over Hope's head. "Bless you, Hope. You've saved my friend from himself."

Hope laughs. "Me? I thought that was you. The training, the running and biking."

"Oh sure. But you got him off the streets. You got him back to work."

Hope shakes her head. "I was worried I'd got him into a debacle!"

"Not from what I hear," Aaron refutes. "He's loving every fraught minute."

Doug is lost in the delicate task of turning mushy eggplant slices without losing any.

"I've got to go schmooze up the birthday girl," Aaron waves and lopes off across the lawn. "Catch you at the cake singing."

"Hey, Hope?" Doug asks, staring hard at the smoky grill. "Thanks for coming to my rescue with Kelly. That extension is really going to help us out."

"It's my job."

"Yeah, but most product people don't get it. They're too busy kissing up to the big boss. You took a risk there with Arthur."

Hope notices an empty margarita glass near the barbecue.

"Drink?" Doug hands over a long barbeque utensil in a mock-ceremonious gesture. "You know your way around a grill, right?"

"Not really," Hope wields the tool dangerously, a fencer without the mask and protective outfit. "You did tell Katie that you invited me?" Hope whispers through clenched teeth.

"Of course, I told her. Don't fret, Hopi. It's a party. We're chill-axing." Doug winks.

"Huh?" Hope fights a wave of dizziness as Doug drifts away toward the house.

134

"Be right back. Gotta get more sauce."

Examining the assemblage on the grill, Hope's altered state intensifies. There are burgers that don't smell like burgers, mushrooms the size of a small beret, and a long line of white squares resembling carpet remnants.

Hope wields the heavy spatula Samurai-style toward Jeff and Julie who lounge in a state somewhere between tipsy and asleep across the lawn. Since the epic fail, new battle lines have been drawn. Arthur and Kelly have been frighteningly silent, she and Meg are the designated cheerleaders, and the engineers have pulled up their sleeves. The past weeks they have existed in a coding coma of Red Bull and coffee, hammering away to meet TAN's deadline. All the engineers, that is, except for Jeff. Jeff simply pulled further into his own personal weather. But Jeff was Doug's problem.

The smell of burnt food alerts Hope to rearrange the searing foodstuffs toward a less fiery spot. Rumor has it that Doug had met Katie not long after he had left Topia, on a massage table. Katie is wholesome. She's got long, straight brown hair, an athletic physique, and a pert nose. Cute. That's what she is. Across the lawn, she cavorts with her pals, coos to her girlfriends' babies. Cute. Accessible. She has always pictured Doug with someone more enigmatic. But opposites attract, right?

Katie's friends are pointing at bellies and giggling. These thirty something tech wives are reproducing like bunnies around the Valley. Three fetching, yoga-strong women lounge on a circle of golden teak chairs surrounding the birthday girl. Hope steals a glance then quickly looks away. Katie's body language has shifted since she arrived. Her shoulders are hiked up and her feet are more firmly planted. The small cluster of women look in her direction. Would Katie have waited until just now to tell her friends that Hope was Doug's ex?

Doug returns, sauce in one hand, icy margarita in the other. "Your turn!" she relinquishes the spatula.

"Cheers!" Doug clicks the spatula with her glass.

Hope sips the sweet and sour drink. Her muscles relax. Another sip and she could care less about Katie and her gal pals. Near the picnic tables, Jeff, Julie, Ryan, and Tran are howling, fully awake, doubled over, watching a video on Tran's phone.

"Remember that time?" Jeff shouts. "Those high head Madonna's that Childs did?"

Hey guys! Julie points to her chest. "I'd like some cred here! At this moment, FearToShred's iconic trick is alley-oop on the wave. Am I right?"

Tran and Ryan whoop in unison. Jeff, looking at Julie with a look of consternation, appears to be pouting again.

"Shit. Guy was upside down," Jeff says.

Doug flips over the seared carpet squares. "Damn," he curses as two fall through the grate and onto the hot coals.

By the third sip, Hope is aching for sleep. Wandering from the barbeque toward a garden of raised planting beds, she reads the delicate, handwritten signs. Beet, radish, and chard.

"I was gardening before you caught me and made me go back to work," Doug is there, out of the line of sight of Katie and the teak chairs, the piñata and the picnic tables. Peppermint soap mixes with charcoal. Hope leans over the planted beds.

"You planted ranunculus?" she hums. "They're my favorite," Hope says, wistfully admiring the orange, red, white, and yellow tissue paper thin blooms.

"I knew that," Doug whispers. "They only bloom for a week or two a year . . ."

Hope leans against a damp redwood, touching her hand to the soft bark.

"So beautiful . . ." Doug whispers, brushing Hope's hair from her neck.

"Hey, Wiser!" Jeff gallops over, a margarita in his good hand, iPhone brandished in the other.

"The guys and me think it's about time we check in a little video of our own. You game?"

"You know the policy. All tweets approved by Product." Doug turns from the flower bed to the smoky grill, leaving Hope wandering through the rear of the garden and his raised vegetable beds.

"Oh, Hope won't mind, right, Hope?" Jeff shouts. "Tequila's blessing," Jeff mumbles. "No one remembers anything!" Jeff nods without a hint of guile.

"I should cut him off, right?" Doug whispers to Hope.

"Feed them."

"Right." Doug piles the grilled mushrooms, tofu, squash and eggplant onto two platters. "Grub's on!"

For a long minute Hope is lost in no man's land, the dreaded party desert. On the lawn, Katie and the ladies are splayed out on teak chaise lounges covered with thick flowered pads, huddled in an invisible bubble of marriage, yoga, and the God-given wonder of infants. Crowding the buffet, her coworkers pile paper plates with baked beans, coleslaw, grilled mystery foods and soft rolls. She doesn't have the stomach for either camp.

She should not have come today, especially after being away last weekend. Work was piling up, James was complaining about being ditched, and Dawn really wanted her to go baby furniture shopping. But when the invitation "Dodgers/Giants: Be Our Guest" hit her inbox, she leapt on it like a lion at prey. Could she finally be reinvented as someone who flew out of town for a ball game?

Opportunities had presented themselves, but she had always refused. Girlfriend's bachelorettes in New Orleans or New York, James' company boondoggles in Mexico, even the cruise with Charlene. Leaving the Bay Area upset her routine, her work rhythm. It wasn't worth it. But Kelly's invite was an offer she couldn't refuse. Besides, she and James had needed some quiet time away from family and making plans. The fact that he was a diehard Giants fan didn't hurt. But when they got to L.A. they didn't synch. Maybe Kelly's parents' apartment was so over the top, piss elegant that it had made her tense, or maybe James was distracted. Not helping matters was this sudden appearance of her father. Twenty years was a lot to catch up on, and it was bringing back a cascade of memories, good and not so good. Either way, they hadn't connected.

By the end of the weekend the highlight was another entry into her Database of Deceits. When Kelly and she went for a walk during seventh inning stretch, Kelly had caught her off-guard by planting a sloppy kiss. Forget whether this was a "me-too" issue (Kelly wasn't her boss – not really) what Hope couldn't figure out was *do girls count?*

Searching for a respite from her current party awkwardness, Hope slips unnoticed into the living room of Katie and Doug's perfect house. Through the sun-drenched shiny tiled kitchen, she does a double take. Either she's been out of the loop, or Doug's been running in different circles, because she has never seen chartreuse used in home furnishings. A circular chair filched from Pee-wee's Playhouse is paired with a wave-shaped glass table. On the table, a four-foot high lead crystal vase is filled with a dramatic spray of lavender tulips. The graceful arc of the tubular stems form the arms of a clutch of lithe ballerinas.

Past a brightly colored floor lamp shooting out red, orange, white, and blue globes like an abstract flower, Hope navigates a long hallway searching for the guest bathroom. Was the kindergarten-styled décor Doug's? Nah. Had to be Katie's idea of retro-chic.

Hope opens the coat closet. A few steps further. She peeks into an office and then a tidy room with a brass daybed. Floral wallpaper telegraphs that this is the guestroom, or a holding place for Doug's progeny. Finally, an identical, redwood door opens into a small powder room. Huzzah!

25

BACK AT the barbeque, Doug's white apron is Jackson Pollock splatter. Red brown sauce, black soy sauce, tomato sauce, and green lime juice smear "Kiss the Chef."

"Everything taste OK?" he asks each guest as he handily dishes up seconds of beans, rice, tofu, and veggies.

"Thanks, Doug," and "Good job, Wiser," from both camps.

Doug wanders toward the mom circle, kissing Katie's head and crouching to whisper in her ear.

"Come back here with that tofu!" Jeff implores.

Doug leaves the mom circle, heads back toward the shredders. "Seen Hope?" Doug asks Tran, soberest of the bunch and winner of the piñata pounding.

"I just saw her a minute ago," Tran shades his eyes to survey the yard.

The day couldn't be more perfect. The early afternoon temperature hovers between a comfortable seventy-three and seventy-six. Clear sky. Monarchs, morning cloaks, and California blues flutter around Katie's penstemon plantings. Daisy nestles next to Katie who snuggles Ethan, the two-month old baby of Celia, a Stanford classmate.

"Hey, Wiser!"

Doug spins around, trying to locate the voice. "Where?"

"Up here!"

On the side of the house, Jeff scampers over climbing rose bushes on a paint ladder, his foot just about to reach the shingled roof.

"New challenge: Free diving off roofs. Quirk: At a birthday party," Julie shouts.

Brett hovers nearby filming Jeff's antics. Doug looks over at Katie, who, handing Ethan to Celia, shoots him a *are you kidding me?* a silent scream audible only to him. Up the ladder, rung by rung, Jeff huffs.

"No one's free diving off of my roof," Doug shouts.

"Hey, big guy? What's up with the roof thing?" Aaron shouts in Jeff's direction.

"Just wanted to prove that I know how to scale."

Twenty feet below, the assembled Shred'ers smack high-fives. Jeff hollers, "Fear to shred! Fear to shred!"

"We're here! We're fed! Thanks Doug!" Jeff points two fingers, gangsta style in Doug's direction.

Doug scowls.

"Now c'mon guys, we're outta here! We're gonna play Cuervo share. We're rocking. We're rolling. We aren't going trolling through TV, or channels for Ethel and Fred—or any of those noodles. We're outta here—we're shredding fear!"

Jeff, with only one good arm, secures his footing and expertly balances on the roof.

"If you jump off my roof Jeff, you're fired!" Doug shouts.

"Don't worry. I'm coming. . . ."

Julie shouts. "Go Jeff! Go Jeff!" She camps it up on top of the picnic table. Holding the barbeque tongs as a mic she sings:

"You think you got it wired. But you got your ass fired. You're going down like the Titanic. I'm telling you, it ain't gonna be romantic! We're FearToShred—we're here, we're fed. We be going down like Mr. Steve. So, don't be getting' no ideas up yo sleeve. We're cramming. We're slamming. We're FearToShred! We're. . . ."

"Tweet for the day! Surfing," Brett yells.

"Past the break," Jeff adds. "At least quarter mile offshore."

"Quirk? With a radio!" Meg shouts.

"Half Moon Bay?" Jeff yelps a rallying cry, flying off the roof in one expert, fell swoop. Landing on his feet, he shoots up his good arm in a salute.

Across the lawn, Katie and her friends exit en masse, a frightened clutch of shorebirds.

"Shit!" Doug falls into an Adirondack chair. "What was I thinking inviting my overworked, barely-legal minions to Katie's birthday?" he moans to Aaron.

"Welcome back to start-uplandia." Aaron says.

"Thanks, Dougy! Happy Birthday, Katie!" Jeff shouts.

Before Doug has a chance to answer, *You're welcome!* FearToShred's assets clamber out the side gate.

* * *

"Hope" Doug exclaims when he discovers her slumped in a chartreuse wing chair. "Did you catch the show?"

"Sorry. I couldn't find the . . ."

"Down the hall," Doug points, the long barbeque tongs now a maestro's baton. "Hope . . . the guys . . . they're gone."

"I heard." Hope doesn't move.

Doug steps toward her. "Come outside," Doug cajoles, "Eat something."

"I was just leaving."

"Hope . . . C'mon. It's Katie's . . ."

"I can't. . . . I have to go . . ." Hope gets up, heading for the door as Doug sidles up. His arms circle her waist and he nuzzles into her hair:

"Thanks for coming," he whispers, lightly kissing her head.

"Doug?"

Hope slips out the front door, securing it tightly behind her. "Was that Hope?" Katie asks, a plate of veggies in her outstretched hand.

"Oh, yeah," Doug says. "She was under the weather, I guess. Said she felt like garbage."

"She sure didn't look like garbage."

"Right, right. Shouldn't we be outside with your pals?" Doug walks past his red-faced wife. "I came in for matches for the cake candles." Doug mumbles, heads to the kitchen, scouring miscellaneous drawers for a book of matches.

"Doug, wait." Katie slips onto the chartreuse chair.

"Found 'em! Let's go light . . ."

"Doug." Katie slumps on the chair, her wan face stricken. "What were you two doing?"

Doug steps over the threshold, clutching the matches. "Huh?"

"When I walked in, I saw you kissing her . . ."

"Wait? What? I was not kissing Hope!"

"Doug!"

Doug kneels by the couch. "Katydid. It's your birthday. Your friends are here."

Hurrying down the front walkway, Hope overhears the heated exchange. She knew she shouldn't have come today. After last weekend in L.A. her suitcase was still unpacked. And, she should not have gone to L.A. in the middle of a code overhaul—clearly the team needed her supervision.

26

AN ANGRILY buzzing phone grabs Julie out of a dream. A bee has been circling, heading straight for her exposed left arm.

"Jules?" Angie mumbles groggily, nudging her to answer.

"Problem!" Jeff 's text glows on Julie's phone, the seven-letter word looming, threatening to upend her day off, poised to ruin the motorcycle ride to Pescadero that she and Angie had planned.

"Just a sec." Julie texts. "Be right back," she whispers to the half sleeping Angie. She grabs a t-shirt, climbs out of bed. The apartment is barely illuminated by dawn's half-light. Alarmed, Julie's heart races. There must be a serious problem because not only has Jeff never texted her on a Sunday, Jeff himself is never even awake at this hour as far as she knows. Coffee. Coffee and sweatpants. Wrestling FearToShred's problems naked was not her idea of a fun challenge.

"Wassup?" she dials Jeff on FaceTime.

"It's bad."

Armed with a double cappuccino, Julie slides open the deck door.

Eucalyptus from above and rosemary from blooming bushes below perfume the morning air. Something bad could mean a downed site, or a foul video that queered their read rates. Something bad could ruin not just her day but her week. But something bad doesn't have to be shared with Angie. Not yet anyway. Julie slides the door closed behind her.

"Kid died."

"Died?" Julie exclaims.

Jeff's slightly distorted FaceTime visage crunches into a tight circle of pain, waiting for a slap, a reprimand, or at the very least, a fiery curse fest.

"Wait. How?" Julie leans over the deck railing, her stomach a tight knot. In the garden, the hot pink azalea bush blooms under a towering redwood. "What kid?"

"Well—our—no, my—tweet yesterday got going in India. A kid on his windsurfing board crashed into a container ship. I'm totally freaking, Jules. It's my fault. Oh, man I shouldn't drink tequila, I shouldn't drink tequila . . ."

"What does tequila have to do with it?"

"I didn't ask Hope, that's why! It was a rogue tweet. It made total sense! 'Windsurf past the break, with time.'"

"Calm down. This is bad, but it's not your fault." Julie pauses.

"No. In fact it is my fault." Jeff covers his face with his good hand.

"We have to tell everyone. Let's meet at the office. We should watch it together."

"Everyone?" Jeff's voice is gravelly, tired, a kid waiting for his comeuppance.

Julie slides open the deck door, a sudden desire to get away from the morning's spring beauty pulling her back into the apartment.

"How's the site?" she ventures before signing off.

"Are you kidding? Epic fail a half hour ago."

"Got it. See you in thirty."

"Gotta go," she whispers into the dark bedroom. She wills herself to get dressed, get in her car. She wills herself off the edge of panic. What did they do? "Windsurf. With time" sounded like any other tweet. Edgy but innocent. Open to interpretation.

Jeff must have telegraphed the tweet after Katie's birthday barbeque when she, Jeff, Brett, and Meg drove out to Half Moon Bay, rented a few boards and rode waves at Pigeon Point until their teeth rattled. Died. Huh. Her stomach aches. *Was it their fault?*

Slouched in her Mini Cooper, all she wants is to go back to Half Moon Bay, rent a board and paddle out past the breakers. What she wants is to hear the sea birds and watch the pelicans swoop for herring. What she wants is to be alone, bobbing on the water like a mindless, empty bottle. But what she wants is of no consequence today. Today, she is a founder. She might or might not be liable, but she is responsible.

Once out of her neighborhood, she speed-dials Hope. "Rally the troops," she says, doing away with niceties. "Problem. Someone died. I'm meeting Jeff in the office in thirty minutes."

Hope sighs audibly, mutters an agitated "I'll be there."

Entering the deserted freeway, Julie wonders if it was their fault if the winds shifted and a player was in the wrong place at the wrong time? Driving toward the office, Julie's leg goes numb, her mind stuck in paralyzed agony, a ghost pain from after the boarding accident that sent her to the hospital. The pain is a nasty, scary symptom that recurs under stress. Her mind races. Accidents happen all the time; she's seen her share in the skate parks and on the mountains. Broken shoulders, arms, ribs, fractured collarbones, legs, concussions, even a broken back. But death? Death was final.

Julie parks the Mini in FearToShred's lot next to Jeff's bike. Doug and Brett's cars are angled helter-skelter, in opposition to the white painted lines as if they had rushed to the scene of a crime. Is it the scene of a crime? Crime or not, it's Sunday. No business park patrols came around on Sunday.

"Where are you?" she texts Jeff. She slides her badge across the reader at the side door of the low-slung building.

"Muir."

Julie takes the steps to Muir conference room two at a time, her bad leg dragging, and dread baked in her stomach like a lump of clay—indigestible, distasteful, and rock hard.

"Hey." Hope looks up from her iPad.

Julie startles; she has never seen Hope without makeup. She's paler than Julie knows her to be, and her eyes are painted with dark circles.

Brett, Doug and Jeff congregate at the far end of the room, cups of coffee in hand, buried in screen data.

A pink box of Psycho Donuts and a second box of muffins are opened on the table, the sweet sugary smell mixing with the strong aroma of coffee.

Jeff is in torn jeans, faded *Thrasher* t-shirt. "Which of you saints remembered food?" Julie asks.

"Saint Hope apparently," Jeff answers, "if you call this arrangement food."

Hope is wearing black jeans, a V-necked t-shirt, and her hair is knotted up in a high ponytail.

Julie takes her place. Meg is missing, but Julie won't ask. Her coworker's somber faces remind her of her grandmother's funeral in Japan. Ashen faces, black clothes, silence. The funeral was imbued with a silence she'd never experienced before, her mother and father pulled so deeply into their private worlds that to speak to them would have been an act of treason.

Jeff looks ragged, chastened—yesterday's bravado a thing of the past.

"Shall we?" Doug asks.

"Let's wait for Arthur." Hope looks up.

"Arthur?" Jeff asks anxiously. He pounds a sugary Oreo-cookie covered donut but his eyes dart around the room like a cornered mouse. When he speaks, Julie hears a low squeak of nerves.

"He's on his way." Hope says. "Listen, Arthur doesn't know anything about yesterday. About Katie's party, about the margaritas. About you guys going to Half Moon Bay. We may want to spin this. Especially since the kid dying was the result of a rogue challenge."

"Do you mean spin the fact that Doug was the host of day drinking and the purveyor of alcohol?" Jeff asks nervously.

"Something like that," Hope answers.

"Here's the story." Julie stands, paces the length of the room. "Beautiful Saturday. Skip the barbeque. The four of us were in Half Moon Bay and decided to issue a rogue tweet. It was bad, but we were feeling naughty. Hope didn't get a chance to . . ."

"And why didn't we pass it by Hope?" Jeff asks, sugar from the donut stuck on his lips.

"We made a mistake."

Just then, Arthur arrives, consternation shadowing his tanned face. He might be CEO of a startup, but family Sundays are sacrosanct. "What's the problem?" he asks, taking a seat and reaching for a plate of fruit.

146

"Bring it up," Hope tells Doug.

Hope, Julie, Brett, Doug, Jeff and Arthur watch as the clip opens. Handsome Indian kid, twenty-something, steers his wind board off the coast. Location checked in at Goa. Turquoise waters are choppy, but the kid's arms steer the board over the waves and out of a small bay into open waters. A plastic portable radio is strapped to his back and his strong leg muscles strain against the water's push and pull. In the scratchy video the group hears the Rolling Stone's "Tiiiimmmmeee is on my side—yes it is . . . Tiiiimmmmeee is on my side . . ." from the radio. A large container ship enters the right side of the frame, but the camera remains focused on the boy. The camera wobbles as the sound of strong wind overwhelms the audio. In a split second, the boy's board veers straight at the passing ship. "Turn your board!" "Jump!" The voices on the audio are desperate. The camera narrows into the sinew of the boy's biceps, the strain of his quadriceps to veer his board. "Jump off! Jump!" The cameraman's heedless shouts are swallowed by the wind.

With a swoosh and a loud bang, the board collides with the ship, knocking the boy into the choppy water. "Get him!" And then the video goes dark.

Arthur breaks the strained silence. "Can we lose this?"

"We don't have to lose it. Site's down," Brett says.

"Epic fail," Jeff moans.

"Fuck." Arthur searches out Hope for answers. "Fucking Strava got sued by that guy who died. What was his name?"

"Kim Flint. But Strava countersued," Hope tells the group.

"But still, his family could come after us," Jeff says. His eyes are wild with fear.

"They could. But according to Legal, we are properly indemnified," Arthur says. "It's a hard call. If we reach out to the family to offer reparation, we could be faulted for admitting blame. I'll get with the lawyers today. By the way, who put this shit out? I didn't see it on Hope's weekly list of challenges."

Silence again, but different this time. Julie's armpits go damp.

"We did," Julie points at Jeff and herself.

Arthur harrumphs. "Got it. Nothing much else we can do here. I'll let you know what the lawyers advise," he announces, turning to go.

A collective sigh fills the room after his departure.

"Shit!" Jeff moans.

"We'll figure it out," Julie says.

"Or, we won't," Hope says.

"Off the topic, for a minute?" Brett says. "We can't go down like this. Epic fails are going to murder us."

"Hacka. Next week," Hope announces.

Julie swears she can see Hope's sabers rattling, an exercise that all uber Product Managers resort to eventually.

"Anyone have a good idea about how we spin this with TAN?" Julie asks.

"I'll get with Kelly," Hope says.

"And we'll get the site back up," Doug says.

Julie texts Angie: "No bike trip today sugarplum."

Julie's gaze turns toward Hope, when, out of the corner of her eye, she catches Doug, wiping away a tear.

27

"Simulation. It's the only way to familiarize yourselves with the height of the jump. The more we understand the distances, the terrain, the more comfortable we'll be when we get out there."

Hope's instructor, Scott, is a cross between a cool triathlete and an ex-Marine. Hip hairdo—longish blond, small ponytail—nice but not movie-star looks—his nose is crooked, and his lips are too thin—cool clothes—expensive jeans, Portland t-shirt—and tight bod. All business.

"We'll also work on speed, a factor you decide. I'll be right there with you on your first simulation. Next session we'll try on our suits in the warehouse and practice jumping from a high platform."

Hope sits stiffly in front of a terminal, third row back. Her avatar is poised at the precipice of a thousand-foot descent. Her fellow classmates in the BASE jump training class are young, very young. And, except for one other woman at the front of the room (Could she be a plant, Hope wonders, hired to help her feel more at ease and make the men feel like pussies if they ditch?), she is the lone representative of her gender.

"You may have heard about the recent death of a BASE jumper in Switzerland. We might as well talk about it. There have been a few unfortunate fatalities this year," Scott delivers the news flatly. "Keep in mind that these jumpers are competing. Their jumps are designed to win sponsorships. They go for the riskiest, most extreme jumps they can dream up. A beginner's BASE jump is no more dangerous than a parachute jump. Most BASE jumpers are already skilled parachute jumpers who want to push their personal envelopes. Questions?"

When Scott had asked why the group wanted to BASE jump, Hope was mum. *Personal,* she mumbled. And it was. Deep down, it was a personal challenge. FearToShred, right? Face the fear. The ice rink had shown her the lighter side of the game. Dream up a wacky challenge and show yourself failing. Everyone could relate.

But what the ice rink hadn't done was get her inside of the reality of risk. When she first came on board, the idea of working with TAN got her juiced. But now she realizes that taking a risk, a real risk, might incite real change even if it were dangerous. And, the more she considered it, the more she felt like she was paying homage to the kid who died. She knew what she was getting into with this company and now someone needed to step up and do damage control. A run of the mill BASE jump might not kill it with their numbers, but it was a clear message that they were behind their product. With Jeff's broken arm, and Julie's bum leg, she figured she was the one able-bodied person left to take the risk. It was more than taking one for the team; it was two feet in. At least it would get them back on track with TAN. Kelly had nearly canceled the contract when the kid died. If it hadn't been for Arthur's brilliant lawyers calming them down, FearToShred would have lost the deal.

Besides, she needs to break out of her personal morass; she can't keep letting Charlene haunt her, or her father disrupt her equilibrium. It was radical, but maybe with this jump she would finally learn how strong she really was, how she could rely on just herself.

With a few keystrokes, Hope's avatar is off of the ledge and aloft. Hope's VR headset holds her squarely in the scene. Her heart beats and her legs turn to Jell-O as she concentrates. Her job is to keep the ground a thousand feet below. Over faux thermals and sudden gusts and rushes of air, she guides her avatar, her stomach in knots. It's like deep sea diving from a bungee jump; it's like dying and cutting. Her stomach roils but behind her goggles, her focus is hawk-like. The ground below looks small and hard, not something she would want to meet with her feet, her shoulders, her butt or her head. Whoosh! A gust of air catches her wing and . . . she has to jostle her controls to straighten her wings.

What is she thinking? There's no way she's going to jump off that ledge, or any other ledge. Well, she came. She simulated. Enough.

Driving away from the BASE class to meet Charlene for lunch, Hope vacillates between telling James about class this morning and telling him that she was out with Dawn. Why bother? Now that she's not doing it. No news flash there. But then again, what if she decides to go ahead with it? Hope maneuvers the 911 through Sunday afternoon traffic.

Hope pulls into the Windy Hill Park and up to Mariposa Circle. The trailer door slams like a tin can behind her.

"Dominic's?" Charlene asks, closing the door and balancing herself on the metal railing. She lowers herself into the seat next to Hope like a manta ray angling through a cave.

"Again?" Hope blurts. "No, that's fine. Sorry." Hope points the car down the hill. Might as well be in place where the waiters are like old friends and Charlene has a good stiff martini in hand when Hope drops the bomb.

"How's work?" Charlene asks, fixing her lipstick.

Work? Oh, right! Which part? Hope wonders. The dead kid? The BASE jumping lessons? Or, how about the failed test? Oh, maybe the botched meetup in Brooklyn where only three people showed? Talk about all dressed up and no place to go. But any of those admissions would lead to *I told you so*. Not today. *I told you so*'s are for babies and adolescents; adults get to make mistakes in private, without their mother wagging a nasty finger.

Enrico escorts Charlene and Hope, with the fanfare owned only by an Italian, to a quiet booth in the back of the restaurant.

"There is one funny story," Hope starts, trying to lead Charlene off the scent of bad news.

Charlene nibbles on sole Meniere like a reef fish nibbles on coral. Her martini, she sips with decidedly more gusto.

"I thought that as the Product Manager, I should try out our product, so I wrote a proposal to snowboard up in Canada," Hope explains. She's tucking into her chicken parmigiana—steamed broccoli, no pasta—and sipping an excellent, deep Barolo.

"That sounds nice, dear."

Charlene is distracted, remote in an odd way. Does she sense Hope's anxiety? Hope powers through. "When I got turned down for the funds to ski in Canada, I decided to ice skate!"

"You used to be a wonderful skater!" Charlene's eyes light up.

"Key word—used to be. It was a fiasco." Hope laughs. "But it got a lot of hits! Oh, mamma! You wouldn't have believed it— wait . . ." Hope pulls the clip up, fast forwards to the downward dog where she rushed the wall, and then her quick flip to the handstand. Mother and daughter are doubled over with giggles when Enrico comes by.

"Hope, show him."

As Charlene slips out of the booth, Enrico watches the video on Hope's screen.

"Be right back," her mother says. "Little girl's room," she winks.

Hope checks her e-mail. James: "Tonight?"

There are messages from Meg, Julie, and Amanda, her new project assistant in Brooklyn. On a Sunday. Rust never sleeps. She shakes her head as Enrico delivers another glass of Barolo for her, a second martini for Charlene, and a piece of Italian cheesecake big enough for a family of four.

"Did she order that?" Hope asks.

"No. That's on the house. For your comedy show at the ice rink. Besides, I'm glad to see you two back."

If this is what she gets for the ice rink, she wonders what Enrico will deliver if she shows him a BASE-jumping clip. A bottle of 1990 Montepulciano and a two-pound Pacific lobster?

With the arrival of dessert, Hope's thinking about the jump morphs, shifts and hardens into desire. Of course, she'll go through with it. She hears Carlos reprimanding her when she wanted to quit training six months ago. "I'm busy," she told him. "No, you're not. That is just your mind taking the path of least resistance. It doesn't want a challenge; it wants to stay in its comfortable cocoon, its comfort zone. To win, we have to fight." Of course she didn't want to jump off a cliff, but now, whether it is Charlene's enthusiasm for her ice-skating talents, or a newly ignited rage at her father for never showing up, the fire is lit. She'll jump whether she wants to or not.

"It's hang gliding, but without all that nasty hardware," Scott said. "The number one fear is heights. That's what we're going to work on over the next few sessions." So what if she's scared? That's the whole idea, isn't it?

"New hairdo?" Hope compliments Charlene.

"Cut the crap," Charlene snips in a quick mood reversal. "Trouble is written across your face like the headlines of the *Examiner*. What's up?" Charlene interrogates. "Breaking up with Mr. Right? Leaving the job? Selling the condo?" Charlene takes a sip of the martini. "Mmmm . . ." Charlene chips off a tiny piece of the cheesecake. "Did you order this?"

"No. Enrico comp'd us for the video." Hope reports.

"So what is it, Hope? Pregnant?" Charlene's questions hit Hope like a spray of bullets from an AK47.

"Mom, would I be drinking two glasses of wine if I were pregnant?"

"Maybe. So what is it?" Charlene rolls her eyes.

"I'll tell you, but you have to promise . . ."

"I won't tell anyone . . ."

"No! Telling is not the problem. You have to promise not to disown me."

"Hope Ellson! What in heaven's name could you have done to have your own mother disown you? Well, maybe if you murdered someone—but even then . . ."

"MOM!"

"Spill!" Charlene sits back, her eyes fixed on her daughter like a turkey vulture searching for carrion.

Hope fiddles with her fork and knife, remembering the small house they lived in before Richard left. Echoes of the fights reverberate. "I saw Dad. He wrote to me and I saw him."

Charlene does a double take. "Wait. Hang on. What? You saw Richard Ellson? Where? When?" Charlene blanches. Even her fresh hairdo wilts with the news.

"Last week."

Charlene rearranges herself, sniffs. "And why are you telling me? Did you think I would care? Hope, you're a big girl . . ." Charlene slides out of the booth.

"Mom!"

"Listen." Charlene leans over the table, her cleavage staring Hope squarely in the face. "Hope. You are a grown woman. You want to see your fucking long lost father? That deadbeat? Count me out." Charlene turns on her heels.

Hope scurries out of booth, chasing Charlene out the door.

"Miss Ellson. I raised you. I suffered. I kept you girls in food and with a roof over your head. You want to shove that all in my face now? See Richard? Fine, but you won't see me!"

"I'm not asking you to see him! What's the difference . . . ?" Before Hope can process what is happening, Charlene is in a taxi.

Hope stands at the curb, squinting into the sun. She heads back to the table to fetch her purse. In the foyer, she pays the bill and texts Dawn.

"Can I come over? Big probs." No answer.

She speed dials James as the wind whips the hay grass on the hills coming out of the valley.

"Doll? What's up?" James was at home this afternoon, working on a tax document.

"Can you come over? I told Charlene about Dad. She hit the roof."

Hope's face is tear streaked when she pulls up to her apartment, but she doesn't bother to repair her makeup. Let James see me this way, she thinks. He wants me? Here I am.

James scans the street anxiously as she pulls up.

"Awful," Hope mumbles. "Charlene just stomped off," Hope's throat tightens. "I couldn't believe it!"

"Richard Ellson is way out of her comfort zone, Hope. Come inside," James takes her hand. "The neighbors . . ."

James leads her up the flight of concrete steps. Unlocking the door, Hope flicks on the light half expecting a ghost to jump out of a closet. Her heart feels like skin after a sunburn, blistered, exposed, and sensitive to light. Even her eyes feel raw. She turns the light off, lights a candle, a ritual that she inherited from Richard who lit candles when the kids were stuck in beds with fevers or flu. It lent an air of magic to their crummy, sweaty nights.

"Drink?" James asks, bending down to pick up Skimpy.

"Fizzy water, ok?" Hope answers, distracted. She stares at the candle flame.

How could Richard be a threat to Charlene now? If their marriage is so in the past, as Charlene insists, why did it send her running?

You're an adult, Charlene admonished. Then why was her mother acting like a four-year-old?

"Water," James offers her a cup, settles next to her with a glass of iced water. "Why didn't you tell me that you'd seen your dad?"

Hope bristles. "Why? Because my family shit is sick. Who wants to hear about single mother families and absent fathers? It was a long time ago. You're busy, I'm busy. Believe me, the last thing I want to be dealing with now is my estranged father. I've got a fucked-up site, a dead kid, and problems with TAN. Oh, and, a thorny founder and a skittish CEO." Without warning, tears flow. All the things that were good seemed to have turned on a dime. "How can everything go to shit so quickly?"

"Family is in a separate category," James rubs a hand gently across Hope's leg. "And it doesn't seem like it went south so quickly. It took time."

Hope holds his hand, waiting for the "I told you so," and how her family might be stressful, but really what's going on is that she is having another bout of PTSS.

"My heart is dark and gnarly, James. I'm not like you. My family is not the one who says, 'let's watch PGA and go for a hike after brunch, babe,'" Hope flings the insult squarely. "Seriously. My family stuff? It's Mt. St. Helens in the middle of an eruption—smoky and spewing and suffocating. It's no hike in the park, hon. It's hot lava."

"Hope? Do you think I don't know? Do you think I don't see you messed up every time you come back from seeing Charlene?"

"You do?"

"Duh. First you go dark. You're all chilly and distant. Then you act like nothing happened. I know what she does to you. I told you. I'm here for you."

"Don't make promises you might regret, sweetie pie. This could get nasty."

"Nasty?"

"Yes. And you? With your country club parents and your horse-back riding and polo? You're not equipped—that's what!" Hope regrets the diss as soon as it escapes.

James slides away. Pacing the small apartment, he's blinking like a near-sighted man trying to read a road sign two hundred yards away.

"I understand. Your family situation sucks. I get it. But can you please not tell me what I can and can't handle?"

Hope watches James pace, astonished. He's still here. He's actually talking to her in a measured, normal tone.

"Seriously. Just because my parents enjoy certain privileges you think I'm a babe in woods? Greenhorn? Naïve?"

Hope sinks into the couch.

"Honestly?" James says testily. "I don't understand you. I'm not criticizing you for seeing your long-lost dad or getting upset about your crazy mom. I just thought we were, you know? Together. People who are together don't go visit their long-lost parents and forget to report back. We're all busy, Hope. But family is important."

Hope circles her hand around her aching chest. That James has weathered her attack is impressive. That he can tolerate her meanness in this moment is a gift. Sipping the water, she tries to diffuse the anger and frustration. It's not that James' upbringing negates his ability to understand. It's that her relationship with her father is so complicated she barely knows how to talk about it. It's love and hate. It's pull and push. Part of her wants to heal things with Richard, and part of her never wants to hear his name again. Bringing James into the equation, his thoughts, his judgements, just felt like too many viewpoints to consider. So she'd gone without telling him. He deserves to be upset. It's just that she threw gas on that fire when she should have doused it. "I'm confused! Seriously. Charlene isn't a mother, she's a nuclear bomb."

"I know, Hope. I know she's untrustworthy and unpredictable and I know that must be hell for you. All I'm asking is for you to trust me."

But Hope isn't so sure. She stares at the candle searching for answers. She didn't mean to insult James but, seriously? How can she take advice from someone who grew up with an intact family? Until his grandfather died last year, he hadn't even known anyone who died. As much as she wanted to dance over to his side, their worldviews were so disparate that dancing over would mean catapulting herself over a gorge.

156

28

"I'm going away," Katie announces.

"Now?" Doug asks, even though he knows. Why shouldn't she? She's not in the middle of a launch. "Where?"

"Healing Hands," Katie says. "A weeklong retreat in Bodega Bay."

"Dr. Rose? Again?" Doug exhorts.

"Why not? I've been on the wait list for a year. Remember?"

"No, I don't," Doug answers, not winning any husband points.

"You won't even notice I'm gone!" Katie mumbles as she packs. Doug is silent.

Since the barbeque, Katie and Doug have co-existed under détente. After Katie walked into the living room just as Doug nuzzled into Hope's hair, no matter how insistently Doug asserted that he and Hope were friends, Katie was spooked. No, more than spooked. If she was just spooked, Doug could deal. He would make love to her with abandon, take her away, buy her flowers. He would be contrite, on his best behavior. But he couldn't get to her. She withdrew. Whenever he was at home, she had her head in a book or was out with a friend.

"I don't think you have much to say, Doug. Not after somehow forgetting to tell me that you are working with Hope."

"Katie. I told you. It's no big thing."

"If it was no big thang, why didn't you tell me?" Katie actually does the 'thang' dance, waving her hand in an angry "S."

Doug had considered telling Katie about working with Hope, and then reconsidered. If he didn't bring attention to it, it didn't count, right?

Doug follows Katie outside, the sight of his wife carrying her black duffel bag, bruising. Daisy pads along behind her, jumping at Katie's command. Doug turns away. No goodbyes, just the car reversing out of the driveway and around the corner.

"Dude. I can't make it." Friday is swim day and Doug had already missed two swim sessions.

Aaron is on him like a marching band at the Gay Pride parade. "Now's the time when your mind starts playing games. 'Give up!' the devilish mind shouts. You can't see your way to the finish line. That's exactly when you push harder." Aaron didn't see missing two swim days as two days—he saw it as symbolic. Doug packs his gym bag.

Diving into the cold, annoying pool, Doug performs the ritual, finishes the swim, beating his last time. Aaron was right; he feels much better. Even if there wasn't a race coming up, the swim had helped him get back into himself and away from Katie's anger.

Driving out of the parking lot of the Redwood Shores Bay Club, Doug is buoyed. He grabs a coffee and dashes out. The last few days have seen him energized and paralyzed by turns. One day, the idea of staying married to Katie forever, having kids and going the distance is a done deal, a no-brainer; other days, he's sure that he would fail as a dad. One minute, he sees himself at the finish line, having biked fifty miles, swum the bay and run the half-marathon. He's exhilarated! Relieved! The next, he's sure he'll never make it to the starting gate. At work, one day he's the hero, pulling it out like he promised Arthur and Hope. Next, he's fielding questions on social media about the rogue tweet and "#WTF FTS?"

29

"WHO'S IN?" Doug asks when he and Jeff settle at the conference table with an espresso and a Red Bull. "Ryan. Tran. Brett."

Jeff rolls his eyes.

"Good, good." Doug ignores the eye roll, but not out of managerial laziness. He ignores the eye roll because he knows Jeff feels upstaged by Brett. Why wouldn't he? And, he doesn't want to sacrifice a spring weekend for a hacka.

"And Julie," Jeff says, leaning as far back in his conference chair as the springs and wheels will allow without a complete failure of engineering. "Where is she? I thought she was with us."

"She had a thing."

Ordinarily, Doug would push back, but since Julie would be working all weekend, "a thing" could mean a parental thing, a health thing, or a girlfriend thing. He won't ask. Not this time.

"Let's call the guys," Doug instructs Jeff. "I want to review our goals." Doug's phone buzzes. "Be right back."

Doug ducks into his office.

"I'm not in school, mom," he protests. "I'm in a startup, 24/7/365."

"Just come for a few days, sweetie. Your brother will be here with the baby. You haven't even met your new nephew."

Since he'd left Wisconsin to work in Silicon Valley, his visits home had become a political football. His nephew's baby naming, a life-cycle event he couldn't get away for, has taken up permanent residence in his mother's rolodex of offenses. And, his Aunt Libby's funeral? "I'm launching a company, mom. I'll come out in the fall."

"OK. I'll wait." His mother's voice is uncharacteristically chilly.

Doug rushes back to the conference room. Brett's standing at the whiteboard: "Middleware: Storm."

Talk about stealing his thunder. But Doug doesn't mind Brett taking over. As long as the team is on board he doesn't care where the mandate comes from. *Own it*, Doug is always telling his engineers. "And bring your teddy bears. We'll be sleeping here Friday night," Doug tells the team. Packing up, Doug notices Jeff lingering.

"We're lying," Jeff starts.

"About the hackathon?"

"No. Not the hacka. The reality show."

"TAN?"

"Yup. The show is so not FearToShred—it's lying. FTS is about passion. People are IN IT. They're players, not watchers!"

"Hello?" Doug counters. "Did you miss something? Everything is a spectator sport now, right? Soccer, football, b-ball, the freaking Olympics."

"But not FTS."

"Oh, now I see!" Doug hits his forehead. "You would rather have people dying!" Doug doesn't wait for an answer or register Jeff's pallor. "Well, now we've got VC's, and let me tell you, Arthur got an earful from them after the weekend."

Jeff looks stricken.

"Jeff, let's be honest. The average person has no stomach for the hairy edge. You saw the WTF FTS after the Indian Ocean kid . . ."

"I'm not talking about the average person, Doug. I'm talking about shredders. Shredders flirt with death, Doug. It's the energy that pulls them to risk every stunt. It's sexy." Jeff says the words, *it's sexy* as if he has held them in his mind for years. "Death is sexy." He says it again, this time with the finality of a thesis.

"Death is sexy? Really?" Doug is incredulous. He turns and sits down across from Jeff at the conference table.

"Hello? NASCAR? Car crashes?" Jeff shoots back. "Sure, a kid died. And, I'm sorry but that's what happens sometimes when people take crazy-ass risks."

Doug searches Jeff's eyes. A kid died and a feeding frenzy ensued. Media hitting them for answers, bloggers in support of the site, and Arthur's tirade about putting out a rogue challenge. But there was no use in rehashing the last week. If he got stuck doing that, how the fuck would he get any work done?

Jeff stands at the door, waiting for Doug to answer. Answer what? Doug feels like this is not a conversation; it's a provocation. Besides what could he say? Could he argue that there is an invisible line that he's drawn in his own life? Walk close to it, push, but don't cross.

Fine. Even if the swim does make him nervous. Push the baby timeline. But don't wreck your marriage. Push the music, but only so far. Maybe Jeff is right. Maybe pushing harder, maybe risking more would be the element that would make FearToShred great. But death?

Sex and death. Risk, sure. Sexy athletes, totally! But death? To Doug, death is a robber, the intruder who had robbed him of his father. In Doug's world, death is beyond scary. Like the bee that stung him swimming at the lake house. Like the reaction to the bee sting that had him near to drowning. If his mother hadn't called to him from the back porch, and the Thompson kids hadn't jumped in and saved him, he wouldn't be here. Death came on sunny days, and cloudy, to the young and the middle-aged and the old. Death was fucking random. FearToShred wasn't random. It had an element of uncertainty, but random, nope. To Doug, FearToShred is quirky adventure, calculated danger. There may be an accident, a broken leg, but not death. If he's hearing correctly, in Jeff's world death is a wall to push against, a threat to tease, tempt, play with. Even if Doug could see his point, even if he could understand the appeal of NASCAR, he still isn't sure he wants to be part of that kind of game.

"Catch you tomorrow," Jeff says. "Hasta."

Seven-thirty. Time. Time is a Mobius strip. Coding, working, training. An endless ribbon of activity; iterations, pushing, perfecting. Doug heads for his car, not sure why he is leaving, or, where he is going.

Since the barbeque, his fights with Katie had crossed all boundaries; they argued over coffee, they argued in bed, they argued in e-mail and texts. Sleeping only four hours a night at best, Doug has been moving through space as if on an automatic walkway; he's moving, but only because something beneath his feet is pulling him forward.

Lake Chagrin is luminous under an early evening sky. It could be sunset, or dawn. July or October. Except for the air, scented with pine-sap and honeysuckle. Spring. Doug walks away from the office feeling as if he's leaving a girlfriend without spending the night. 'I should work with Brett on the rewrite,' he mutters. He wheels around, then thinks better of it. Giving the team independence is the first step to success.

The sky wrings the last bit of pinky-orange glow out of the sun before melting into blue.

Why go back? Brett is doing exactly what he was hired to do—tearing down the old code, replacing it with his new design, and testing the crap out of it. How Jeff and Julie got this far on flaky code is still a mystery.

Today is his day off. No training. The house is empty. This morning, he had planned an evening of peaceful solitude, but now, the idea of cooking dinner, sneaking a glass of Pinot, noodling with a few guitar riffs and watching old episodes of *The Wire* suddenly seems as appealing as a dentist appointment. He's on edge.

Is it leaving Brett with the half-finished code? Is it the bugs Brett will certainly encounter? Or is it that stupid test? Arthur's diss reverberates like a thunderclap: *We agreed on a patch job, Wiser.*

"Patch won't work," Doug insisted, but Arthur wasn't listening.

Snaking up 101 North, his head is lousy with voices: Arthur's anger, Katie's ultimatum, his mother's disappointment, Aaron's lecture on mind games. In just a couple of months since he's started at FTS, he's disappointed everyone he loves and respects.

He's cruising north when, without warning, his blood starts running in a different direction. A few bars into "Hotel California" the restlessness intensifies. *What was I thinking? Eating alone? Watching reruns? What am I? An old lady?*

The *A Game* bar is his old haunt. It was exactly far enough away from Topia that he and Hope were safe from running into co-workers, but close enough that they couldn't get too cozy. Their routine was a beer and a bite then back to Hope's place in two cars. Cool, they thought. Discreet. But now he realizes people knew. Everyone was having affairs. Jennifer and Ted. Carl and Helen. Joe and Lindsay. Sex was in the air, or in the coffee. Looking back, Doug realizes that sexual attractions were the engine that fired the company. Topia was Web 1.0—not like now with brogrammers and sexual harassment lawsuits. Topia was the result of throwing the best and the brightest into a fishbowl. No problem. We'll hold hands and we'll all get to the top.

Now, he's heading for the bar like some heat-seeking missile, even if he did pinky swear with Aaron. Aaron had warned him about alcohol after Doug bonked on a hard ride. A block from the bar, Doug speed dials Aaron. If Aaron will come over for dinner and *The Wire*, he will skip the *A Game*, turn around. He will skip whatever trouble he is heading for. "You've reached Aaron Cohen. At the tone—" Duh! It's Tuesday. Single people date on Tuesday. No need to wait until Friday to score, right? Where's my sex life? he wonders, heading for the bar.

The Giants vs. the A's plays on a big screen. The bar is packed with voluble Techies talking shop, guys meeting friends for a beer and to watch the game and a few gal pals out for a little fun. Doug orders a beer.

The A's score and the guys at the bar shout a collective Arrrggghhhhh!! He understands. Theories and sports lore abound that the team that scores highest in the first three innings is going to win. For himself, he's never been with a winning team; first, he loved the Toronto Blue Jays, then the White Sox. He'd never been able to get on board with the Giants or A's, just one of the many hazards of his relocation.

He's hungry but he's sick of eating. Veggies, fruit, nuts. By a quick calculation, he is sure that he has eaten eighty percent of the San Joaquin Valley's output.

Enough. He orders a basket of curly fries and a hot dog. On the big screen behind the bar, the game turns around as the Giants pummel the A's with a grand slam. Half an eye on the TV and half on his fries, Doug ponders Jeff walking out in a huff: *FearToShred is more than giving people vicarious thrills. That's what TAN wants, Doug. Not my scene.*

He's sipping the hoppy, cold beer, eating the curly fries—taste better than he remembers—and nibbling at the hotdog—worse than he remembers—and blissing out into his own little bubble of grease, carbohydrates, and salt. He's drifting into a TV and alcohol dream when Hope appears on TV. Well, not Hope exactly, but her doppelganger. On screen is an auburn-haired goddess with a less pretty smile, but with the same long, cattail legs. Maybe Hope has missed her calling. Should have been an anchor on TV, that is. Maybe that was why she is so hell-bent on making TAN work. Knowing Hope, she was angling for an on-air job on a local news station, or maybe even a silly gig as a game show host. Why not? How the heck did Hope Ellson end up in tech anyway?

Doug catches the bartender's eye. Another Sierra Nevada should erase Hope, right? But there she is again. There's Hope in that dress she had on the other night. That was blue also. Doug's sure it was a strategic choice; Hope was the most deliberate dresser he knew. Yeah, Hope as a game show host! That's why TAN. Duh.

Draining his second Sierra Nevada, Doug starts down a road he doesn't really want to go down. Hope. And not the Hope at Katie's birthday party, or Hope at work yesterday, and not even Hope today, but Hope when they were together. He's thinking about a time—just a few months really—when things were sailing along. A time when he was starting to think that things might work out. But he had never dated a beauty queen, or anyone like Hope before. He didn't understand the distance she kept, a distance that Doug finally understood wasn't personal, but rather a learned and necessary behavior. Still, when she disappeared, he didn't know why.

He signals to the bartender. "Tequila shot? This beer needs a chaser."

The bartender slides over the small glass of clear liquid. Why is he going down the Hope road again? He's married. Besides, there's no new information. Even when Hope showed up to recruit him, she acted so cool, like nothing unusual had happened. Like she disappeared all the time.

Katie might be angry at him, but she usually gets over it. He should go home and call her. Figure their shit out. She wants a baby? Fine. There's really no reason to put it off any longer. He searches the baseball game for a sign. If the Giants hit it out of the park, he'll go home.

Doug leaves the bar even though the game is in overtime, score tied. He leaves the noise, a few fries, and most of the hot dog. The idea of hanging out in his den, alone, watching reruns or noodling on his guitar is as far from desirable as a long swim in a cold pool. He's not sure how he morphed from "Mr. I Love My Solitude" to "Lonely Guy Watching TV," but there it is. He gets into his car, backs out slowly. Turning onto El Camino, he heads south.

30

Hope's lights are on when he pulls up to her apartment. She's not living with James, is she? He cringes. He stares blankly at a light mist falling under the streetlamps, trying to remember if she's ever said, "our place." No. He doesn't think so. What he does remember is that he forgot to post his training stats on the site yesterday. Aaron hates that. "Keeps you honest." Man, the guy rode him.

He posts today's swim time and wonders what exactly he's going to say when Hope answers the door.

"I'm here to talk?"

At the moment, idling under a rustling sycamore on a cool evening in front of Hope's apartment seems not only perfectly normal, but a good idea. He hasn't sat outside of a girl's house since he was, what? Fifteen? Except that he wasn't married then.

A chill wind blows through the open car windows. He should have called—what if she's in pajamas?—but the two Sierra Nevada's convince him that it's okay to just walk up the metal and concrete steps. Besides, it's Tuesday. Hope is always home on Tuesdays.

She opens the door revealing a mess of papers on the dining room table and classical music playing on the stereo.

"Doug Wiser."

Is he imagining it, or does she look like she's expecting him? Is this why she recruited me? To get me right here? The disturbing thought is like a wrestler's hold. Stop thinking so much Wiser. You're losing it.

"Drink?" Hope asks, heading for the kitchen. Her backside is smaller. Much smaller.

"Water," Doug follows her into the kitchen, hands stuffed in his pockets.

"Water?" Hope asks. "Where have you been?"

Doug examines his sneakers, wishing he'd worn real shoes today. Hope cares about stuff like that. "You mean tonight?" He stalls, not about to tell her that he went to their old haunt, even if, suddenly, being in Hope's apartment seems awfully sentimental and puerile. My wife's away, so I go looking for my old girlfriend! "I was just out with Anthony at Bay Bar up in San Mateo."

Hope nods, hands over a glass of water—three ice cubes, the way Doug loves it.

"Can we talk?"

"Shoot.

"I hope you don't mind that I just showed up here, Hopi," Doug blathers.

Hope looks at Doug askance, points at the club chair across from the couch where she has now settled, legs curled like a cat's.

"No worries. But first I have to show you something." Hope flips open her laptop. "These videos came in today. Jeff posted: 'Every survival kit should include a sense of humor.' We got some really crazy clips in." Hope clicks on one disaster scenario after another. Pakistan. Footage from the tsunami in Thailand and India. Mexico. Chile. Haiti.

"People are pissed!" His voice is scolding, though he knows he's shooting the messenger. In clip after clip, disaster workers flip the finger at the camera.

"You think?" Hope asks, taking no offense at his terse tone. "What the hell is Jeff trying to do? Have a sense of humor? Lame." Doug's beer-induced happiness fizzles. "Did he really not know the hackles that joining the words 'survival kit' and 'humor' would raise?"

Hope raises her eyebrows, flipping through Chilean earthquake videos, drought-ridden fields in Africa, and the tsunami in Japan.

"Does he really not think past the skate park? Is he really that shallow?" Doug posits.

Hope shakes her head.

"Did you approve that?" Doug asks rhetorically.

"Nope."

Jeff went rogue, again. In one clip, a beefy guy in a flak jacket yells, "Is this funny enough? Is Silicon Valley laughing?" Chilled, Doug reaches for the sweatshirt he had tossed over the arm of the couch when he walked in.

"Maybe Arthur is right, Hope. Maybe we should just stick with the skating tricks. Dial it down."

"Doug!" Hope jumps off the couch. "You can't tell me you don't remember us getting our lashings when we launched Topia? Good enough to criticize, remember? Headlines smoke out your detractors like bees from a hive. We're still beta testing, right?"

"I know," Doug moans, that happy beer bubble finally bursting. He's remembering the bloggers that came out of the woodwork when Topia took on expensive luxury items.

Doug frowns. "I'm not sure if it's the rewrite, or the pressure from TAN, or Jeff's antics, or the accident, but this is starting to feel dark."

Hope pets Skimpy, settled on the arm of the couch. "Dark? Really? We're trying things; we're being bold." Hope walks to the kitchen. "Besides, Dougy? It's not like you to worry."

"I'm not worried. I'm confused. I mean what would you think if Jeff told you that death is sexy? And how FearToShred is about pushing the razor edge and how sexy that is?"

"What's that about?"

"He collared me today, really bummed me out. I never saw the company that way. I signed up to build a fun site for wannabe X competitors, not the next NASCAR."

Doug hears the refrigerator open and close, metal on glass. "So, Jeff's off the wall, but the company isn't only about Jeff, right? This challenge got through the cracks—but hey it got four million hits!" Hope returns, two beers in hand.

"Brewski?" She hands him the beer, the familiar moment sparking a déjà vu.

"Why not?"

Hope hands over the beer like a reward, but for what? For showing up at her place on a Tuesday night, inebriated? For his "what's FearToShred all about rant?"

"Listen, Doug, here's the thing: We're all in love with the company. Jeff for his own wacky nihilistic reasons. You for the tech challenge. Me, Arthur, Julie, Brett. I think there's room for everyone."

"I don't," Doug shakes his head in the negative. "I'm starting to have second thoughts, Hopi."

"Now?"

"I'm not sure."

Doug sips the Lagunitas, Hope's house beer. Being alone with his ex, in her apartment at nine P.M., his mood shifts again. Being here is no longer sentimental; it's the most natural thing in the world. Hope scans more disaster videos. Suddenly, Doug's wary feelings give way, unleashing a landslide.

"But what if Jeff screws the company? What if we never get the rewrite done? I'm a hired gun. Sure, I'd like to make a killing as much as the next guy, but I always know my chances—50-50." A line of poetry pops into his head: "So much depends upon a red wheelbarrow."

"Huh?" Hope looks up from her laptop.

"Poetry. Go figure."

"You worked out today, right? No, that was yesterday."

It takes Doug a minute to catch up. Aha! His Strava update popped up on her Facebook page when he moronically checked in yesterday's workout status from his car. The fucking app has GPS! Duh!

Hope snaps the laptop shut.

Doug pries himself off the overstuffed chair. Suddenly, he's very hot. "Don't laugh. I think I have it. I think I have a way that will get Jeff over his panic that we're going vanilla with TAN."

"Like?"

"It's something between the stunt the guys pulled over the weekend and the show." Doug puts the beer down, starts pacing. "We leverage what we have to do good."

Hope sighs. "If we pivot now, we're toast. We'll never . . ."

"It's not a pivot," Doug says, though they both know that it really is. "We're going to save FearToShred's soul. We'll put out challenges that will inspire our community to greatness. Drop a dime for humanity? Don't you love it?" Doug paces, an animal energy surging. "If we could make doing good into a game—we get to capture the energy of the people obsessed with working out our dorky scenarios with flags and fake babies and fake blood and wacky tricks that gets Arthur excited because it's zany and creative. Who needs zany? Zany is so 2010. Nope. We're going for real, Hope!"

"For real?" Hope stretches her legs out from under her, wiggles her toes. She had forgotten to stretch after her workout and her feet were staging a rebellion. Her calf muscles were shouting for ice, but now didn't seem like the best moment.

"Hope. Focus. Seriously." Doug sits down on the floor next to the couch, grabs her laptop. "What's your password?"

In five minutes, Doug's hacked into the system and posted his test tweet.

"Hey, I passed it by the Product Manager, didn't I?" he jibes.

"But the Product Manager did not approve." Hope's bent over, rubbing her feet. Doug notices a new line around her mouth.

"One more thing. Then we'll drop the shop talk," Doug averts his eyes from Hope's bare feet and lovely arches.

"Fine."

"Arthur thinks Jeff's wimping out. Arthur thinks Jeff's afraid of going big. Thinks Jeff's a pantywaist. I don't agree. He just wants to save FTS for his homies. But as much as I love Jeff, I'm with Arthur on this. I think we should go big."

Hope throws her long legs over the side of the couch. "OK, let's try your idea. But don't get too pumped! Just 'cuz you're posting do-good tweets, don't assume our users are playing. Remember, I just ran around the whole country doing meetups. I'm not so sure shredders are do-gooders. Besides, FTS is uber-cool, sure, but in the end, it's just a game."

Doug listens, a dealer sorting a deck into suits. The need to make sense of what he's doing—with the company, with his life, with Katie, comes over him like a storm. He can see a whirling mass of clouds; he can smell the rain coming.

On the credenza (Since when did Hope have a credenza?) is a photo of Hope with James. They're dressed to the nines. James is handsome in that magazine sort of way—sculpted cheekbones, perfect pools of brown eyes, perfect black hair slicked back. His eyes are wide set in an exotic way, but everything else about him, pure WASP. The slicked back hair, the wide, carefree smile—all scream financial security, prep school. They look good together, actually. Kind of like they were made for one another. For a second, Doug is happy for her.

Doug turns his attention to Hope. "Forget work for a minute. How are you?"

"Me. Sort of alright, sort of weird. With Charlene. Well, not just Charlene."

Doug nods. "Tell."

Hope hugs her knees to her chest, pulls her feet up under her. "Well, out of the blue . . . no you don't want to hear this. Doug— you're all pumped about the company . . . it's distracting."

"Hope," Doug says sternly.

"OK. So, my dad . . . showed up out of nowhere. He saw an article about the company. Now he wants to reconnect. Charlene's gone AWOL."

"Really? Your dad? Like after what? Twenty years?"

"Yup."

"That's why Charlene is AWOL?"

"Yup. She said, 'If you see Richard Ellson, you won't see me.' She said that me seeing him is the ultimate diss. 'I'm the one who raised you, in case you forgot, Missy.' It's insane."

"Shit."

"The problem is I love my dad." Hope's lips quiver and a hot, giant tear escapes down her tired face. "He gets me."

"Oh, Hope," Doug bounces down onto the couch next to her. "Of course you do! You only have one . . ."

"I know he was a jerk for leaving but things are different now . . ."

"I get it."

A silent breach opens. It is a busy, vibrating silence because Doug's filled it with ideas. *I should leave. I should stop drinking*, he thinks, but for some reason, Doug can't do either. It's as if some gate has opened and he's spewing—he's not sure if it's truth or bullshit— but whatever it is, he's saying things that he's wanted to say for a long time.

"I think the do-good stuff is about me." Doug swallows a swig of beer. "I think I've been myopic. I was doing my thing; I was heads down.

Give me a problem and I'm going to fix it—and I have—to the exclusion of everything. But for what? What was I fixing? Arthur's dream? Jeff's fantasy? My bank account?"

Hope picks at sunflower seeds in a small raku fired bowl. Doug joins, munching, carefully putting the shells into a second, plain white bowl. He is working at it, maintaining a sense of decorum, or common sense, or at least the dignity of keeping some thoughts to himself, because the other question he's grappling with is: had he come on board because of Hope? Was he trying to fix some unfinished personal business at FTS?

"Questions? You always have questions, Doug. But at the end of the day—so what? We're here to fix the site, get it to TAN on time, and move on. We're not so in control, right?" Hope gets up, disappears into the bedroom. Doug slides over to the credenza thinking to get a closer look at this guy who Hope must like enough to keep in her living room, when his eye catches the glint of something sparkly. It's a small Swarovski bird, a tiny cut-crystal bauble that throws off rainbows like a Tiffany diamond. Doug knows Hope's got a thing for birds—she loves them—thinks she was one, once. *That's why I fly off all the time,* she whispered time and again.

And what kind of bird are you? A heron? A dove? A scene from their dating life comes in as clear as day. He picks up the bird. Hummer.

"What else did Jeff say that landed you in the bar?" Hope is back with a different shirt on—or did he not notice the blue V-neck?

"Jeff didn't 'land me in the bar,' remember? I was out with Anthony."

"Oh, right."

"We were going at each other about content, about danger, and then we started talking about sex and death. When he said death is sexy, I had a meltdown."

"Ah. Well, how about this? I think that in the face of death, people realize how much they love life. In that way, death juices them. It's not exactly that death itself is 'sexy' in the way we think about looking at someone we're attracted to and getting turned on, it's on another level. And most people don't hang around on that level. You forget that, Doug."

"I don't think that's what he's saying, no."

"What do you think?"

"I think he's saying that he wants to keep danger lurking, even if people die. I think he's saying death is sexy not because it makes people realize that they love life, but in a lascivious way, the way that people rubberneck car accidents. He really wants us to be NASCAR, daredevils."

"Huh."

"Right? You're being generous. Your take is life affirming. Jeff's, I think, is just dark."

Doug and Hope sit with those two opposing ideas while Skimpy crunches kibble.

Doug muses, "Maybe when death comes to you early in life, you accept it as a guest at the table. It doesn't have time to lurk outside the door. I'm just not sure that I want to invite it in."

Hope nods.

That is what he loves most about Hope. Shorthand. "Sex, death. Forget about it. It doesn't matter. If we pull this game off, and I'm sure we will, we are going to make that second part of your millions you've been waiting for." Doug catches himself, thinking that what with Hope's good luck with money, she's probably already doubled her million from Topia.

"Oh, now you're sure?"

"Yes. I crunched some numbers last night. Right now? Today?— the company could sell for eighty million. That gives you a big fat six million you didn't have yesterday. Fuck Jeff and Julie. Let's take a risk and go big. It's our chance!" Doug holds himself back from grabbing Hope for a bear hug.

"Are you sure, Doug Wiser?" she exclaims.

"I'm sure," he says, his blood running fast. If they can pull off his do-good challenges, bring Jeff back into the fold, get his founder off his obsession with sex and death they could do it. But he needs Hope on his side.

Hope is in the kitchen doorway, her eyes bright. Is it the beer or the money talk? Who cares?

"It's going to push our schedule back and Arthur's going to have to schmooze up TAN, but what else is new? Rome wasn't built in a day."

Hope grins mischievously. She's already gotten an extension from Kelly, but realizes now that she hadn't told Doug.

Doug paces. "If we can pull this off with TAN, if we get our 5x users, our stock skyrockets."

Hope does a little dance on the carpet, a cross between the twist and a break dance.

"I'm ready, Doug. In fact, I worked a little magic. I got the extension."

From the twinkle in Hope's eye and her wide smile it appears that she doesn't mind Doug's musings or his being here late on a work night. Katie, on the other hand, would have a fit if he came home smelling like a brewery.

"Here's the thing. Jeff wants to putter around in his little rarified corner, creating a cult site for fanboys. But most can't get into his rarified corner or the *Thrasher* gang. FTS is Arthur's vision. He was the one who figured out how to make it commercial."

"You're right," Hope nods. "The company got away from Jeff."

"Exactly."

They sit in the semi-dark living room, the sycamores outside rustling in the night wind. He picks up Skimpy and lifts her in front of his face with one hand.

"OK. We'll try your do-good idea."

"See if you can make it fly with Arthur. I'd better go. It's late." Doug places Skimpy on the floor next the chair. And then, Hope isn't across the room anymore, but over him, taking his face in her hands. Her long hair falls on his forehead like warm water.

The first sensation of Hope's lips on his sends his stomach through his shoes. Or is that dread sending his heart spiraling downward? You would never know by looking at them, but Hope's lips are the softest, juiciest, most kissable lips ever. She thinks they're nothing special, just like she thinks that most of her outstanding features are standard operating equipment, but someday, Doug will tell her—hers are the lips men kill for. Hope's smell and her body are familiar and unfamiliar at once—like a whisper, or a dream. She perches on the arm of the chair, leans in. Her back is more muscular, her arms thinner than he remembers. None of it matters. He loved her then and he loves her now.

Without a word, they're in her bed, a tangle of hair and arms, tongues and lips. Her bed is warm and is like sinking and being raised up from the dead. Doug is happy and sad, grieving and excited, guilty and abandoned, all at once.

Clothes stay on. Making out with the urgency of teenagers, they do not need a reminder that Doug is married, and Hope is in a committed relationship. Still, neither questions the logic of the moment. Even with clothes, they can't help it; they remember the way to pleasure. "Like riding a bike," Aaron once said about getting back with an old lover. Doug never quite understood how he could compare a woman's body to a bicycle, but he gets it now—the body remembers how far the pedals are, the angle to lean over the handlebars, how much pressure to apply.

Hope is on top of him, her eyes closed, her head back. Doug knows her body, but he never thought he would know it again. Now, he realizes that it's taken up permanent residence in his fantasy, embedded into his memory. Being in her bed is like being home and being far away—an adventure and a failure, a conquest and a surrender. Then, they are naked.

Slipping into Hope is like being in junior high school and like being old enough to die. It's wonderful and terrible, thrilling and scary, it's his fucking life going down the tubes.

After, he's not sure how he can still feel this way for Hope and love Katie the way that he does. The question hovers like plastic ribbons from a cruiser's car antenna or the tail of a kite—afterthoughts that follow him through the night, but never divert his attention. There are questions hovering, but they are questions for later, when he's alone.

At two A.M., Doug slips out of bed. Four text messages blink: 11 P.M., 12 A.M., 12:30 A.M. and 1 A.M.

He gets into his car; heads for the nearest McDonald's for a coffee.

"Are you still in the office?" he asks Brett.

"At my desk, even."

"What happened?"

"We made a code change and all the unit tests failed. We set it up so that all the engineers get paged, remember? Anyway, that was at 11:00. I took care of it."

Doug heads south. The comfort of the night falls away like a warm coat and suddenly he's cold and tired. He drives fast, suddenly frantic that he had not talked to Katie tonight.

He drives toward the office, hoping he'd remembered to leave a clean towel in his desk drawer. He'll need a shower before everyone shows up. He frowns, trying to unravel how he got into Hope's bed. Alcohol certainly, but he's had other chances. The launch party for sure, or even Katie's birthday party. Not to mention the nights they had worked late these last months. Why tonight?

Doug slides his badge, noticing the time: two A.M. He's walking up the steps, worrying about the new bugs. Heading through the fluorescent lit hallways, he winces at his own lack of fortitude. There he was, alone with Hope, talking shop. But that wasn't really why he had driven to her apartment. He had driven there to confront her once and for all. Why did you leave? But once he got there, it was as if time had collapsed and they were their old selves working at Topia. They were pals—two over-achieving, over-ambitious, over-responsible big thinkers chasing yet another dream. They were on a mission. Really, all he wanted was to be in her presence. And so, he had not ruined the moment with his whining. And when the moment rose up and they kissed—well, he certainly wasn't about to ask her then. It may have been a walk down memory lane, but it was the best walk he'd had in a while.

31

"Got a minute?" Arthur stands in Hope's office doorway looking beyond tired. His face is wan, his eyes dulled. Even his blond-grey hair looks lifeless. *Maybe this is Arthur looking worried*, Hope considers. But she really wouldn't know; she's never seen him worried.

"Sure. But I've got a date in the City tonight." Hope checks the time. "I have until six-thirty."

"Quick stop at Trinity. Promise." Arthur raises two fingers. "Scout's honor."

"Check."

"Buzz me. I'm ready when you are."

Hope wraps up her day. E-mails, texts, posting on social. Showing up in her office at five on Friday afternoon could mean one of three things. A: Wiser's do-good challenges flopped and she's to blame. B: TAN's deadline. C: He's got a new plan up his sleeve.

Doug has been in the hot seat ever since Arthur discovered his rogue tweet. "You can do anything, but not everything." The challenge had gotten some traction, but not enough to rationalize a pivot. A quick drink could give her the intelligence she needs to extract Doug out of a tight spot.

"Lobby in ten," Hope texts, turning back to the blog post she's been struggling with all day. Arthur can wait. That should level the playing field.

Downloading today's last videos, Hope gets stuck on Arthur's words. *Buzz me.* The words, issued with disarming familiarity revealed volumes about Arthur! Familiarity with your inferiors was a New York game she never learned—how to take subordinates into your confidence, make them feel . . . special. But who trusted their boss? Surely Arthur knows that "buzz me," is not her style. It's too cozy. She is a Californian; give her a wide berth.

The blog had been flooded with negative comments ever since the accident. "WTF?" and "FTS=Death" and "Dial it back guys!"

The new communities that Meg had been bringing into the fold: Burners, Makers, Mutant Fest'ers, were all checking in videos, from the sublime to the ridiculous. "Every survival kit should include a sense of humor" had gone over like gangbusters with the Burners. Even if the disaster workers shot the finger at the camera and snarled with disdain. She runs one more quick check of her mail.

MSTRBLDR: "Beer next Tuesday?"

Doug. Did meeting for a beer mean a work talk or a reprise of the other night?

Since last week, her mind had been racing on multiple tracks. Why had she made the move on Doug? What about Katie? Was she going to tell James? Most of the tracks she knew were useless obsessions, worries, and fears, but she castigated herself along the way. She knew it would be a slippery slope with Doug since she saw him at lunch last month. She was attracted to him, her shards pulled to his magnet. She always had been. Not only was Doug the only one who could take FearToShred big time, he was the epitome of stability that calmed her perennial self-doubt. Still, he was married. One of the tracks that was especially noisy was James. It wasn't fair. She certainly wouldn't like it if he was sleeping with his ex. At the same time, she hadn't made any promises. A beer next Tuesday wasn't just a beer. It was a landmine.

Visions of Topia come flooding back: Doug passing by her office at six P.M. with a box of Chinese takeout, alone in the office when he needed a sounding board, Doug arranging an off-site with hotel rooms that shared a common, interior door.

While she is rooting around for her MAC Diva, a last message pings on Hope's desktop.

NMBRCRNSHR: "Babycakes. Dinner tonight at La Folie! You dressed? It's HAUTE!"

Her boyfriend must have gotten a raise, or, he's in trouble. James never splurges on French restaurants. Did he suspect that she had slipped, and this was his way of pulling her closer? James wasn't always completely in tune.

"Tuesday . . ." she texts Doug without checking her calendar.

She'd clear it if anything interfered. Maybe she'd have the beer, or two, and finally muster the nerve to tell him why she left. But she won't sleep with him again. Coming clean with Doug would clear her conscience once and for all. She needed closure. That was yet another track that her mind ran on. Had sleeping with him been a silent apology? Either way, if she clears things up with Doug, maybe, just maybe she could move on with James.

Before Hope heads out, she checks the analytics, types a last note into the FearToShred blog: "Play Within the Play."

Digging out a compact from her purse's nether reaches, a tattered Chinese fortune from her last Chinese meal:

The tides of your life are about to turn. Can you keep a secret?

Big plans are in the making.

Hope tosses the fortune that Charlene had ceremoniously handed her into her mesh metal wastebasket. Five-twenty. She dabs on face powder, swipes on dark eyeliner pencil, and packs her laptop into the briefcase. She might be going to La Folie tonight, but Sunday was catch-up day.

"Tuesday?" James texts.

Shit. Wrong fucking thread!

"Sorry that was for Meg . . ." Hope fudges. "Pick me up at Trinity @ 6:30? I have a last-minute meeting with Arthur."

"Fine :) But . . . Meg is NUMBRCRNSHR?"

"Later," Hope signs off of the thread with James and shoots a quick word to Doug: "Tuesday." She double checks the recipient before hitting "Send."

A little extra blush, a swipe of powder. "Mmmm. . . ." She purses her lips in the reflection of the compact mirror. "Better."

"Question?" Annie, her community meetup assistant's dolphin icon pops on her text.

Hope texts back, "Tomorrow. Finished for today," immediately regretting the offer. Saturday is her sacred day off.

"Sure."

"I'll call you at 4, OK?"

Hope makes the note on her iPhone, noticing that at three, she's got a shopping date with Dawn.

Taking the steps downstairs, Hope sucks down a few deep breaths, bracing herself for Arthur. He wouldn't take the time out of his precious Friday night if something serious weren't brewing. Now, she wishes she had taken longer. Time diffuses things.

Arthur points toward his Tesla Model X. "Ride?"

"Sure," Hope checks her watch. Five-thirty. Talk fast, Arthur.

Trinity, the bar that specializes in saketinis, is packed to the rafters with VC's, startup execs and on-the-make wannabes in for that last adrenaline hit before heading home. Hope waits at a tiny table while Arthur orders drinks.

Usually when he wanted to pick her brain, or pass something by her, or criticize her for the schedule or someone's performance, he didn't request a private date. Had he gotten wind of Doug's nocturnal visit? Is he upset about Brett and Meg? Or is he on her case about Jeff nearly queering the deal with TAN?

Waiting for Arthur, she sketches out her weekend list: Speech for CrunchCon: "Games People Play" READ: *Reality is Broken* and *Trendspotting* WORK: Arrange engineering team meeting on Monday afternoon. What else had she just promised to do?

A parade of cobalt-colored pinpoint lights flickers above the bar. Hope's gaze gets caught on the bar itself, a glass top lit from inside. Colors change every ten seconds; red fades to pink; blue to green; lavender to rose, like a mood ring for a crowd. "Call Annie."

"Cheers!" Arthur hands Hope a Cosmo, sets down a Scotch for himself. She slips her phone onto the table, the alarm buzzer set for 6:26. She should have ordered Vittel water, but Arthur never asked.

"Did you see that . . . ?" Arthur points across the room. Following the arc of his arm, Hope notices the thick gold wedding band on the left hand, the Harvard ring on his right. At the end of his arm, she sees Fred, a colleague from Topia. Her heart skips a beat, her pulse quickens. Calm down, there's nothing wrong with going out for a drink with your boss.

"Who? Fred? Do you know him? I used to . . ."

"No—the sculpture of the trapeze . . ."

Hope strains to look above the cobalt light. On a thin wire, a miniature figurine perched precariously.

Arthur sips the Scotch, the color returning to his face, the light to his eyes. "Something's up."

Hope leans in. "Oh?" her voice drops an octave; it's that shaky bird.

She must have looked alarmed, because Arthur pats her arm. "Not about you. You're great."

"Good to know."

"How much time do you have?"

"Forty minutes."

"Plenty."

Forty minutes might be plenty for him, but it's close to wrecking Hope's plans. What she can't tell Arthur is that she just wiggled out of their Friday night date tradition, a drink and a quick romp before going out. She'll make it up to James this weekend.

"Kurt Balsa is interested in us."

"Kurt Balsa from YUMI? In FTS?"

"Yup."

Hope listens, her mind skidding off two simultaneous tracks. "LIKE," and, "Don't recommend." With a reputation for mindless, addictive video games, YUMI is one of the least liked gaming companies.

"Don't we have a contract with TAN?" Hope asks. There it is again, that broken bird voice. Why does it only sing with Arthur?

"Yes, there's a contract. But it's predicated on our delivering. Which at this point is a big question mark, correct?" Hope blanches. No secret there.

"Back to YUMI. The reason I'm telling you all this is not to burden you." Arthur's voice is more subdued, gentler than she's ever heard it.

"But because, even to entertain this notion, even to get our ducks in a row, we'd have to fulfill their due diligence requests. Like now."

"Now?"

"Not to worry. No one's getting married. Plenty of deals fall apart after due dil."

Hope sits back, time suddenly opening like a cavern, dark and scary. "Arthur, wait. YUMI? Seriously? Everyone hates them! Besides, Doug's team is almost finished with the rewrite. We've got Meg on Chicago, and I'm going to Austin. Our users are through the roof and The Adventure Network is behind us 100%. Why give up now?"

"It's not giving up—not at all. This is my job, create opportunities and build value."

Hope gulps the Cosmo so fast that her knees go weak. Why me? Why now? This was the part of business life that she had never gotten used to, the out of left field problems, fire drills, and emergencies. You're moving, laser focused on a goal and then, BAM! Buyers come out of the woodwork, key people quit in a huff, opportunities sprout like wildflowers after a spring rain.

"I hear you. We all want the show to come to fruition. Hey, if it's not YUMI, it will be another company. But they asked. I have to give them a chance."

Hope frowns.

"Don't worry. I've got you covered. If this works out, I've got pre-approval from the board to accelerate your vesting. You won't have to wait four years, Hope. If we can pull off a sale to YUMI, you'll be not only rich, you'll be free."

Ah, so now it isn't just due diligence. Arthur is plotting. "Detail?" Arthur trains his icy blue orbs on Hope. "I'll need your and Julie's votes."

Hope nods, the new information piling up like leaves in a fall windstorm. The data is there, all fire colored: red and orange, yellow and gold, but she's having a hard time keeping the facts in in one place. Votes, Julie, Doug, due diligence. Kelly. TAN. Hollywood. Doug. Selling out. Jeff. Doug. Meg. Kelly. Doug.

She listens as Arthur lays out a new plan for her life. How did this happen? How has she morphed from Miss Uber Product Manager into Arthur's pawn? The offer he is laying out is appealing, seductive even, but free? Free? Exactly how much money would it take her to ever really be free? Besides, is helping Arthur sell the company part of her job description? Would it be considered insubordination if she refuses?

She's listening to Arthur talk about YUMI and trying to recall, from memory, her contract.

Arthur leans in closer. "You've done a great job. But between the rewrite—which as we say, 75% ain't nothing till it's done—the team's antics last weekend, and Doug's little hack job of do-good shit . . ."

"They're just messing around. Arthur, remember? You're the CEO of a game company?" Hope wonders why he doesn't mention their uptick in numbers after the surf trick or the ink they've been getting as a result.

"True. But all games have rules."

Hope doesn't know why, but she suddenly falls into that chasm of time, headfirst, her legs flailing behind her. Damn! Why did she think that FTS was going to be different? Why did she think that she could skate through without having to manage the jockeying, the power grabs, the ego trips, and the money grubbers? What made her think that this one was going to be a cakewalk? Hope sips the Cosmo hoping to get back on track and out of the hole. It's no use. The interrogation ramps up.

Why did she even trust Arthur? It was that first meeting. His eyes, his sincerity, his dimples. Argghhh! Now he's asking her to help him sell the team out. From that first meeting, he was so smooth. So self-assured. So, so, calm. Her nerves jangle like she's just downed a double espresso. Arthur is asking her to join his team—his team of one that means betraying Doug—not to mention Jeff and Julie, Kelly and TAN.

". . . In a way that no one at FTS will know what we're doing."

"How?" Hope checks her phone. "Two minutes."

"That's where you come in." Arthur says, his usually basso timbre voice lowered conspiratorially. "Think about it over the weekend. We'll talk on Monday."

Hope's phone alarm goes off. A wave of exhaustion shudders through her body from her toes to the top of her head. I shouldn't have come. I shouldn't have come.

Wending her way through the end of the week crowd toward the front door, a memory of a particularly nasty fight between her parents floods in. There was some whispered talk about management asking Richard to do something that he didn't want to do. "I'm not their lackey," she remembers her dad shouting.

Charlene, "So what? They're paying you right?"

What is it with the Ellsons? Do we look like we're for sale?

Hope steps out into the dusky, still-warm evening. Level playing field. Who was she kidding? Arthur 1. Hope 0.

Just an hour ago, she was a thousand percent excited about FTS. Things were lining up. The rewrite, the show. Even the rogue tweets were encouraging. Except for Jeff, it seemed like everyone was on the same team. But now she feels sullied, guilty.

Why is Arthur talking to YUMI now? And why does he think that she would be such an easy mark? Acquiescing to Arthur's request to help him do the covert due diligence might mean a quick and easy payoff, but what about the team? What about the engineers? What about Doug? Her stomach does a flip, thinking of how she jumped ship at Topia and how, after hearing through the grapevine how caught off guard the company was, she promised herself that she would tie up loose ends before she left another company. She's not the type who can slip out the back. People notice her comings and goings, measure her likes and dislikes, and monitor her moods. Being high profile was the flipside of moving up the food chain. There is no place to hide.

Swiping on a fresh coat of lipstick, she catches sight of James in the new white Lexus. Jesus, she hates that car. It's as if she is already Mrs. James, two kids already strapped into the back seat. She isn't ready for a four-door, soft leather seats-bourgeois- mobile. As soon as she could afford it, she had bought her own cars; she likes them fast, agile.

Slipping into the car beside James, she kisses him with all the heat she can muster.

"And happy Friday to you too, Miss Ellson!"

Hope flips on the radio. "I'm starving!"

"Did you forget to eat lunch—again?"

"Hmmm. I think so." She takes his free hand, holds it in hers. "Shit."

"Shit what?"

"Shit, Arthur just bummed me out."

"Let's not talk about work tonight."

"Deal."

Hope relaxes into the leather upholstery, remembering some buzz around the office about Kurt Balsa from YUMI being an old friend of Arthur's. Where was that? Oh right, in an engineering meeting Jeff mentioned something to Doug about YUMI's R&D. "They know they're about to get scooped," Jeff dropped one day. How did he know that? Even Doug looked surprised.

"I'll make it worth your while," Arthur had said as he was helping her with her jacket. And how do you plan to sell the X *Games* crowd, skaters, Makers and Burners to YUMI? Hope wonders. She turns up the radio volume.

"So, was that really work, or was it a seduction?" James asks coolly.

"You turkey! You can't be jealous of that guy! He's married!"

"Married? Ha! That never stopped anyone. Ninety percent of extramarital affairs are initiated by married men." James is a statistics fanatic, a trait that carried over from his CPA training. Numbers fascinated him, gave him a framework for understanding the universe. In a flash, she realizes that Doug is one of those statistics.

Doug is a numbers guy, too, but where Doug and James part ways is that Doug is not interested in numbers to prove himself correct. He is interested in numbers as exploration, as a philosophy. James is interested in them only insofar as he can prove himself an expert. One of his favorite parlor games is quoting made-up statistics with the very same gravity as proven ones and seeing who calls his bluff.

"And 37 percent of statistics are made up on the spot," Hope blurts, "You want statistics? Here's one. How many women have you dated that were multi-millionaires?"

James shoots her a bewildered look.

"Ignore me. That drink got to me." Hope kisses his neck. "You're right. I should have had lunch."

Stepping over the threshold into the hushed *La Folie*, Hope quickly forgets work and Arthur. A sonorous violin saturates the atmosphere with gentility, romance.

Generously spaced tables are impeccably set with china, crystal wine glasses, and silver.

"Right this way." A suave, dark-haired man takes Hope's jacket, directs them to a quiet table in the back, his guttural 'r' trilled. "Mademoiselle?" He pulls out a generously upholstered chair for Hope.

Two glasses of champagne are on the table when they arrive. Friday night is date night, but not this kind of date. Her menu doesn't even have prices on it. Is she forgetting something? Is it their anniversary? His birthday? Are they celebrating a promotion? Thoughts swim in her head, a school of silvery herring, all in a great circle, and so close she can't tell one from another.

"Cheers!" James gazes at her with love, warmth, respect and seduction. There's a sparkle in his eye. James? James who didn't even read her the riot act about missing their usual Friday night pre-game? This is James, delivering her to a rarified atmosphere and champagne?

Her chest tightens, and an urge to cry begins slowly forming in her throat.

"Cheers!" She clinks her glass gently with James'.

She sips the champagne, her eyes trained on the menu that reads like poetry, but she can't concentrate for thinking of Doug, Meg, and Arthur. The strands of the people she works with—and cheats with—seem to have just been tied into a tight knot, a trick knot that she can't begin to know how to untie. Would Arthur really sell the company out from under them? Now? When they were so close?

The sparkling wine tickles her nose. She extends a long finger to stroke James' arm. Sipping the elegant, dry bubbly she prays that the gathering storm of emotions isn't the beginning of another crying jag. Because under the happy liquid, she's panicking. What if she says no to Arthur? What if she were to tell the guys? Did he really trust her that much? What if she told James?

She peers over her menu, steals a glance at her boyfriend. James looks beautiful, peaceful. Maybe he's just treating her to a night out. It's no secret she's been working double overtime.

The waiter returns, no note pad in evidence.

"Seafood ravioli and the filet, please." The hell with her diet; she hasn't been out in weeks. In fact, she doesn't think she's eaten lunch all week either. For that matter, her dress size was down to a size four. That was worth celebrating!

James is speaking, safe subjects that allow Hope space to feign full attention. He speaks in a gentle voice, and of nothing dangerous. No buyouts or hostile takeovers, no sexual improprieties, no pressure, or stress or self-doubt. He speaks about his volleyball friends, asks about training and Carlos. He asks after Dawn, her due date, and even after Charlene. She answers. She is kind, careful. They speak, looking for all the world like two happy, well-adjusted, successful, hardworking, well-dressed, well-educated lovers, out for a celebratory meal after a long week.

When the *crème brulee* arrives, Hope leans back in her chair. "Thank you so much. I really needed this." The scene of Swinton in the young chef's restaurant flashes across her mind.

"I know how hard it's been over there for you. I've been worried," James admits.

"The job I can manage. It's the politics that are killing me. Arthur against Doug, Kelly on our case, Jeff's insolence and Brett spurning Meg's affections . . ." Hope pauses, realizing that every one of these conflicts has the potential to conflate even further. As the waiter nears with after-dinner drinks, she takes a moment for herself. It's Friday. The week feels like it's been three weeks long. She realizes how emotionally spent she is from managing not just the gnarly, time bomb of a project, but her co- worker's emotional ups and downs. She pauses, holding the things that James doesn't know close, the kiss with Kelly, the night with Doug. She hears Charlene shouting at her and Dawn to keep quiet because "I haven't had a minute to think all day!" Out of nowhere, she thinks of Jeff with a tenderness she hadn't been able to summon since he'd missed the TAN announcement. She'd been too busy being angry at him. But now she realizes, that like her, Jeff is a fish out of water. Jeff may have liked the idea of getting rich, but he had no training in what it would mean to be accountable, responsible.

"I get it," James says. "You get three people in a room and there are politics."

Hope nods, grateful for his understanding, even if he doesn't know all of the details. "I'm too full for dessert," she protests, gazing at the small ramekin.

"Oh, c'mon. Just one bite. I'll share it with you."

Hope picks up a silver spoon. She digs into the pudding, tapping her spoon repeatedly on the bottom of the ceramic dish. "Isn't crème brulee smooth?" Hope slips her spoon in and stirs. She pulls out a round glob the size of a lychee. "Whaaa?"

"Here," James says, popping the nut into his mouth and then dropping something shiny into the palm of her hand. "Looks like . . . a ring?"

32

THE MORNING of the jump, Hope wakes up alone. In a lucky break, James is off golfing with his dad in Paso Robles, a long-held spring family tradition.

Since last weekend, once the first flush of James' proposal had begun to fade, Hope's ambivalence reared its ugly head, an angry sea serpent breaking the calm of a serene pond.

One minute she couldn't wait to go wedding dress shopping with Dawn, wedding dress, and veil, and shoes! Now, that was a time she could wear some Blahniks! She couldn't wait to walk down the aisle, meeting James at the end, kissing him in front of their friends and families. The next, her nerves were so jangled she broke out in a rash. James is the best! He's kind, he's thoughtful! He was going to make a great husband. Not to mention that he's very hot, a fact that caught her off guard when weighing the marriage pros and cons. In the beginning, when Celine introduced them at her engagement party, she knew she would sleep with him, if not that night, then very soon. His blue eyes and black hair were enticing, and the way he looked at her was a combination of irony and desire. He was one of those guys that was so natively smart and so worldly that he had earned the cred to look askance at anything banal, or, as Hope would come to learn, corny. But when he said he was a CPA, it was like a cold shower. A CPA was the guy stuck in some dark back office who hunched over a company's spreadsheets. Boring! She had a lot to learn. James was no number cruncher, or rather he was, but only in the largest sense. He was all about strategy and forecasting, about keeping one step ahead of economic eccentricities. Even if his job wasn't the sexiest, he won her over. Her loves had been all about the engineers, the guys who got crazy, never-created-before shit done and made it all work. But James commanded his own corner of the world, and boy, did he make it work.

Sex and thoughtfulness aside, she still had that rash. Every day, whenever she found herself with a spare minute—driving, at the gym, in the shower! She tried to parse why she was anything but joyful. Finally, last night, falling asleep, the night before her jump, she thought she just may be on the verge of understanding.

"Go like the wind. With a red flag." Julie's tweet had already been favorited and re-tweeted this morning. She alerted the BASE-jumping community, the GoPro guys. They did everything but tell Arthur.

✳ ✳ ✳

"I am now landing. Smoothly and safely. I am now landing. Smoothly and safely." Hope repeats the mantra her teacher recommended. It doesn't calm her nerves or steady her shaking knees, but it does focus her brain. Standing at the edge of the Secaucus thousand-foot cliff, Hope's past and future collide in a photo collage of should haves, could haves, might never be's. Graduating from Cal. Landing her first tech job at Topia. The affair with Doug. James. His parents. Doug in her apartment. Kelly. And, now, engaged to James. A bride-to-be. Has she lived long enough? Has she lived the life she was meant to live? Who knows? Whoever knows how long is long enough? Will she have children? A real home? Or, will she always wander, searching? Did she plan this jump to sabotage her future? If she dies, she won't have to face the hard questions. Who is Doug Wiser to her? What is money in the bank? Is James really her guy?

"Remember in the warehouse?" Scott, her field instructor breaks her reverie. "Eyes down. Focus on your landing, but don't forget to enjoy the ride. That's what you're here for, right?"

"And, to fly the flag," Ken, the cameraman, reminds her. Hope nods. Her mind commands her to back away from the edge.

She doesn't have to do this. She could walk away. The voices in her head are certainly working hard to convince her. "You are surely bat shit crazy, Miss Hope. And, Are you on a suicide mission? *The mind. She plays tricks*," Scott had lectured the last day of training. "There are few tasks that require as much discipline of mind as jumping off a cliff. BASE-jumping is not for weenies." Hope cringed. Was she a weenie? "But just in case, we're here behind you. We've got your back."

Hope sucks in a deep breath.

"Ready?" Scott's baritone is comforting. It's grounded, sure of itself. "Just in case you forget how to land," Scott chuckles, securing the headphone under her helmet.

He pats her back. "When you're ready."

Hope closes her eyes, whispers a silent prayer, quiets the voices. This isn't about sabotaging her future. It's not about suicide or crazy. This is about learning how to live.

Hope tips her body forward, opens her arms, and kicks off of the ledge. The draft of wind that lifts her feels like a hand holding her in its palm. For a moment, she adjusts her form—parallel to the earth. "Lie as flat as possible. Parallel will give you the best lift," she recalls Scott's instruction.

"Good liftoff, Hope! That's great. You've got nothing but net now girl!"

Hope trains her eyes on the dusty valley. She'll float for about a half a mile before adjusting the wings for the descent.

Whoosh of air. Hope hears the wind whistle against her helmet like the rush of a swollen river; the sound is thick and deep. It's her friend, the thing that will keep her aloft. She's learned about shear, and thermals and gusts and the ways she can get thrown off course. A hawk appears, dangerously close to her wings. She marvels at the bird's architecture, its grace.

"Relax." Scott's words echo in her headphones, and the muscles in her neck let go. The sun is warm on her back. Being up here, a thousand feet above ground is like surfing a good wave, and in a way, less scary. She's alone and it's quiet. Except for the peril of a rogue gust, she can land whenever she wants.

Alone up here, Hope thinks about randomness, about how sometimes things just happen. There are no reasons. Life unfolds. Up here, the need for answers falls away. Why did she sleep with Doug? Up here, she's enfolded into a beautiful emptiness, a quiet moment. Trees pass in a green blur below. Sparrows and bluebirds flit in and above their branches. To the west, a small pond. Trees, hillocks, even the freeway in the distance look heartbreakingly lovely. In airplanes, she always takes the aisle and never looks out of the window. The ground feels impossibly far away, but Scott's voice is near. She knows how to do this.

Hope releases the FearToShred flag just before beginning her descent.

"Looks great!" Scott's baritone in her headphone is as reassuring as a sandbar to a sinking swimmer. "Release the brake."

Hope presses on the lever that will deliver her back to solid ground.

Time speeds up as she descends, the ground now morphing from a beautiful pastiche of shapes and colors to a threatening landscape of obstacles and obstructions.

Slowly, with utmost precision, she straightens her body, feels her feet in their protective boots. Slowly, the ground comes toward her, until the last when it rises very fast. Hope hits the ground, her body taking over where her mind has gone blank. Thank god for those simulations, she thinks, once her neurons fire again, and her legs are firmly planted.

"You did it," Scott whoops, embracing her in a warm hug. She needs that hug like she never needed one before; she is shaking uncontrollably.

"Don't worry about that," her instructor says, hugging her close and walking her to the van. He wraps her in a warm blanket. "It's chilly up there at a thousand feet, yeah?"

Hope wants to tell him she didn't even feel the chill. That all she remembers is the floating sensation and how she thought that the whole jump was worth everything just to feel herself suspended, and yet held by the air. She wants to tell him that at first, she wanted to close her eyes, but forced herself to stay alert.

"Thank you so much." She shakes Scott's hand when he drops her back at her parked car.

"Stay cool," he says. "By the way, your clip already has a hundred thousand hits."

33

"I'VE SEEN this movie before." Doug strips off his sweatshirt and heads into the woods. "In fact, I wrote the script."

"You mean *Night of the Living Dead*?" Aaron quips. "Cuz you be looking like shit, Wiser."

"Something like that. We got snagged at the part where we had to go two steps back. So what? Why did Arthur throw a fit?" Doug shivers, shaking off a pre-dawn chill. Grey brightens to blue as the sun peeks out from just below a dense fog bank hugging the horizon. The forest floor is damp with night dew dripping from low-hanging redwood branches. A raspy jay gives a call, then another.

"Pick it up, Madame!" Aaron bellows.

Doug is bumming. Today is the first Saturday morning in over two weeks that he could have slept in, and Aaron has him in the woods at seven.

"From what I can see, Arthur's bet the farm on FTS," Aaron huffs.

They head up the first small hill of their ten-mile training route. The fog breaks up, revealing puzzle pieces of clear blue sky. Doug breathes, the cool air icing his throat.

"Maybe not the farm, but his reputation," Doug snips.

Aaron a few steps ahead, Doug takes advantage of the lapse in conversation to go over the failed test one more time. *Can't you guys just find the bugs and fix them?* Arthur excoriated. Does Arthur really believe we can build a world-class service from scratch under extreme time pressure and not have a few hiccups? Doug fumes. The sun edges up, peeking out now from just behind the trees.

Doug huffs as they hit a level stretch, "I'm not sure Arthur has a farm to bet. Since his last company tanked, he's been a working stiff. A salary man."

"C'mon, Daisy!" Aaron calls.

Daisy sprints up, heels to Aaron, the picture of perfect canine behavior. Doug's legs feel strong, less achy and stiff. He's running in synch with Aaron, his lungs wide open to the cedar-scented air.

"I wanted to do a little independent research," Doug huffs, picking the work thread back up, the breath from his mouth forming a small cloud. "Sent out a few do-good challenges. I went rogue. I thought I was on to something cool. . . . But Arthur's pissed."

"Independent research? Now? When you're so close to the race? You missed two workouts this week."

Doug ignores Aaron's question, breathes deeper. Be here now. Why not? I've sure been everywhere else this week, he chants silently.

"Oh, yeah. I've been meaning to ask you something." Aaron slows his pace until Doug catches up. "Why were you checking in your stats from San Mateo?"

"Oh that? I'll tell you on the downhill side."

Aaron pulls ahead. Doug hangs back, watching his best friend run with his dog. It's a beautiful sight. Daisy's shaggy hair blows in the wind alongside Aaron's strong calves. The pair strike the trail with the measured beats of a metronome.

"Why doesn't Daisy heel when I call?" Doug complains. He keeps time from his position five yards back. What the hell? He'll do the race and the hackathon, and it will all work out. Maybe if his dad had done more of this and less work he would still be here. Right. It is his birthday tomorrow. Doug makes a mental note: call Mom.

"Oh, man," Doug pants, catching up to the happy couple. "Did I tell you about my protégé?"

Aaron looks over his left shoulder for Daisy, slaps his thigh. Daisy heels.

"Tell me."

"Brett, from MIT. I swear, he's me—when I was in my twenties, I mean, even down to the weird family stuff. His dad's a fancy corporate lawyer, M&A, that kind of stuff. Had it all planned out—Brett was going to work for the firm. Just like my dad, grooming me into Mr. Commercial Real Estate Developer."

"Yeah, but your dad wasn't around to breathe down your neck when you left town."

"True." Doug peels off another layer as the sun climbs higher.

"When are you going to start taking my advice? Nylon's cooler."

"Don't get all smug on me." Doug jabs Aaron's rib. "I told you—I refuse to wear anything that I can't trace back to a plant." Climbing the first steep hill, Aaron slows the pace. Sweat drips down Doug's scalp, neck, and back. He curses the three beers of the other night. It wasn't the miniscule weight gain that he'd seen this morning, but they seemed to have slowed him down. Or was it staying up until two in Hope's bedroom? He banishes the illicit memory then remembers that, on a whim, he'd invited her out on Tuesday. Katie being away had been having a decidedly deleterious effect on his good-husband role.

Four miles later, they're back at Town and Country caught in the frenetic web of Saturday morning: kids to soccer, couple food shopping at Trader Joe's, bikers, yoga babes, espresso drinking runners and diehard bookworms haunting Books, Inc.

"So, what were you doing in San Mateo?"

"Huh?"

"Inquiring minds want to know."

"I went to Hope's. There's been so much shit going on—with the rewrite and the show. And, Jeff is going nuts. I needed a reality check."

"A late-night reality check? Hello? Earth to Wiser? You're in training. Is that why you've missed your workouts?"

Doug bites into a warm, chewy bagel, ignoring Aaron slipping Daisy pieces of bread under the small wrought-iron table.

"I slept with her."

"WTF Wiser? I thought you were married!" Aaron's wide eyes scan the table as if searching for answers in cappuccinos, bagels, and orange juice.

"You could have saved me!"

"I am saving you! I've got you out here, don't I?" Aaron pushes his half-eaten bagel away. "And why do I have to save you?"

"Look—I was on a tear. Jeff and I had this weird conversation about sex and death. Katie was away on some kind of retreat with this guru doc that she has the hots for, and after you left the barbeque, she caught me hugging Hope, and went nuts. On top of that we were fighting about the baby . . ."

"Slow down. What was that about Jeff? What do you mean you had a weird conversation about sex and death? At work?" Aaron looks at Doug, puzzled.

"Oh yeah. Work is no boundary in Jeff's mind. He was on this rant about how FearToShred is all about death and how death is sexy."

"Right, the kid . . ."

"It wasn't even about the kid who died. Anyway, I left work and I didn't know where to go. Katie wasn't home; you weren't around . . ."

"Not used to being on your own, eh?" Aaron flashes a superior smile. "It's not that hard."

"Well, maybe for you. OK, truth? I got drunk . . ."

"Man!" Aaron throws his head back in dismay. "I thought we agreed . . ."

"I told you! I felt kind of weirded out and lost."

"I'll give you that—but to Hope's? That's Daniel walking into the lion's den."

Doug busies himself with his bagel. How can he tell Aaron that in that moment, after two beers and a tequila shot, after the curly fries, and the Hope lookalike on wide screen TV, he just had to talk to her? IRL! He needed her take on Jeff, on FTS, on what the fuck was going on with the show, with Arthur, with the company.

"Listen, I did not go there to sleep with her," Doug says. "But now that I did, I'm clear. Katie's my one and only. I'm going to settle down, have the baby. I'm jumping in with both feet."

"Do tell."

"Look, Aaron," Doug hops onto the empty seat next to his friend, leans his arm on the back of his chair, getting as close as possible without whispering into his friend's ear, "Hope isn't the right woman for me. She's hot. She's sexy. And, she's 100% ambition. She wants me to go down that path with her, but I'm still thinking about my music. Katie gets it. Besides, Hope isn't going to change . . ." Doug chomps the doughy bagel, savoring his weekly dose of comfort food.

Doug sits back, takes a long swig of fresh-squeezed orange juice. Just talking about the other night is making him woozy. "Close cover before striking," Aaron quips. "Try that on FTS."

"With a guitar?" Doug poses, leaning over to fill a portable water bowl for Daisy.

"Be right back," Aaron holds up his hand signaling "time out" and walks over to the next table to chat with a yoga-hot-body thirtysomething who has been angling for his attention.

Doug sips the tepid coffee. It was a stretch that Aaron would understand sleeping with his ex could help his marriage. Aaron's not married. At Topia, Doug was in awe of Hope. He had never worked with anyone who cared as much as he did. Now, they both really wanted to make FTS work. Sure, the money was great—but it was the creation of something new that got both of them jazzed. That was what brought him to Hope's in the first place—the idea that he could talk through Jeff's rant, TAN's pressure, and get real answers. He needed that the other night, badly.

Aaron reappears. His eyes have narrowed, and even his mouth is tight.

Doug asks, "Old flame?"

Aaron squirms.

"Anyway, that's how it happened—how our affair started in the first place—at Topia. One night, I'd finally run a successful load test. I'd never built anything so massive. I knew it was a game changer for me—and there Hope was, really excited. We were in it together. I think I went to her place last week to see if what happened at Topia really meant something, or if it was just a fluke. A day or two later I realized that what was then was then, and now, we're on different tracks. Yeah, we're at the same company but we're running on different platforms!" Doug chuckles at his own joke.

"Funny, Wiser. You can joke, but this is muy serioso." Aaron says. "You went down the road with Hope again? Hope? She broke your fucking heart! While Katie is here, loyal, grounded, earth mama Katie! It doesn't get any better than that! Hope's a train wreck, and you know it!"

Doug and Aaron walk around the corner to the car. Aaron is right, of course.

Voice of reason. Hope wouldn't be happy with him—him with his failed band, his engineer's brain and constant searching. Him, with his dorky home projects and raised vegetable beds. Hope is wired for action, excitement. Man, she's already the next BASE-jumping hero. What's next? Show runner? TV anchor? Who knew with Hope?

"Epic slip," Doug admits.

"Hope is a striver," Aaron says as they part ways. "Katie's your match," Aaron says, his face as serious as on the one day a year he schleps himself to synagogue to atone.

Doug gets it.

"Choose life," Aaron says, embracing Doug in a brotherly hug.

And he will. He knows that he, too, could easily live the rest of his days as a malcontent. Well, no. That's not what he wants. "I'm going to live," Doug affirms. "Well past my father's tender age, well past FTS, even past this triathlon."

"How you gonna 'splain this to the wifey?" Aaron asks, beeping his car door open.

"I'm not."

✳ ✳ ✳

On the way home from California Avenue, Doug plays "Offering," a sublime cut of Philip Glass and Ravi Shankar. It's a composition for glass bells and sitar, complicated rhythms, sonorous drones and high, angelic pitches. He's not sure if it's the depth of sound from Shankar's sitar, or the magical sound of the glass bells, or the way the modern twelve-tone scale counterpoints the ancient instrument, but something in the music opens him up to the eternal. With the ring of the glass bell, the whine of the sitar, he's suddenly all about being good, trustworthy, reliable.

With this wave of positivity, he understands why he could never be with Hope. And not because he doesn't love her. It's not because he doesn't admire and respect her, adore her for her moxie, not to mention her talent for diving into half- baked situations and making them work. It's not that he won't dream about her body and the way they fit together for the rest of his life.

The reason he can't be with Hope is because for him, work, any work—a startup, Topia, anything, as much as it excites him—and it does—is, in the end, a means to an end. Being an engineer is cool and it's gratifying, but it's not music. It's not that riff that took him to another world; it's not life in the backyard with Katie and their pals.

For Hope work is life. She will chase rainbows for the rest of her days. No matter how much money she has in the bank. What Doug sees now, the sun shining high, his body pumped full of endorphins, caffeine, and carbohydrates, is that Hope's catastrophe of a childhood will never stop informing the choices that she makes, the way she sees herself in the world. Her scars may be fading, but they're there to remind her. She was numb once, and she could go there again. Because he can see it now. Even when Hope has every reason to be content, she can't be.

What Doug sees now, on this perfect Saturday afternoon is that he's going to jump with two feet into his marriage not just because he made a commitment, but because Katie is about life, and living and all that that implies: children, and family, the house and Daisy. She's about wondering, and examining, and changing horses midstream if something isn't jibing. And even though he called her flaky a few years ago, he gets it now. She's *open*.

Doug grabs Daisy's paws and wipes them across the mud mat. The shaggy dog heads for her bowl, lapping water across the clean kitchen floor.

Doug pulls a dry sweatshirt off the top shelf, tosses his soaking t-shirt into the laundry basket. The dry fabric against his damp skin is like being wrapped in a warm towel after a long swim.

A twinge in his leg announces a muscle spasm. For once, he heeds Aaron's advice. He pulls an ice pack from the freezer, lies down with it resting on his thigh when Aaron's text pings:

"You alright?"

"Great. Off to work. TTYL"

Doug speed dials Katie. "Can you talk?"

"Yes. I'm in between classes."

"How long do you have?"

"Five minutes. Ten if I stretch."

"Stretch."

"What's up?"

"I'm sorry things have been tense. Just the job and the race, it's been a bit much."

"I understand."

"I want to get back on track,

"Me too."

"Wanna make a baby?"

"Now you're talking. Mwah," Katie says, ringing off.

Two P.M. Shit. He's late. He had set up a progress meeting with Brett for two. He hustles into his office, the ice pack tumbling. He quickly scrolls down the thirty-seven new messages that arrived since last night. On Friday night? Keys in hand, he pats Daisy, fast asleep in her bed in the living room.

34

THE HEAVY glass door to *Il Fornaio* swings open. Arthur, bright- eyed is on the other side.

"Good morning, Sunshine."

Hope smiles weakly.

"It used to be we came here to see who was up to what," Arthur whispers. "Now we just come to see who's got time for breakfast meetings!"

Arthur's humor just misses the mark. Hope calculates at what point in the proceedings it was acceptable to excuse herself. She needs a quick make-up check; the fog has just about melted it off.

Arthur's humor might miss the mark, but his outfit nails it. An ice blue Lorenzini shirt, its fine cotton weave accentuating the shade of his eyes; black tailored pants complimenting his long legs, and an expensive leather belt to show off his thin waist. Well, at least she made the right shoe decision; her heels might be brutal on her instep, but they are the perfect match for Arthur's expensive business casual.

"Just to clarify," Arthur says sotto voce. He looks around, cautious of being overheard by another VC or even by the waiter delivering their cappuccinos.

Mansplain, is more like it, Hope thinks, but doesn't dare interject.

"We are full steam ahead with The Adventure Network. No matter what happens today."

Hope listens.

"Having TAN as a client makes us that much more valuable to YUMI."

"Got it."

"And mum to Kelly. Does she know where you are today?"

Hope swallows hard. Shit. She had forgotten to send Kelly the Monday status update. "I'll text her."

"The man to worry about is Christian, YUMI's M&A guy. He's going to grill you like a skirt steak. Don't take it personally."

Hope nods, swallows a slug of bitter espresso. She hates Italian roast; it gives her a stomachache and tastes like motor oil.

"He'll sidle up to you, smooth as silk. He'll act like your best friend. Then, he'll interrogate you. This guy doesn't want bullshit answers; he wants the truth. And he gets it. As far as YUMI is concerned, our technology is flawless."

Arthur breaks into his plate of poached eggs. A shiver runs up Hope's spine and she shudders, as involuntarily a movement as a pollen sufferer sneezing in a garden.

Hope half-heartedly works through a flaky croissant, searches Arthur's eyes. "Question."

"Shoot." Arthur stabs a section of yolk, slides it onto a square of fresh-baked brioche toast.

"What if we do make deadline? You see, last night, Brett filed his report. He says we're only a week—two at the most—away. The other day, you said that YUMI was our backup plan. I assumed you meant if we miss the deadline."

"Not your problem." Arthur cuts into a piece of pale melon. "There are always offers and counteroffers. Nothing's over until the contracts are signed and sealed." Arthur looks up from his breakfast. "We're just going over to see if Kurt is for real." He spears a square of glistening papaya on his plate where potatoes should be. "If YUMI wants in, it's more money than you'll ever see with TAN. Besides, the deadline is moot, don't you agree? Even if Doug delivers the rewrite in time, we don't have time to test it; we don't have time to put it under The Adventure Network's load."

Hope's heart sinks. "Quit the cradle when the craft becomes a cage?"

"What's that?"

"A situation appropriate tweet?"

"Quirk: With a shark." Arthur winks, but she's not in the mood. "Just be careful. Don't show our cards. We give YUMI no real information. Sometimes these guys just want to sniff around. They just want to see if what you're doing competes with what they're doing."

Hope slips into the ladies' room while Arthur pays the bill. Her face in the mirror looks better than how she feels. What she feels is like crying—but this time there's no mystery why.

The two walk to the car, their bodies in synch, but their strides hitting the pavement as variously as a parade and a funeral procession.

Hope slides into Arthur's Tesla, trying to feel her numb toes in the too-tight shoes. Her mind is a kaleidoscope, all colorful, broken pieces, all falling and rearranging themselves moment by moment. *You're out of your league*, Charlene upbraided her when she took the job at FTS. *And besides, why would you leave now, when Chuck's been so good to you?* Hope braces herself for YUMI's polished M&A sharks.

* * *

"Nice art," Hope comments on the ride back to the parking lot. "I wonder if Kurt knows the artist."

"There is no artist," Arthur sniffs in reference to the corporate art gracing YUMI's walls. "That shit is made in China. YUMI's boardroom is no place for an Art encounter," Arthur chides.

Hope reddens, flustered. They are back in the parking lot in Palo Alto. Hope maintains her poker face.

"Now, the tricky part is getting the architecture specs." Arthur recounts a request from the meeting. "You might have to go in through the back door."

A memory of Doug in her bed flashes across her mind's screen. The YUMI meeting had been a mash up of bravado, posturing, and familial niceties.

"See you back at the farm. I've got a quick errand," Arthur says.

"Right."

Registering Arthur's subterfuge, her heart skips a beat. She hasn't played this game since sneaking around with Doug at Topia.

The fog has lifted since this morning, giving way to a cloudless, blue sky. Back in her car, she flips off the too-tight heels, slips into a pair of backless sandals. Shit! Kelly. Another person for her database. Fuck it. Kelly can sweat the numbers update for an hour. Backing the Porsche out of the spot, she hears a dull, doomed sound.

Hope gets out, searches under the car for a flattened animal or a dented fender. Nothing. Getting back into the driver's seat, she notices her right, side view mirror collapsed. Righting the mirror to its proper position, she catches a reflection of herself. She recoils. The blush she chose in the *Il Fornaio* bathroom is horribly contrasted with her pale skin. How could she forget that those damn *Il Fornaio* lights made her skin tone two shades darker? Damn it, Hope. You're in too deep.

Back in the car, and out of the lot, her throat tightens, a sure sign that a vortex of sadness is circling. *What am I doing helping Arthur sell out the company? I love these guys!*

Heading out of Palo Alto toward 101 South, Hope decides.

She'll tell him no.

She won't be his lackey, won't help with due diligence, won't sneak around. She thinks of her mother, across the bay, working her shift in the office at Alpha Beta.

Hope flips her right directional. Merging quickly into the late morning flow of traffic, she catches sight of a CHP cruising up the northbound lanes, slows to legal seventy mph.

When James handed her the ring, she'd been flummoxed and flattered. Now, whenever the subject of wedding plans came up, the conversation ended in deadlock. Hope couldn't manage any disruptions, not now. The company and her role in making it successful was 24/7. James countered that he would take care of the details—packing, finding a place for them, moving—but still she resisted. After equivocating twice, she questioned if she was just making excuses, using FearToShred to figure out if she could be Mrs. James. Was moving ahead quickly James' way of saying that she might not figure it out? His way of saying, "Look, I'm solid, I'll mind the fort and you can worry about the company." His way of reassuring her? But marriage, making a commitment, had been ferried to a dark corner in her mind. A corner she would get to later. But now later has arrived.

At midnight, after James falls asleep, she stares at the ring, hard. Laser rays of orange, green, blue, and yellow light mesmerized her until the glow of the evening receded and the dread of the next day encroached. Would she come clean? Could she tell James every-thing? Now when she may—or may not—help Arthur sell? If she knows James at all, he would make a case against helping Arthur. Is she ready to defend herself? And, what about Doug? Is she dreaming? She can't tell him about Doug! Ethically, she's all about coming clean before a wedding but telling him about Doug could very well be a deal breaker.

She'll have to decide—fast. Stretch out an engagement too long without good reason and people get suspicious.

Heading down the freeway, past University Avenue, a red Leaf cuts her off. The bumper sticker on its left rear fender gob smacks her like the sight of a comet in broad daylight. "If you tell the truth, you don't have to remember anything."

Hope reviews her own Database of Deceits when Doug appears, clinging to the side of her thoughts like a limpet. *We're going to the races*, he had said, dancing around her living room that night. There it was again. *We.*

In a quick inventory of her mischief, she tallies up nine lies, or, if she was being kind, secrets: not telling James about interviewing at FearToShred, not telling Charlene about leaving Manuserve, not tell-ing James about Doug, not telling anyone about YUMI, not telling Arthur that she's not for sale, not telling Doug about why she left, and finally, not telling James about kissing Kelly, not telling James about the BASE jump. Oh, and not telling Charlene about Richard —but that ship has sailed.

Hope blinks back a tear, the catch in her throat, tighter now. Fuck! Doug! *For old times' sake*, she'd quipped, unzipping his pants, but the next day, and the days since, she hasn't stopped thinking about him. About what could have been. About how she'd been scared, and so she ran off. When she leaned over him to kiss him, she wasn't thinking of the consequences or the hazards. She only knew that she was drawn to him, dancing around her living room, jazzed about FTS's prospects. How Doug 2.0., Doug thin, Doug energized, even if he was a bit drunk, was joyous! Cheerful! Upbeat! Doug, looking boyish again and like his old self, pulling her in like a magnet. It was as if time collapsed and they were their former selves, stoked about Topia.

No. Sleeping with him wasn't about *old times' sake* at all; she still wanted him, wanted to be with him. Not going to happen. It's too late. She might have transgressed last week but Hope Ellson is *not* a home-wrecker.

Familiar scenery blurs by at sixty-eight miles per hour. Past the Dumbarton Bridge, past Moffett Field. Redwoods planted on the side of the freeway, the mountains to the right. Grey, green, blue. Echoing in her mind like a hiker's call for help, the desperate cry—Why? Why me? Why everything at once—YUMI, TAN, the rewrite, the reappearance of my dad and Doug 2.0? Her head is spinning with Arthur's request, Kelly's hard driving on the show, Doug, James. Married? Single? Hope is in a limbo of epic proportions. Not talking to Charlene. Dawn now pissed that Richard didn't call her for lunch. The company poised for success. But was it too late?

How to navigate this minefield? Step this way, hurt Doug. Step that way, hurt James. Step over here, screw the Shredders.

A tear escapes, and then another, and then she's lost in a fit of convulsive sputtering. The first tear is for FearToShred and how vulnerable her coworkers are. The next is for being engaged, but the rest, the hot release is not just about today, or last week, or last month.

The tears are for all the grief of her life. Doug. The lost baby. The affairs. The lying. Richard Ellson. Charlene's histrionics. Arthur's manipulations. Jeff's antics. Jeff derailing Katie's birthday. Katie! Another person that should be on the Database of Deceits, but under what? Work or personal?

Hope sobs, driving, dabbing her cheeks and eyes with a Kleenex. The hazard of sleeping with Doug again was that it reminded her of all the reasons she had fallen for him in the first place. With Doug she had permission to be not only her great self, not only her highest, most radical, most creative, most experimental, most innovative, explorative, wild self, but also her sad self. He was so confident, so fascinated with his own world, so comfortable in his own skin that he could give and give gloriously and generously and unselfishly. He never saw her unhappiness as a reflection on his ability to be a good boyfriend. And that touched her. It touched her beyond the sex, beyond the professional connection, beyond the friendship. He touched her soul, a place no one had ever touched before, or since.

The first time they made love, she'd spent twenty minutes in the bathroom sobbing. With Doug, she discovered something she didn't even know that she had been looking for her whole life. But how was she going to handle it? How was she to trust herself that she wouldn't fuck it up? Not to worry. Fuck it up, she did.

Eyes on the road, she blows her nose, hard. One exit east of Mountain View, the tide of grief recedes.

Even though he'll never say it, she knows. Doug sees beneath all of her Hope-ness. He sees her all the way to her white-hot rage, and her fear. What Doug doesn't see is that most of the time, it's too much to bear, and that really, when everything is stripped away, she is just as scared of what life dishes up as the next person, that inside she is that Swarovski hummingbird, displayed so innocently on her credenza, all light-reflecting surfaces and fragile as glass.

35

JEFF IS hacking away at Brett's fixes, his brain on fire from the past days pouring over stack overflow. In school, he loved nothing more than taking on a new language. But now, his focus is way off. After the kid died in India because of his rogue tweet after Doug's barbeque, and the failed test, he can't help but feel he's a pariah, marginalized from the team, barely tolerated.

"For fuck's sake." Jeff stands over Julie's desk pleading his case for slipping away for an hour of skating. "We're going to be here all weekend for the hackathon, right?"

Julie's eyes are rimmed red. "How can I go skating when I'm in the middle of wiring up the new backend?" she asks, incredulous.

Outside, the summer sun is high.

"Jules! It's almost Equinox. Don't you guys always celebrate that?"

Julie rolls her eyes. "Oh, that's right. I forgot you're the expert on pagan lesbian rituals."

"C'mon." Jeff turns to go. "Besides we can put out a cool tweet: Equinox! Skate-in at five P.M. with 5 pop-shove-its. Quirk: With a candelabra."

Julie guffaws. "New challenges! New challenges! I've been dry as bed death in that department. Forget about me—how are you going to skate with that?" Julie points at Jeff's arm, still in a cast.

"The same way that you skate with your busted-up leg." Jeff peeks around the side of her cube. "Nothing behind me, everything ahead of me, as is ever so on the road." Jeff wags his good hand at his co-founder. "Later!"

The skate park is buzzing with so many skaters it's like a hive in honey season. The sun is still high. The shadows that got Jeff into trouble are long gone. Jeff jumps on his board, takes an easy spin around the park.

"Hey." He waves to Jeremy and Brian already up the high ramp. He's making his rounds, high fiving his homies when Julie rumbles up on her new 500 Ducati. Pulling her board off of the back, she jumps on, skating a gentle loop around Jeff. A few loops and Julie heads up toward the low ramp. Jeff follows. Up the ramp, Julie does her first ollie. Jeff circles her like a deft butterfly collector, stalking silently.

Julie heads for the high ramp. Brian and Jeremy turn to watch as she does two pop-shove-its in a row, catching the air that made her famous. She lands, circles Jeff, shredding the side ramp until they are in a delicate ballet. Jeff follows, holding his arm above his head and watching Julie's turns. In just two rounds, he's imitating her moves, the way she twists her waist, turns her right arm out for balance. Skating around the park, the low glides around the side, and back again. They're skating and they're gliding, and the tricks don't really matter; they are movement and kinetic energy.

Julie heads back up the high ramp. Jeff stops to watch. Now he gets it. She's been warming up for a trick that Jeff doesn't attempt, even on his best days. Jeff stops, flips up his board and steps away from the ramps. Julie goes down, then up. Down, then up, executing her ollies to perfection. For an instant, Jeff thinks to stop her—"We have a hackathon," he wants to yell and almost calls her down. But there! Blam! The board takes off, liftoff. Julie catapults up to the top of the high ramp, flips her board, catches it, and comes down as gentle as a cat.

"GTG!" Julie gives Jeff the wave as she ropes her board back onto the Ducati. "Girlfriend night."

"K—Hasta, chica!"

Heading downtown for a beer with Jeremy and Brian, Jeff stops on the way to text Julie:

"Grt skt. BTW, something stinks."

"What?"

"Saw Hope coming into the office at a weird time the other day—noon. Looked like she was crying."

"You know how girls get. Give her space."

"Hey, Jeff. Long time no see." Nancy, Jeff's old girlfriend, sidles up to him at the bar.

"Hey Nance," Jeff gives her a warm hug. "What's shaking?"

Nancy, a petite, five-foot-five redhead with a fair share of freckles is a favorite of Jeff's. But he just isn't boyfriend material. Still, he misses her, or for that matter, misses having anyone around to check in on him, sleep with him. Care. Jeremy disappears, pulled into a conversation down at the other end of the bar. Jeff and Nancy are still talking when the sun goes down and the after-work crowd has thinned.

"Wanna stop by for a bite?" Nancy offers. "I just made a killer pasta sauce." Jeff follows Nancy up the front steps to her apartment. He's following her but it's not dinner he's got an interest in.

After, driving home in his 2016 Mazda, he wonders how the fuck Doug and Arthur manage. Work and wives? Work, wives and kids? Work, wives, kids, and mortgages?

He shudders at the thought.

36

Now, INSTEAD of juggling three balls in the air, Hope is juggling five. Delivering to TAN, overseeing community, and managing the hacka had been challenging enough. Now, add sleuthing around for YUMI and figuring out when to come clean with James and her stomach goes into spasms. It's no secret. One of those balls is going to drop.

"Hope! Thanks for coming." Brad Chasen is waiting for her in the vestibule of Sushi So Good.

Walking through the dimly lit eatery Hope has a déjà vu. She's been here before—but with whom? Or why? Was it last year? Five years ago?

Brad sips iced water, trains his dark eyes on her. "Ordinarily, we would invite the Engineering VP, but Arthur advised against getting Doug involved."

"I understand. How can I help?"

Bento box lunches and hot tea arrive speedily. Hope prepares to take notes. "Didn't you work at Seven Arts?" Brad asks.

Hope nods. "Yes! Why?"

"I was there when you were the Product Manager. I reported to Luke Smith. I was a lead engineer. I remember you—you did that cool thing with Twitter, getting our users to vote on their products. Everyone knew you. How did you land at FearToShred?"

"I was recruited, why?" Hope asks testily, steam rising from the black lacquer bento box.

"It's out there. All those skater dudes and surfers. I love it."

Hope raises an eyebrow.

"To tell you the truth, I think YUMI would be a better fit," Brad says.

Hope doesn't let Brad know that part of the deal is that she will not be going to YUMI. Arthur promised to accelerate her stock, no handcuffs. Hope breathes in a whiff of jasmine rice, salmon, and pickled vegetables. If only her life were like this—each part neatly compartmentalized, beautifully constructed, complementary but separate from the other.

"Here's what I need. And don't worry, it sounds worse than it is." Brad tucks into the teriyaki steak while Hope silently runs through the engineering group at Seven Arts. The face in front of her is good looking, but beefier than she remembers. The eyes are strangely familiar, green with gold flecks and beautiful, hooded lids. Was he the one who? No, that was George. Or the other one? Damn! She'd had a little fling with Brad. She fusses with her iPad, stalling. That department Christmas lunch—here! She'd gotten hammered and . . . well. . . . There was definitely some blow involved and a bit of surreptitious necking. Jesus, Hope!

"Technology stack, architecture documentation . . . and some narrative on the plan to deal with scalability."

"Got it." Getting the tech stack and architecture meant getting it from Doug.

Hope slams the lid of the iPad that has morphed from a benign work tool into Pandora's box.

The two eat in strained silence. Asking Doug would mean cooking up a story about why she suddenly needs his narrative on scaling. Maybe Brad can help her out there. A bead of perspiration drips down the back of her shirt. What the hell is she thinking, asking Doug for proprietary information?

Brad looks at her with a hint of lust as gold flecks sparkle in his eyes. Hope realizes in an instant. He remembers that Christmas lunch and the misbehavior that ensued.

"I've got an idea," she starts. "Everything should be in our internal GitHub repo. IT can give me the password."

"Good thinking. And we'll need that narrative. Scaling is integral to the deal. I'll need everything in two weeks."

Those balls in the air just got a little heavier.

✳ ✳ ✳

Hope walks down a small stretch of office park trail out of the line of sight of the office.

"Sorry I'm late. I got a phone call." Doug reaches out for a hug, then pulls back in a spastic move.

Hope starts off down the path, shoes crunching noisily on the gravel. A fountain in the middle of the fake lake muffles the sound of the freeway nearby, the cries of gulls, honking geese, and planes landing and taking off, landing and taking off.

"No problem."

Hope waves her hand quickly, a cat swatting an unsuspecting fly.

"You're pissed about my do-good tweets, right? They flopped." Doug searches Hope's face expectantly.

Back at the office, everyone is working as if they are just about to cross the finish line.

"No, that's not it. I didn't exactly have high hopes for that idea, if you recall."

Doug's face colors slightly. Was he remembering what happened after their conversation about the do-good tweets? "Still, I'm sorry they didn't fly."

"So to speak."

"But you!" Doug turns to slap a high-five, "Your BASE jump was through the roof. You demon!" Doug exclaims. "I can't believe you pulled that off. You're nuts!"

"Ahh. . . . FearToShred right?"

"I'm impressed, Miss Hope. That was really taking one for the team."

"It wasn't all for the team," Hope says. "The skating stunt, maybe, the jump, not so much."

"Between your BASE jump, the silly ice-skate and the surfing alley-oop we're almost there."

"A lovely side effect," Hope says wistfully, remembering her knees shaking uncontrollably before she took off from the ledge.

"So what's up?"

"I thought it might be nice to get fresh air," Hope says. "You know, take a stroll, watch the geese, get some sun."

"Hope."

"Well, two things actually. One, I need some info on the scaling and everything you're planning for the hackathon."

"No prob."

"Listen, Doug," Hope stops in her tracks. "We have to talk about the other night."

"I'd say so. Looks like you've had some changes." Doug points at the ring on Hope's left hand.

"Yup." Hope wants to but she can't bring herself to meet his eyes. Instead, she watches a white egret land gracefully on the lake's edge.

"Do you think he knows that the lake isn't real?" Hope asks, her voice far away.

"You mean does he know that under the surface no fish could survive? That it's all chlorine, pumps and mud?"

"Yeah."

"Honestly? I don't think he cares. He needs a water landing, a water landing he gets. Listen, Hope, I don't know what to say." Doug leans his newly designed biker's body against a young redwood, his face shaded. "It was intense, I know that. But I'm married, and you . . . you're engaged!"

"Yes. I guess I am."

Doug waits. He can't really tell Hope he showed up at her apartment because he was at loose ends after Katie had stomped off for her retreat. And the talk with Jeff had provoked his fears about the company. He wanted Hope's reassurance. All that talk about death and sex had rattled him. He went to Hope's apartment to hear from her that he wasn't crazy or to remind him that crazy just went with startups. He went to Hope's apartment for a reality check, not a roll in the hay. Was it his fault she kissed him?

Hope turns away from the white egret, looks at him directly. "Doug," Hope starts, not sure why she's said his name, or what is going to come next. The egret takes off, white wings spread across the perfectly blue sky. "I didn't want to leave Topia, or you." Hope blinks back a tear. The last thing she wants to do now is cry. "The other night . . . it was a mistake?"

"No. It wasn't. We just can't keep that up."

"Agreed. But why haven't you said anything?"

Hope stops herself mid-sentence when she hears her old frustration surface. The frustration that was bottled, stored and put on a shelf for three years.

She was always the one who had to bring up their relationship. Even when she left, she never stopped hoping that he would confront her, ask her why she left, but he never did.

"Um. . . . In case you haven't noticed . . . we've both been a little. . . . How did you say? Preoccupied?"

Hope shakes her head. "Preoccupied isn't the word," she laughs sardonically. "I've got my mother MIA, my father wanting to see me, TAN . . . and . . ." Hope stops short. She can't tell him about YUMI. "Yes, it was intense. So now what?"

"Hope? Earth to Hope? Now we rewrite. Now, we keep the company afloat. Now I train for my race. Agreed?"

"Agreed."

37

JEFF'S OFFICE looks like a cross between the overnight camping trip of a preternaturally rambunctious Boy Scout troop and an X-rated pajama party for a sect of animals for which there is no genus. What it smells like is more easily recognizable—dried-out pizza, stale beer, and sweat. Empty cardboard boxes with congealed cheese and vestiges of pepperoni, orange juice, Red Bull, and Coke cans are scattered about the room, the colors and shapes colliding in a messy Robert Rauschenberg collage. Coffee cups with old coffee, fresh coffee, and water litter the desks and floor. Copies of *Thrasher* are strewn around, and the white board is smudged from layers of erasures. Blue recycle bins are filled to overflowing with empty beer bottles.

"I've called housekeeping. They're due any minute," Jeff jibes.

Julie, Brett, and Doug pile in for a pre-meeting, arranging themselves on the mismatched chairs filched from cubes and offices to form a loose semi-circle.

"Another test?" Julie asks weakly, anticipating Doug's request. Her eyes are red, and her hair stands up like the Leaning Tower of Pisa.

"Yeah, Wiser. What the fuck?" Jeff implores, his mouth screwed up in a way that recalls a jellyfish. He's sprawled on a short sofa pushed up against a file cabinet.

"We did what you asked. We were here all weekend. We checked in our code. It's testing out. So why is Arthur hassling us?

Or was that you, Wiser, pretending to be Arthur? You know, good cop, bad cop. . . ."

"Hang on, let's not start a bitch session." Julie pulls the FTS site up on Jeff's monitor.

Doug sits back, awed at Brett's command of the team and the architecture. He's not here to demand another test; he's here to congratulate them. He accidentally picks up the wrong cup, swallows a sip of Tran's cold coffee. "Arrggghh!!"

Hysterics ensue. "Wiser! That should wake you up!"

All weekend, as videos were posted, Brett, Tran, and Jeff were watching the code check out, bird-dogging the logs. Doug is about to join in on the guys' whooping about videos and user spikes and leader boards when Hope squeezes into the melee wearing her fighting clothes: black pants, a yellow buttoned-down shirt, a jean jacket, and Fluvogs. Doug worries; she only wears those shoes when she is up to no good.

"Your numbers are up—way up." Hope turns a second screen toward the group. "Except for this one . . ." Hope shows a recent challenge to the group:

> FearToShred @FearToShred: Life is either a great
> adventure or it's nothing #fts

Jeff sits up, looks at the screen Hope's pulled up. "What the hell?"

"Oh, just a little experiment." Doug replies.

"An experiment? While we're here slaving over the freaking rewrite?" Jeff's voice quavers, a cross between a crow's nasty caw and a wave breaking.

Doug knew he would have to come clean with the guys sooner or later. Just not today. Arthur had called a meeting that Doug was sure was not going to be meeting of the minds. More like a beating of the minds.

"After our little talk about using the site to do something good, I wanted to see if we could leverage our uptick in numbers, branch out, as you've said, to the do-good camp. Apparently, not so much," Doug explains.

"Have we not told you, dude? Shred'ers want to play what they want to play. They're not so much about making the world a better place."

Hope checks her ringing phone.

"Great, everything's great," Hope says, winking at Doug. "The team did what they were supposed to do. They're tired, but good. We'll run a test on Monday."

"Good to hear. Give Doug my congratulations," Arthur clicks off.

Hope wonders at Arthur's upbeat mood. Did a successful hacka change his mind about YUMI? Well, why not? As he said, *it's not over till it's over.*

38

"CAPTAIN'S ORDERS," Doug sends a Slack message to the team: "Go home—see you all on Monday." He postpones the load test until Monday afternoon. He'll run through the code himself. If the new tweet "It's the FUTURE, guys" gets the heavy traffic he expects, the site will be tested plenty.

Hope's butterfly icon pops. "Meet me at the side entrance."

Winding through the hallways, Doug can't hide a shit-eating grin. He passes Arthur pacing in his office, talking on his Polyphone.

He waves but Arthur doesn't wave back.

At the side door, Hope leans against a small pine, her shoulders slumped, her hands limp.

"We did it!" she says wearily, returning Doug's fist bump.

He hugs her, then realizes that just as he has spied friends and colleagues out here at the lake, those same people could see them now. He pulls away. "Great idea for the hacka!"

"Hey, I'm not taking a lick of cred for this one—it was all you." Hope turns to walk the path toward a small stand of young redwoods.

The day is late-spring brilliant. Wildflowers dot the shore of the fake lake—poppies and sour grass, purple spiny ice plants and azaleas. The sky is cloudless, painfully blue. These kinds of days are a challenge for Doug. Even though he knows it's fruitless, he spends half his time calculating how he can get away for an hour on his bike, squeeze in a short training run. After three solid months of training, his body has been re-engineered to move.

"You might not want cred," he says gently, "but you set it up. You approved the pizza and beer."

Hope shakes her head. "Can you really possibly still be such a Midwestern cornball?"

They walk in silence, breathing the salty bay air, a moment of victory mixed with extramarital shame.

"Are you moving to L.A.?" Doug asks, slowing his pace.

"No. What makes you think that?" Hope turns to him, alarmed.

Near the shore, two Canadian geese wind their long black necks around each other.

"I thought Kelly might be lobbying you to defect," Doug waves his arm around the lake. "You know, offer you a cool job? TV anchor? Game show host?"

"In your dreams, Wiser."

Doug and Hope circle Lake Chagrin, rounding the part of the lake where the pampas grass and shrubs grow tall. Doug closes his eyes, takes in a long breath of the sweet hay scent. "I miss my cabin," he says. The sage, and herby scents, the sun and cobalt sky. He'll be up there with Katie and Daisy after the race.

"Not to belabor this," Hope starts.

Doug's mouth goes dry. "Wassup?"

Hope turns, a calm look of pure admiration on her face. It opens a door.

"You did an awesome job back there, Doug. You really pulled it out."

"Much appreciated, boss. There were a few dark moments, but the team made it happen." He's about to launch into a long spiel about how her leadership had been nonpareil. He's about to say all of this when he notices that her cuffs are rolled up exposing the familiar network of pale scars, a tic-tac-toe board on her left arm.

"What?" she says, seeing him looking at her tenderly.

"Oh, just that I just made you look good for TAN—really good. Meeting deadline when you're up against it with a multimillion-dollar contract is no small matter, my dear."

"And I want to thank you."

In the shade of a redwood, out of the line of sight of the office, Hope hugs Doug tightly. This time, neither pulls away.

39

HOPE WAKES in a sweat. Beside her, James snores lightly. The digital clock blinks 3:48. Slipping out of bed, Hope tiptoes into her kitchen in a dreamy daze. Where was she? Who was the shooter?

She flips on the kitchen light, puts the kettle to boil. Skimpy pads in from the living room, rubbing up against her leg and mewling softly. What was it? She leans against the counter, trying to gather pieces of the dream that woke her, but the fragments slip and pop and disappear; they're shards of glass hurtling, reflecting, spinning.

In the bathroom, Hope changes into dry t-shirt and sweatpants. Brad. Brad was there. But why?

In a landslide of images, the dream comes into focus, each muddy detail sending a sour taste from her stomach to her throat. Something noisy and final and her stomach clutches.

She is in the office. Brad calls her office line. "Meet me in the conference room." A larger than life shredder has replaced the conference table. Brad pushes her toward the shredder. "Stop pushing!" She shouts. He hands her her briefcase, makes a shaking motion. She empties papers into the shredder. "Quickly," Brad shouts. She's sweating—the room is suddenly crowded with FearToShred staff, Brett and Meg, Julie and Jeff.

She can't breathe. She pushes her way through the Shredders toward the door. "POP!" Hope feels a sting in her back, in her lung. "Hope Ellson! We are FINISHED!"

Hope massages an ache in her back, paces on the veranda. Above, a full moon illuminates the tops of trees, angled roof lines, and small backyard garden ponds. "What have I done?" she moans, a discomfiting mantra.

"Babe?"

Hope turns, startled. What category does lying about your dreams fall into?

In the bathroom, Hope shakes out a Valium. It's Sunday. She'll have time to sleep it off. She snuggles back into the warm bed. James strokes her back.

At ten, James is there with hot coffee and juice. On the tray, a small crystal vase with a white rose, and under a cloth napkin, a chocolate croissant, her favorite Sunday treat. "Aw . . .. you didn't have to do that!"

"I slipped out while you were sleeping. Rough night?"

"Bad dream," Hope says, sipping the hot coffee.

"Tell." James sits on the edge of the bed.

"Nah. Why ruin our day?"

"Alright. You can tell me later. Our appointment is at eleven. I thought we could go out for lunch afterward."

"I'll be ready."

In the living room, James turns on the TV. He's been following the basketball playoffs with the heated passion of a loyal fan. Today was "wedding venue" Sunday. Was she ready?

Should she tell him about the meeting with Arthur? About YUMI? About how she manipulated Doug to give her the intelligence YUMI needed for due diligence? About sleeping with Doug? Not today. Pulling apart a croissant, her hand trembles imperceptibly. But even considering all of the misdeeds she had committed, did she deserve to be shot?

The driveway up to the Peninsula Country Club is long and lined with yellow rose bushes.

"Mr. Pearson. Welcome."

"Hey Ritchie," James says, slipping the valet a bill. "This is my fiancée, Hope Ellson."

"Lovely to meet you," Ritchie says. "They're expecting you at the front desk."

The club was James' first choice for a wedding venue. Hope went along, her enthusiasm for an elegant venue waxing and waning. Part of her liked the idea of full-tilt glam, and part of her wanted a small, quiet dinner on a remote hilltop.

After a tour of the grounds, the chapel, the reception area, and the bride's and groom's changing areas, Hope was convinced. The Peninsula Country Club was not for her. How could she invite her mother, sister and the Shredders here? Besides, she couldn't exactly ask her father to walk her down the aisle. What kind of lie was that?

40

"WE'RE IN trouble." Hope says, rearranging a stack of sandstone coasters that Dawn brought back from her "babymoon" in Sante Fe. Kokopelli stares back at her from her new Roche-Bobois concrete and glass coffee table.

"Trouble?" James asks. "What trouble could we be in that a CPA hasn't seen?" James grabs a beer. "Are you late on your taxes again, Hope dear?"

Thursday, seven P.M. Not an ideal time for a confrontation, but what time is?

"Don't you think we're in trouble?" Hope asks. She twirls the shiny two-carat engagement ring around. After much deliberation, she couldn't decide whether to wear it, or place it, secure in its tiny blue box, on the coffee table.

"Well, something is wrong," James' words are short, clipped. "First, I find out about the BASE jump—but not because you told me. No. I find out because my FearToShred notifications alert me to a video that's got a million hits! Ahh. That's great, I'm thinking yeah! But—it's you! Waving a flag."

"James. I'm sorry."

James shakes his head. "No doubt. We're in trouble." James sips the beer while Hope pours a St. Pauli Girl into a cold glass. Outside, the sun is just setting. Dusk. Her favorite time to get into bed and make love. She loves necking and then napping through that liminal time.

"I didn't tell you because I knew what you would say."

James shakes his head. "Oh, really?"

Hope leans against the credenza, the picture of the two of them at his sister's graduation, mocking.

"Hope, we're in trouble because if I'm going to marry you, we need to tell each other everything." James pets Skimpy rubbing herself languidly against his leg. "We need to be transparent."

Transparent? What is this? The Federal Government? Facebook? The insurance industry? Hope doesn't recall signing "James' Rules of Engagement."

Outside, the night cools. Hope unglues herself from the credenza, closes the sliding door and the window, and slouches against the couch cushions. Skimpy, purring in James' lap, is the only sound. It's a pleasant purring, "yes, yes." Has she lost her mind? Here is James, stable as the day is long. He's angry now, but he's a great fiancé; he's sexy, confident, even-tempered. He wants her. He's fighting for them. Transparency. Is that too much to ask? It's a rational request, the stuff of marriage.

"Hope. You're stressed. Let's wait on the wedding." James places Skimpy gently on the chair, settles on the couch next to Hope. They collide as he reaches for her hand reaching for the beer.

Hope's lip quivers. "Oh my God. I'm so stressed. But I'm not too busy to plan the wedding. It's this," Hope waves her hand back and forth. "*This* isn't working. It's not about transparency or secrets . . ." Hope is mumbling, her voice pouring out like water down a spring mountainside.

James inches away, settles on the far end of the sofa. "There's someone else, right?"

"Huh?

"You're in love with someone else, right?"

"James? What are you talking about?" Hope tilts the beer and then tilts it away. "No."

"Men's black socks behind the bathroom door? Hello?"

Did Doug leave his fucking socks? Had she not found them for a week? Where the hell was her cleaning lady? Her mind races. She'd paid Merry Maids for a cleaning, hadn't she? Maybe James was right. She does have PTSUS. She's losing track. Hope swallows hard.

"Really?"

James leaps off the couch, leans against the credenza in a proprietary posture. He had bought Hope the piece of furniture for their first-year anniversary. "OK, even if you aren't seeing someone else — why won't this (he draws air quotes around Hope's this) work?" James looks crestfallen.

Hope fiddles with the ring, ignores her buzzing phone. She sinks lower into the cushion.

"This can't work because I'll never stay home. This can't work because I don't want kids. This can't work because I still have shit to work out. I'm just not ready."

James' disappointment morphs to fear. Hope can see his cheek muscles twitch, the light in his eyes go dark. She wants to reach out, remind him that she had warned him. I'm dangerous, she had told him. She said it that first month, when he was cooking her gourmet dinners, courting her. Apparently, he wasn't listening.

How can she explain that this is not about him? It's about her. About the whole package of being James' wife. One day, she told herself, she would try; she would be a good wife. The next, she knew that she never could. Because the idea of domestic bliss made her anxious, sad. She knew she would pick fights; she would find fault; she would be restless. She would blow it because that was who she was. She was more at home with chaos than comfort, more at ease when things were unsettled. She couldn't blame him; he thought he could fix her. "This could work if I wanted to have a wrapped up, neat and tidy, transparent little life," Hope ventures. "If I wanted to have the country club wedding, push out babies, dial back my career." Hope flops on the sofa, spent.

"What are you talking about?" James asks, losing patience.

"James. We love each other," Hope squeezes back a tear. "We just don't want the same things."

His face rearranges itself, a kindness reignited. "Tell me what you need! We don't need a country club wedding. Or babies. And what makes you think you'd have to dial back your career?"

Hope is silent.

"As long as there's no one else. As long as you still love me, I'm in. That's my best offer."

"You say that, but when I was dumped by Seven Arts and had two offers—one from Manuserve and one from Zillow? Remember?"

"Yes. I remember."

"I wanted to go to Zillow. I felt it. I knew they would hit. They sold for two fucking billion! Not two hundred million, James! Two billion!" A nasty demon pulls Hope to rehash the past.

James winces.

"You insisted. You were a hundred percent sold on Manuserve—you insisted it was the right move. You said if I went to another startup it would be a deal breaker."

James moans. "We all make mistakes, Hope. But was it fatal? Here you are at FearToShred. Just what you wanted. And by the way, you didn't bother to consult me."

"No, I didn't. Because honestly? I don't think I've really forgiven you. The BASE jump was like Zillow. A risk, but a risk I felt I could survive. I'm still young, James. This is the time for risks."

James grabs his jacket. "OK. I get it."

But what about the small, lost Hope? What about the confused Hope, the messy one who never fit in? That was the part of the "this won't work" that she couldn't explain. "This isn't about you," Hope says, taking off the ring. "I can't do it, James. I'm really sorry."

41

A FOUL air, like a cabin in a deserted wood where untoward business is being conducted, an air of guilt and avarice, fills the conference room.

Brett, Tran, Ryan, Meg, Jeff, and Julie are gathered around the table, their faces tired and sallow. Dirty t-shirts can be laundered, but the dark circles under their eyes are going to take time to erase. Doug scans the table, wondering whom to send home, and how soon, when Arthur bursts through the glass door.

"Big changes," Arthur scribbles on the white board. He turns to face the assembled. "We've been acquired."

A stunned silence fills the room; air buzzing out of a popped balloon.

"One hundred and twenty million," Arthur adds, smiling. "Two million for each engineer. Julie, Jeff," Arthur says shortly, "We'll talk." Arthur beams, a proud dad telling the family about a raise.

"Whoo-hoo!" A weak yelp from Ryan breaks the silence.

Brett and Tran high-five. Ryan and Tran pump their arms: "Yes!"

Jeff shakes his head. "No. No."

"Acquired by whom?" Doug asks.

"YUMI. They have big plans to incorporate our technology . . ."

"But what about the game? What about our users?" Brett asks.

"They like the game," Arthur answers.

Jeff jumps up, circles the table, a jaguar in a cage. He pounds his fist on the wooden table. "Forget the game! How the fuck did this happen?" He points a finger at Arthur. "Since when do you have the right to sell the company out from under us? You can't do that without me and Julie . . ." Jeff stares hard at Julie. "You gave your vote for this shit?"

Julie's eyes fill. "Jeff . . ."

Jeff stomps out. "This is unbelievable. Just fucking unbelievable."

The door to the conference room exhales. Julie gets up halfheartedly. "I should go . . ."

"Stay," Arthur says. "I'll get with him later."

"And TAN?" Doug asks.

"TAN is off," Arthur explains. "The contract terminates upon change of control."

"How convenient," Doug sighs. "But why now, Arthur? We were so close!" Doug suddenly notices that Hope is missing. But then again, why would she be here? Product Managers wouldn't be invited to a meeting with founders and lead Engineers. Right?

Arthur, looking buoyant, scribbles critical dates on the white board. A hundred and twenty million is fifty percent more money than Doug ranted about in Hope's living room two weeks ago. That means her six mil just turned into nine.

"Who goes and who stays will be handled by HR," Arthur says soberly. "As far as you guys—you're all invited to YUMI."

"Invited?" Brett mumbles. "It's not really a choice is it? We don't get our payout if we don't go, right?"

"That is correct." Arthur asserts.

Could Doug tell them it doesn't matter what Arthur says? It doesn't matter because it all comes out the same in the end. It's bad. It sucks. It's like losing your first girlfriend. You get the news that she's through with you, and you're dumbstruck, you're stumped. You think, what signs did I miss? And how did this happen? It doesn't matter that she still wants to be friends. It's over.

The terms of the sale are better than good, but most people can't really hear anything except that it will be two years before they get their payouts.

"A hundred and twenty mil," Julie shakes her head.

"I didn't see that coming. It's good. Very good." Doug nods.

✳ ✳ ✳

Julie and Doug walk down the empty hall to his office. "Why didn't he tell everyone at once?" Julie asks.

"Protocol. You tell the founders and engineers first—they're the ones who will profit the most. You separate them from the ones who are getting laid off."

Jeff's office is empty. Doug knows what he's going through. Jeff could be out skating, orchestrating his move to Kauai, or trying to figure out what to do with all his money.

"Wanna hide out in here for a while?" Doug hustles Julie into his office. "I think we can steal a few minutes . . ."

Before Doug closes the door, Julie is supine on his stained red office couch, her legs dangling over the arm.

"When I didn't see Arthur around for the last couple of weeks, I thought he was playing the 'don't talk to me until you have something good to say' game."

"He probably was. And, he was talking to YUMI and the board," Doug adds. "But you. You must have voted your stock, right?"

Julie unfolds from the couch, paces Doug's office with her limping gait. "Yes. But I'm not sure I did the right thing. When Hope came to me . . ." Julie stops herself short.

Doug raises his eyebrows.

"I mean . . ."

"Don't worry. I've been around this block, Jules. Hope was probably in on the deal with Arthur. He couldn't have gotten the votes otherwise."

"Whew." Julie rubs her leg. "This voting problem's been bugging since I went skating with Jeff."

"I think we were all a little shaky with Jeff."

"I feel bad. I mean, I should have warned him, maybe?"

"Julie. Listen," Doug puts his arms around the small woman. "No guilt. You both just got an awesome payola."

"Payola? I dunno. I actually feel kinda sick. Like after a birthday party sick. Like too much chocolate cake and champagne sick." Julie searches Doug's eyes for empathy.

Doug nods. He gets it. Julie was a pawn in Arthur's game, but at least she gets out rich. He opens the mini fridge, grabs a beer, hands one to Julie. "Fuck training. We are day drinking now."

"Really?"

"On the day of the sale? *De rigueur.* On the day my net worth shoots up," Doug replies, "doctor's orders."

"Well, for the record," Julie says, her screwed up face relaxing, "I'm stoked. I don't care if it's two years from now, eighteen fucking million is more money than I ever dreamed of."

Clink! The two tap bottlenecks and chug long swigs.

"Doesn't making Angie happy counter some of the guilt?" Doug says playfully.

"No question," Julie says. "She's been dreaming about houses for a year now."

Doug pats FearToShred's co-founder's back. "We did good. And, in case you're wondering, I'm not angry."

"Whew."

Doug shakes his head wistfully. "Truth? We built a great app, and now it's going to live someplace else. Even if YUMI is evil."

Julie frowns. "Does Arthur really think Shred'ers are a good match for YUMI?"

"It's not that he thinks we're a match. It's a talent acquisition," Doug says.

"Which talent?" Julie says absentmindedly gazing out the window at Lake Chagrin. Is it her imagination or is the lake shimmering today? The geese have flown, the gardeners have cleaned up the shit, and the redwoods stand regal in the sun.

"I think," Doug points at Julie, and then himself, "us."

42

ONCE HOPE had committed to helping Arthur, all she wanted was to press "Restart." Had she even ever really said "yes?" No. She simply had never mustered, "no." Helping the sale to YUMI was worse than sleeping with a married man, worse than lying to Charlene about Richard's reappearance, worse than lying to James about Doug. Hell, lying to Charlene might be on her Database of Deceit but it wasn't on her guilt meter.

"I can't do this," she had committed to herself last week, walking into Arthur's office with the resolve of the born-again to convert the masses.

Behind his desk, the large screen runs videos from last night's challenge: "It rises. With roses." Loaves of bread rise in time lapse photos, rose petals scattered around freshly baked muffins. Crazy guys flying jet packs with bouquets, a bride held aloft on a chair at a Jewish wedding, bouquets of roses in her arms. Vultures, hawks and hummingbirds flying from treetops, rose bushes in various stages of bloom fill frame after frame. English roses, tea roses, tiny Cecil Bruners, yellow roses in full bloom.

Arthur has prepared her. "Life is long, Hope Ellson. The team will get over it. Besides, they'll be paid. Don't forget, a sale to YUMI is a win for Jeff and Julie."

And so, he had convinced her. But by the next morning, she was down again, berating herself for betraying her team. She was so down that she almost called in sick. Hope Ellson never calls in sick. No, she would have to carry this burden alone, just as she had carried all of her other burdens.

She'd had her reasons for not countering Arthur's sell job. Secretly, she reveled in the fact that Arthur had enlisted her. It was naughty, it was disloyal, but it was also irresistible. Being taken into the confidence of the CEO was about as close as she had ever come to an insider. Being taken into Arthur's confidences was warm, cozy and insulated with a cushion of power that was as sexy as fucking her ex on a school night.

Except that today, she's over it. Over hurting people. Over the betrayals. Over making messes.

So, she'd gone to work, wondering how she would square selling the company out from under the people who built it, who loved it, who had put their hearts and souls into it. And not just selling it but selling it to a sleaze ball company with no moral compass, and no ethics except "Profit."

So *why* had she capitulated? Was it the money she stood to gain that threw her into a tizzy? Was she blowing any and all future chances with TAN? Was she tarnishing her reputation in the valley? An endless loop of questions with no answers harassed her.

What does a person do with nine million? Start a foundation? Buy a horse, a Tesla, a country house? Set up retirement plans for her mother and her sister? For herself, this wasn't just her retirement money; this was a lifestyle upgrade. How would she spin it? Or did she even have to spin it? Would people know that she helped Arthur? "The Valley— she is small" echoes.

She would figure it all out later. Now, she was hoping for divine intervention or at least the hand of grace.

43

THE LONG hill, along the Embarcadero, up to Fort Mason, around and under the bridge, is the first in a long series of hurdles.

On the way in this morning, Julie had texted:

"This one's for you, babe! You go!" Then she added:

"There is no dishonor in losing the race. There is only dishonor in not racing because you are afraid to lose."—Garth Stein.

"Isn't that true about nearly everything?" Doug muses. Life is a race. The company was a race. The music had been a race. Katie's baby clock is a race. A race against time.

Sometimes, like his father, you lose. Time moves forward, never back. Time improves wine, but damages beauty. Moments in time. The magical alchemy of things coming together. Things that fall apart as quickly as they coalesced. The company, Hope, a bike ride.

Doug pedals past the Ferry Building, listening to cars and trucks thrumming over the metal deck of the Bay Bridge. Ahead is Alcatraz, that politically sticky island that draws tourists by the boatload. Training had had its challenges, but completing a triathlon is a different animal completely. Doug has the sense of having practiced riding a horse, albeit an unbroken, slightly wild horse, on a trail in Woodside, but today, he is taking a ride on an elephant in the jungles of Thailand. He had considered running through the entire course once, just to allay the fear, but Aaron discouraged him. "Hey, you gotta save some surprises. Think of the training like dating. You know what it leads to, right? Race day is going for it with your favorite girl for the first time. You want to leave a little mystery."

He drank the Kool-Aid. The sexual metaphor helped. *Turn the anxiety into desire,* Aaron counseled. *Remember, it's all a mind game, Dougy. And you're the boss of it. You wrote that game. In fact, think of it as one of your little work games. You're the master of the universe, man.*

He didn't argue. Still, he should have come up with a series of challenges! He was so brain dead after the hacka, his brain on mute.

So, all weekend, instead of running the course, he rested his muscles, babied himself. He took naps and laid hot and cold compresses on his feet, back, neck, and shoulders. He ran through the bike route, the swim, and the race a million times in his mind.

The only part of the training he neglected was the cold-water swim, and he's sorry now that he hadn't forced himself. Besides, who had time? Hundreds of competitors had trained in the frigid water of Lake Tahoe. But unlike his fellow competitors, Doug is not doing this to win. This race isn't a business deal; it's an act of faith.

The first long hill ends at a vista point. The east-facing hills, bleached a pale yellow, bake in a blinding morning sun. Ridges and folded contours rising from the bay are a sweet baked Alaska flaming on a silver tray. Knife-sharp cliffs are tinged with green and gold; the view is clear all the way up to Napa.

Doug has seen the sight before, but today it takes his breath away. Coming up on the Golden Gate Bridge after biking along under the Bay Bridge is like seeing your gorgeous girlfriend, who just minutes ago was in sweats, dolled up for a Saturday night date. There's a way that the iconic bridge ties the two landmasses together that never ceases to feel, well, downright glamorous. The deco design, the towers, the sheer expanse give the whole tableau an MGM movie-set feel. You expect to see Clark Gable strutting out in a top hat and tails with Carole Lombard on his arm in a long, slinky gown.

Forget Hollywood. The way the orange bridge reaches out from San Francisco to Marin, almost against all odds and imagination, inspires awe and wonder in all who travel in its vicinity. Experiencing such a grand feat of engineering inspires people to dream their own dreams. Isn't this what every great architect hopes for? The raising up of the human spirit. And the best part was, the Golden Gate was a piece of architecture that could take its time, have a long tangential conversation before making its point. Hello ships, sailboats, ferries, cars, bicyclists, walkers, joggers! You're not entering some backwater slough. You are about to enter San Francisco Bay, gateway to the Far East, entrance to the United States! Stand up! Be proud!

Doug rounds the corner, keeping the bridge in his sight for as long as possible. He makes the turn south, thinking how his own personal conversation had been short and sweet: "Wiser. You have arrived." And maybe in his own way, he has arrived. He hadn't gotten as far with his band as he'd hoped; he would go to work for YUMI. So? He's still here, isn't he?

He circles back south, the high-rises of downtown coming into view, spread out like some magical village, like a misplaced, mystical Oz. Tall buildings are all glass and shine, class and civility off in the distance. Between hills, the Transamerica Pyramid and Salesforce Tower puncture the blue sky like urchins puncture the sea.

Doug's legs shout. Mile eighteen. Two more hills ahead, the two that are not as forgiving as this last. Down and up onto the next grade, Doug thinks about the company. *Was my insistence on the rewrite a deal breaker? Is that why Arthur lost his confidence? Don't go there, Wiser. Today is my day off, right?* Besides, what's done is done. There are always missteps, things take longer than you think, co-workers butt heads. Nothing new, really.

Doug tackles the next uphill stretch, his mind drifting back to work like a homing pigeon. He knew that joining FearToShred was a risk, but once he made the decision, he went in with two feet. He gave it his best shot. He couldn't have done it any other way. Like Jeff said, *We were all in love with it, with the dream of it.* There was no other way.

So YUMI won. So what? My heart's been broken before! I'm not even talking about women, not even Hope, or Katie. I'm talking about work, music. *You care too much,* his dad once said when he moped for three days after losing a soccer final to the high school across town. Doug was crushed. *Lighten up! It's a game,* Dad counseled. *Losing one day doesn't mean you can't win the next.*

The problem in life, his dad said, was that most people were afraid to get back on the horse. He made a roller coaster curve with his hand.

Doug bought it, but from then on, he kept his dreams and his inner life private. He might get back on the horse, but before he did, he needed to tear things apart, figure out the missed signals, the bad plays. In the end, it's really all about faith, isn't it? We start something that we know is a long shot, muddle through, give it our best, and pray for a break.

How else can you live? No, the better question is, why else live? Doug coasts down a short hill. We heal. Mostly. And when we don't heal, we're changed. And change is what we're here for, right?

He's coasting, a three-mile respite. He pedals on, taking a long sip of water from the pack pasted to his back and checks the field for Aaron. Doug pedals on, sweating bullets about the swim. Focus, he admonishes himself. Wasn't it I who pronounced myself over my fear of the swim last month? That was then, this is now, he'd announced to Katie.

The day is young. Eight more miles of biking followed by the one-and-a-half-mile swim, finishing with the thirteen-mile race. Pace yourself, Wiser. Pace yourself. He's on the next to the last downhill, when he starts thinking about the band. It was about timing. And not timing as in the beat, but timing as in, he had been ready. Could he be ready again? The band failed, but hey, that was then. This is now.

Cruising back down toward the Embarcadero, his brain fog lifts. He realizes that although he thought he was ready for a new life when he left Topia, he wasn't. He puttered, he tried the band, but he should have tried harder. So what if his guys defected? There were more musicians he could have auditioned. He could have reinvented the group. What the fuck, Wiser?

Another uphill ahead, and he's back rehashing the FTS launch party, time looping back three long, complicated months but feeling now like five minutes ago.

Doug pumps up the last hill, through the deep green of the Presidio. He sucks a deep lungful of eucalyptus, listening to the bike wheels crunch through brittle leaves. He veers right, remembering the redwood needles and how they derailed him that day on Skyline.

He pumps up out to Arguello and left onto California Street. He relaxes into a groove, his breath strong and measured, his heart pumping hard. He bikes under the grand sculptural branches of old cypresses. He's on a cruise now, watching fog wisps from the ocean brush the top of the trees.

He's pumping to make up lost time from the long uphill grade, watching the road, watching another pack of riders pass. He's pumping and tiring. But why now? He wonders. Now, when there's a clear coast downhill. He checks his pulse. Elevated but within range.

There's a moment, coasting down the wide boulevard, when he starts to reconsider the day's challenges. What if I don't swim the Bay? What if I don't change into my wetsuit? I could turn right, break away from the pack. Who would care? The quitting tape grates on his nerves. His heart beats faster with the thought of escaping—but the thrill of quitting doesn't match the thrill of seeing himself at the finish line of the foot race. Considering the options, he pedals on. Up through the doubts, up through the misery. He barrels through like a submarine or an aircraft taking off.

Face it, Wiser. The Bay is your Holy Grail. Open water. Doug pumps hard now, edging out of the pack toward the front where he can get a view of the Bay. The whirr of gears downshifting and athletes breathing a particular music of metal and flesh, sharp notes and deep basses.

Katie is there when Doug pulls into the changing area. She's holding out a clean, dry towel and his wetsuit. Her eyes are lit up like the old days, lit with the pure pleasure of seeing him, lit with something that if everything that had happened this past month had never happened, if they hadn't fought about the baby, if she hadn't seen him with his face nuzzled into Hope's neck, if they hadn't almost lost one another, he might say the look is something like love.

"You made great time. Hurry up!"

Doug proffers a quick peck.

Great time?

In the changing tent, shimmying into his wetsuit he searches for Aaron. "Don't think, Wiser! Just go!" Aaron's command echoes in his mind.

Doug tears out of the tent like a man from a fire and runs toward the boat that will take him out into the open water.

"All in!" the captain shouts into his bullhorn.

Doug dives in. After a few shivery minutes, his body adjusts to the temperature, and he begins moving well. The water, much as he hates to admit it, is actually refreshing after the heat and sweat of the uphill bike ride. He thinks of a tweet: Swimming in the bay. Quirk: After an eighteen-mile bike race. Will they still be issuing challenges at YUMI?

If they're still going to do extreme sports, this is about as extreme as he'll ever get. He makes a mental note to involve Escape from Alcatraz organizers next year.

The race pacer, a sturdy guy about Doug's age, shouts encouraging remarks: "Looking good! The water's easy today—we lucked out. Great weather! No wind! Just give us a sign if you need anything!"

The *clichés* are more helpful than Doug could have ever imagined. Swimming in the bay is more like rappelling off a rock face and less like hang gliding than he had feared. He swims, organizing his thoughts around the lift and dip of his arms, the kicking of his legs. He swims close to the boat, in his own lane. He doesn't want to worry about other swimmers the way he did with the bikes rushing behind to overtake him. On the bike, Doug kept his ears tuned for the whirr of invading gears.

Now, he can't hear a thing beside the megaphone and the intermittent deep hum of the foghorn. Push, dip. Kick. Push, dip, kick.

He considers the slimy, creepy, scary creatures circling his legs and his heart beats faster. Anxiety. Not good. "It's all about the arc," he hears Aaron. And so, he focuses on his arms, bringing his elbow up and over at just the right angle, turning his face at just the right moment. Breathe. Kick. Dip. Breathe. Kick. Dip.

"Halfway!" the pacer yells.

He may not be in the zone but he's in the flow. Kick, push, dip. Kick, push, dip.

"Three quarters, guys! You are so close!" The pacer roots them on with blasting salsa music. His feet are kicking but he can't feel them. He's focused on the hot towels and chocolate Aaron had promised are on the other side. And then, he's thinking about the run. Not yet. Be here, now. Focus.

For the last stretch, arms aching, feet numb, legs exhausted, he breaks the movements of the swim into an engineering project, fashioning his body into a projectile. Kick, dip, kick, dip. In the pool, he was all about timing and overcoming the hurdle of submerging his warm body into the cool pool. At the pool, his workouts were about overcoming his fear of open water. Here, it's about getting to the other side, and getting to the other side only.

"Angle the torso when lifting the arm, turn the head while propelling forward, and kick the feet while focusing on the arm angle."

"Twenty yards!" the pacer yells. Doug is dizzy from the waves, the bobbing up and down, the circular movements, something he could never have prepared for in the pool.

"Five! Prepare to stand!"

A volunteer is at the beach with warm, dry towels, helping Doug out of the water. He wants to hug her, call her savior, but his teeth are chattering, and his legs are shaking so hard he can barely stand.

"Drink this!" Another volunteer rushes him into the changing tent. He slams a cup of hot chocolate while twisting out of the sticky wetsuit.

"You did it!"

"I did?"

"Yes! Fifty-two minutes!"

Doug is drying and rubbing and blowing and stamping to keep warm, and at the same time, trying to stand still to sip the warming drink. His teeth chatter. "I didn't train hard enough."

A cute volunteer rubs his back, warming him. "No one does." And then he's pushing his legs into dry shorts.

Outside of the clutch of swimmers lacing up running shoes, Doug catches sight of Aaron heading off for the trail. "Aaron!"

"Hey! I bonked! They pulled me out of the Bay! I'm only doing the run to say I finished!" Aaron yells.

Doug can barely hear his friend over the loudspeakers, music and chaos of hundreds of gyrating, shimmying, and jumping up and down athletes.

"I rode with the pacer the last quarter mile! Fuck!" Aaron shouts over his shoulder.

"No!" The news that he survived the swim, but his coach didn't is an unexpected dose of schadenfreude. "My pacer was fantastic! I think Ron Howard trained him. You know, the motivated by kindness thing? I was a freaking science project out there, man!" Doug is rambling, tired and cold, but talking a blue streak.

"See you on the other side!"

A volunteer hands him a dry t-shirt and warm-up jacket. Tying on running shoes, he wishes that Katie were here, rubbing a dry towel over his head, but no spectators are allowed on the beach.

He suits up into dry running gear. Volunteer #278 shouts, "GO!!"

Doug slams a Power Bar, sips a last drop of hot chocolate. Then, he's off. He charges out of the changing area, a bull to the red flag. He's almost finished! Thirteen miles? A cakewalk! Yeah!

He starts the run, glad for dry land. He heads out to the park with the pack. The noise of the city—cars alarms, sirens, and race music are a welcome change after the watery whoosh of waves and shrieks of gulls. He's still a bit dizzy but the ground meets his feet at every step. It will pass. His feet slowly warm, the nerve endings vibrating back to life. Water rushes in his ears; he's an astronaut just landed. With his feet back on solid ground, he has the sense of having been hurtled through space—dark, black, huge, mysterious space. It's almost over, Wiser. You're almost done.

On the trail, Doug wills one foot in front of the other. His legs are sore from the swim, his arms drained. Runners, fleet as Winged Mercury, pass on his left, but he doesn't care; he's so over the competition. His stomach grumbles. He's running past cheering crowds, running past a few limping athletes, dreaming about a big pizza with mushrooms and grilled onions. Meatballs and peppers, too! He realizes that he hasn't eaten anything decadent in almost a half a year. Okay, forget the curly fries and hot dog, because that whole night is erased. Hope buzzes back into his vision, but he brushes her away. Pizza.

Miles one, two and three go without a hitch. At mile four his right foot begins protesting. It starts in the heel and then pain shoots through his arch to his toes.

He's running, but really, it's more of a slow jog. His left knee starts yelling; his right femur shouts. Mile five brings a backache of new dimensions and by mile six, his back is harmonizing with his hamstrings.

"I am a harp constricted by its woody nature, a Stradivarius with too taut strings," Aaron had lyrically mused. The image stuck.

"I am spirit, constrained by vein and tendon, heart-pump and lung bellows," Doug had sung back. Who knows where this stuff came from? Sometimes, when you are lucky enough to hit the zone, you get out of your own way; sometimes you are channeling God, sometimes poetry.

Talk about God! Doug is running, when all of a sudden, he sees his father—or his doppelganger—in the crowd of cheering people. "Go Dougy!" he hears. "Go Kyla! Go Kevin!" He hears names, but he doesn't want to slow down. As he passes, he can't help but turn his head for a double check. Out of the corner of his eye he sees his father's beefy cheeks, that shiny hair, that paunchy middle. He's smiling, too.

He runs on. The backache is worse, more intense. A siren screams; the high-pitched chord jangles his nerves. He thinks of Daisy, waiting at home. He wishes she were here now, running with him, cheering him up. Mile seven. He resists the urge to slow, to limp. When I hit that finish line, I want to look cool. Stay cool, Wiser.

He's jogging, slowly, navigating through the throbbing feet, the backache, thinking about his dad. The thought comes from nowhere: Why didn't my mother stop him from working himself to death? All at once, he's filled with rage against his mother. Doug had believed that his father's relentless working was for himself, his own ego gratification. But now, Doug is seriously wondering if it wasn't for his mother and everything she wanted—no, insisted on!

The house at the lake, private schools for three kids, the luxury cars, the country club.

Maybe that's exactly why I should have a child! The thought blossoms like a crocus breaking ground. I've spent enough time thinking about myself! Have I ever, really, truly, honestly, cared a whit about anybody? All at once, Doug sees his life in stark relief, and all at once, it seems . . . ridiculous. The striving, the myopic focus, the obsessions.

Is this what everyone is feeling, homing in feverishly toward that finish line? Was this the "mystery" Aaron had alluded to? This doesn't feel like a first date at all. Unless your first date is watching a horror movie! Did he know that a triathlon not only broke your spirit, but also threw your life into stark absurdity?

A pacer holds up a paddle: "Mile eight." The shouting of the crowds drowns out a weak whoop from the pack. "You're almost home! Keep it up! Go runners!" Runners? Doug has lost touch; he's numb from his toes to his shoulders. He's jog-limping, slogging through molasses. Five more miles? No fucking way.

His whole body aches, his life is absurd, and everything has been a mistake: from Topia, to the band, to the reinvention of the band to FearToShred, to sleeping with Hope. The only thing he is certain is not a mistake is Katie. He's running and questioning. Has his whole life just been organized in opposition to boredom? In opposition to the Midwest, to the easy life, to the status quo, to the flat expanse of Michigan that everyone he had gone to school with loved with all their hearts? Had he organized his life against everything Midwestern? Against a staunch regionalism, loyalty to his home state? Those qualities he had dismissed as naïve, simplistic, now seem so sweet. The way his classmates planned out their lives in high school, set their sights on a good job and a house on a lake.

Long summers. Cross-country skiing in the winter.

He'd bailed. Left the Midwest for the land of endless summer. California was his island, his lake house. He was so cool; he didn't even go back to lord it over his old pals. Now he wishes for a life where not every single person wants to be a rock star. It is exhausting.

"Mile ten!" the pacer runs by. "You guys doing OK? Sag wagon?"

Doug can't summon the energy to respond. Three more miles. He sniffs away tears. Or is it sweat? Mistakes have been made. He will have to square it all after the race. A surge of energy shoots up from his legs. A training run with Aaron comes into focus. The soft dirt. Sunlight filtering through towering redwoods. Three miles. Exactly the distance from the beginning of his and Aaron's run to the intersection at the creek. He runs, numb to his body, numb to his thoughts.

"Mile eleven!"

Only two more miles! Doug's mood shifts. He's giving it his all, a valiant show, keeping up a slow but steady pace.

Suddenly, despair hits. Out of nowhere, he begins to feel that things might not go well. Not just with Katie or the code, the game and YUMI, but also with the Bay Area and California. Suddenly, he's obsessing about plane crashes and terrorists and then about not finishing the race. His heart starts racing in a different way than it was when he saw his "non-father father" in the stands, and in a different way from when he stamped out of the cold water. He jog-limps, dreading the finish line, dreading even seeing Katie.

One more mile! Wiser! C'mon. It's a mini triathlon, not an Iron Man.

It's a mental game, Wiser. You do games! You're the game guy! Again, Aaron's voice. So he's doing the game, trying to convince himself that he's gone the paces, that this is almost over. He's wondering again if this is the surprise, the mystery Aaron meant. That the end is harder than you can even imagine? He searches out the field for Aaron, but all of a sudden, he doesn't just want to see him, he needs to. Doug is about to call out Aaron's name, uselessly, when a dark field starts creeping into his peripheral vision. I should stop, I should call Katie. He stumbles, then catches himself.

And then there's this crazy slideshow. Doug runs, or at least he thinks he's running, but he's not sure. Strangers and family, well-wishers and kids from elementary school, people are everywhere, in front of him, on the sides of him, in the stands. Running or jogging, jogging then limping, he's moving and watching a slideshow.

There's his father, and his mom, and there's the lake house. He's swimming in the lake, and he's watching himself on stage at the Knitting Factory with that first crazy riff, and then again at the FearToShred party finding that riff again. He's training, and there's the guy as big as an elephant seal. "Did you make a killing?" There's Katie, and Daisy at the beach. He's at the barbecue, hugging Hope, and then he's getting drunk in the bar. He's in Hope's apartment. He's in her bed, and he's looking over Brett's shoulder as he shows off his winning code, and he's watching himself training, those first weeks. He's watching Katie fly away on her bicycle, ringing the bell, and the echo, "Did you make a killing?" There's Arthur raging about the rewrite and Jeff ranting about sex and death. There's Lake Chagrin and then nothing.

The screen goes black. Doug wonders, *where are the credits?* They're gone and the cheering section is gone, and the pack is gone, and the pacers are gone, and his legs are gone, and his back is gone and he's thinking "What the fuck?" And then he gets it.

I didn't make it. I'm gone.

44

A THICK, pale yellow folder rests on the leather seat next to Hope. The folder, and what was inside of the folder, had caused her two sleepless nights. Driving across the San Mateo Bridge, Hope rehearses. "We're good now, right?" Hope would ask before presenting the folder. The break with Charlene had been hard. As much as she dreaded her evenings with her mother, she missed her!

Figure that one out, she asked Dawn. "Love-hate. Most common family relationship," Dawn had offered up the dime-store psychology. But Hope knew what it was, loyalty to the woman who had kept a roof over her head and food on the table. Bitter fights aside, it was in that small house that Hope had studied, planned, and schemed. That counted for something. Even if, in her despair, she did take a razor blade to her arms. It helped. Watching the blood drip, smacked with pain. Her father might have left, but she still had a pulse. And a life. A life she wanted to live out. A life far away from this valley, a life with smart people full of ambition and dreams. She knew they were out there; she just had to find them.

Pulling off the freeway at Pleasanton, Hope is half an hour early. She cruises Main Street, past the old tack shop, the hardware store. Down the street is the football stadium where she used to neck with Steve, there, Main Street Theater she and Dawn would get lost in Saturday matinees.

Stopping at Dottie's Bakery, Hope orders a non-fat latte and resists her favorite treat—a gingerbread cookie with maple icing. At a quiet, tiled table, she grabs her iPad out of her bag. List making for a talk with Charlene is silly, but it serves a purpose. It calms her. It also helps her sort out where to start.

First, there's the FearToShred sale. But would she tell her mother about her winnings? Or how she helped Arthur? Then there was breaking her engagement, and the BASE jump. She would have to prioritize. There is only so much Charlene can take in at once.

The door to Charlene's trailer opens without a squeak. Charlene is dressed, made up and looking regal in a white tunic embellished with gold chain.

"Hope! I'm going crazy!" Charlene is at the kitchen table, pouring over bills.

"Obamacare?"

"Yes, but I can't figure these damned forms out."

"I'll take them." Hope slips the papers into her briefcase.

In a quiet booth at Il Cortone, Charlene sips a martini, Hope a glass of Justin Cabernet. "Hope, you have made me a happy woman."

On the table is the folder with signed mortgage papers for Charlene's new condo. Hope grins happily. *You have made me happy* are words she never expected to hear, not now, not anytime, from Charlene. When Hope went with the broker to buy the spacious one-bedroom unit, when she wrote a check, when she pictured Charlene sitting in her white living room with the expansive grassy yard beyond the sliding glass doors and the bronze table and chairs and umbrella where she could drink her morning coffee, she was dead sure that Charlene would push back. She steeled herself. But here she was, content, happy, and grateful for her good fortune.

"It was too much." Charlene toys with the heavy silverware. In the way that Charlene fingers the spoon, the knife, Hope senses her fragility. Hope can see in Charlene's sad eyes, the effort she had to make just to control the chaos of being a single mom, the weight of that responsibility. "I just couldn't wrap my head around Richard showing up."

"I'm listening." Hope sits back in the leather booth, a bead of sweat launching a slow roll down her spine.

"I don't want to say this but I'm going to. Because we're getting too old to not tell the truth, right?" Charlene takes a sip of the martini. "When you told me that you saw your dad, I lost my cool . . ."

"Yes, I was there."

"But I want you to know why, Hope."

Hope gulps. Maybe she's too old to not be telling the truth, as Charlene insists, but she might be too young to hear it. Maybe lies are better. Lies had gotten her this far, hadn't they?

"Hope, you and your dad were inseparable. You worshipped the ground he walked on. If he came back into your life, where would I be?"

"Charlene Ellson!" Hope exclaims.

Charlene blinks back tears.

"Where would you be? Where you always are. My mother!" Hope leans forward in the booth. "No one could replace you, mom," Hope reaches for her mother's hand. Charlene squeezes.

"Hey, where's your ring?"

"That's another story."

She would tell Charlene about why she broke up with James soon, but what she won't tell her is that after weeks of private deliberation, she had loaned her father twenty thousand dollars. The loan was high on her Database of Deceits; if her mother knew, she would have a cow; Dawn would probably disown her, and James would have been apoplectic. Besides, the way Richard presented it, the loan was an investment.

The story her father told was that his company had tanked, he was trying to save it, and, he saw an opportunity for her. "This is not money down the drain," he promised. "Not only am I going to give you your principal back within twelve months, I'll make sure you are written into the deal when we sell."

She'd heard it all before. "I'll think about it," she had told him. And she did, for three weeks. But after breaking with James, after the BASE jump, after she got her payout from FearToShred, it occurred to her that this might be a karmic debt to pay.

Maybe this would balance the scales for selling her team out, for sleeping with Doug and nearly crashing his marriage and for breaking her engagement with James.

Whether Richard was a scoundrel or a saint, she didn't know. Her feelings were clouded by love. Whether he was a loser or a gift, she really didn't care. Having him around to cheer her on these days had made her happy. As she'd said before, he loved her like no one else.

45

PULLING UP in front of Doug's house on Waverly, Hope's heart skips a beat. The last time she visited was Katie's birthday. Was that only a month ago? Has she been aging in dog years? Can this much happen to a person in one month? How did she wake up and drink coffee, go to work and show up as the same person on the outside but totally changed on the inside? Hope listens to the creaking metal of the engine cooling. The convertible top is down and a soft, fragrant breeze wafts across her face. She leans her head against the cool leather headrest. What if Aaron hadn't taken Katie out to the beach, as he promised? What if Katie was here? She texts Doug: "Coast clear?"

"Clear."

Up the rose-strewn path to Doug's front door, she recalls their last talk, at Lake Chagrin. "What now?" she had asked.

"What now?" Doug answered testily. "Now, we work. Now, we get the company launched. Now, I finish my race."

Hope knocks gingerly on the redwood door.

"Open." Doug's voice is strained, weak.

Stepping across the threshold, Hope breathes a sigh of relief.

Doug's face breaks into a happy smile. She hugs him lightly. He's pale and gaunt.

A sweating pitcher of water and his iPad rest on a small TV table. An acoustic guitar leans against the wall. Daisy is at the foot of the narrow couch, dozing.

"Doug." His name catches in her throat.

Doug's hand quivers in his lap. Doug sucks a sip of water from a chilled glass. "It was crazy. It was the end of the race. The finish line was right there! I'd done the swim! Hope! Remember I told you about how I almost drowned as a kid when I got stung by a bee?"

"Yes."

"I was petrified of the Bay. I could barely get myself to the pool twice a week."

Hope's face twists into an empathic smile. She knows about facing fears now. Doug leans back, his wide chest shrunken.

"Really, Doug. Don't strain yourself."

"No worries, Katie's kicked into full tilt healer mode; she's taking great care of me. Green smoothies. Pasta! I'm getting better."

Katie's on it. Caregiving is her raison d'etre.

"The bike ride was harder than I'd expected but the swim was easier. I was in a good mood. I was all about finishing! Besides, running was my favorite! I was fighting leg aches, but I was fine. I guess I blacked out. I don't know, I saw my father, and my whole life."

"Seriously?" Hope wonders if she was a part of that slide show but won't dare ask.

"Doctor says I had a minor heart attack. I don't remember anything. The docs did emergency surgery—put a stent in. Can you believe it, Hope? I'm fucking thirty-seven!"

Hope frowns. "I'm so sorry." She wants to take his hand, to hug him hard, kiss him! Anything to bring the blood back to his face, to see his old pudgy self.

Instead, she sinks deeper into the soft velvet chartreuse club chair, her mind wandering back to how she'd sat in this very chair, imagining Doug and her living together.

"What about you?" Doug asks softly, bringing her attention back to the room, to the sunlight pouring in through the lace curtains, geometric shapes dancing on the rug.

"Doug? Really?" Hope frowns. "We'll talk about me later. Now, I want you to get strong. To be your old Master Builder self . . ."

"Hope. I'm not dying. I'll be OK. I just want to know. What happened?"

Hope squeezes her lips together. Where to start? Back in high school when she was hell-bent on making her millions? That having her own money, once and for all, was her way of saying fuck you—but not to work, because she knows she is built to work—to Charlene! She won't tell Doug that. Not today.

Hope leans in, faces Doug head-on. "I thought Jeff was about to implode. I talked to Julie. She wanted in on the deal with YUMI. She was afraid of Jeff's resistance to TAN. TAN had big ideas, but that's Hollywood. I got caught up . . ."

"And Kelly no doubt . . ." Doug says softly.

"Maybe," Hope blushes. "But mostly, I thought selling to YUMI would be good for us financially. You included."

"Even after I busted my nuts fixing the damn thing?" Doug lets out a cynical laugh.

"Doug. You were brilliant! I was so proud."

"Don't worry. I was angry at first, but after I got a good look at death, I could care less. Arthur is a player. No surprises."

"It all happened so fast. Before I knew it, I was in YUMI's office agreeing to do due dil."

"Yeah, that part I still can't totally square." Doug gazes at Daisy. "We were pals, Hope."

"Be right back." Hope heads for the bathroom. Didn't she say she was going to come clean? But what happened with Arthur and YUMI wasn't a lie; it was business deal that demanded discretion. That's not lying. Right? In the bathroom mirror, she reapplies Diva and composes herself. Is Doug really asking her about YUMI?

"Doug," Hope starts. "Let me just go over the basics. We can talk more when you're feeling stronger."

"That's fine. The basics."

"Arthur lost confidence. He saw Jeff 's antics, the dead kid. Kurt made an offer. He asked me to help. I was conflicted until I realized it might be a good thing. But I had to keep it on the QT." Hope top levels the reasons, leaving out the crying and her fears that Arthur was manipulating her.

"I get it."

"It wasn't that I kept it from you. I had to be discrete."

"But what about Jeff?"

"Can we talk about Jeff later?"

Quiet falls over them like a light mist.

"But wasn't it fun being in Arthur's good graces?"

"Maybe a little."

"So why did you do the jump? Arthur must have had a deal in the works by then, no?" Doug asks.

"I did it for myself."

"Seriously?"

"Yup." That was true. The moment Hope jumped she knew that it would change her life. "I did it to get over my fears. Even this very moment," Hope blurts.

"Which moment? Seeing me in my jammies?" Doug laughs, his cheeks coloring for the first time since she's arrived.

"No . . ."

Hope waits a beat.

"Why didn't you ever ask why I left Topia? Why I left you?"

"Hope," Doug says, his face tender, his eyes soft. "I wanted to be with you for as long as you wanted me."

"Oh, really?"

"Yes, really, Hopi. You are the Queen of Big Dreams. I'm Master Builder. But that doesn't mean I want to sacrifice my life the way that you . . ."

"Right."

"And now?"

"Now? No clue. I broke up with James if that's what you're asking."

"I wasn't asking, but really?" Doug asks, alarmed.

"Don't worry. It's not about you. It's about me. He wasn't the right guy. Well, not for me."

"I get it."

"Actually, James is great. It was the whole James package. It was too neat. Marrying James would have been fitting into a box. A nice box, a fancy box! But still, a box. He said he wasn't pressing, but I knew he wanted kids. Kids? With my crazy parents? What would I do with Charlene? With my shitty past? There was no room for me there."

"Hope, I love you." The words roll off Doug's tongue with a sweetness and spontaneity that crack Hope's heart. "But I'm married. I need you to know I adore you. I always have and I always will."

Doug shakes his head, a saltshaker setting free demons, ideas, plans. "We could never be together. You know that," Doug says wistfully.

"I do?"

"Sure you do. You could never be happy with me. You know what I really want? I want to mess around in my garage with my guitar and my tools. I want to fix the broken door, rebuild the bathroom, and clean the gutters. I want to walk my dog and plant my vegetables and flowers and throw backyard barbecues. I'm a back-end guy. My life wouldn't make you happy, Hopi! You're Miss Excitement."

"You've been pretty exciting lately . . ."

"Hope." Doug reaches out his hand.

Together, they sit, silently, holding hands, errant tears freely flowing.

"Doug. Get well. We'll talk."

46

"ORDRD U a nfat double latte :)" Julie texts. Why are they meeting in this crowded, caffeinated buzz box? Shouldn't they be in a quiet place to lay their hearts on the table and dissect them in peace? Besides, she hates Italian coffee. But this is Julie's meeting.

"Hope!" Julie waves.

An Italian barista shouts, "Non-fat cap, doppio espresso, mocha!" The words echo off white tiled floors and stucco walls, mix with the steam hissing in a steady stream from an industrial espresso maker. Hope feels like she's in an airport waiting area. She drops her brief-case, folds herself onto the hard, wooden chair.

Kissing Julie, Hope eyes a plate of croissants that her former co-worker has placed seductively in the middle of the small table.

"First, let's clear the air," Julie starts.

Hope settles in. She can tell the air is clear already, but she'll hear Julie out. She can tell because the black circles under Julie's eyes have faded, her eyes look brighter and even her jet-black hair glows. Is she having more sex? Moved to a bigger house? Had a vacation?

"Absolutely," Hope agrees. "But first, let me say that you look wonderful!"

"Oh, yeah! Took the wife to Maui for two weeks. I think I slept a hundred hours. I surfed and downed who's knows how many rum cocktails." Julie nibbles the croissant.

"Did you decide about YUMI?" Hope asks expectantly.

"I'm going. It's fine. I negotiated a month break. I'll be out in two years."

Hope picks at the crusty end of a croissant. "Totally. Or before if their stock does well and you're feeling rich. What about Jeff?"

Julie reaches a slender hand across the table.

"We'll get to Jeff. I just need to say something. That day you asked me to consider voting so Arthur could do the deal? It was the right thing to do. Don't ever for a minute blame yourself. You did good. I'll work things out with Jeff."

Hope nibbles the croissant, the sweet, buttery pastry buoying her mood.

"He's pissed. *You pulled the rug out from under me*, he complains. He's really gone ballistic."

Hope nods, sips the latte for strength.

Julie's face turns wistful. "*We were fucked!* It's his mantra. He texts me every day. I threw my phone into the Pacific. I got tired of trying to calm him down. His thinking is so *cliché*."

Hope waits. This is Julie's meeting; she called it. Julie sips her mocha and munches on the croissant—with peach preserves. Hope's head pounds. The barista's shouting grates on her nerves. All the way over here, she was dreading that Julie would say she regretted her decision, that her relationship with Jeff was a mess, and she couldn't live with her own disloyalty. Julie polishes off her breakfast with a quick dunk of the croissant into the hot coffee, licks her lips, smiles guiltily.

"Hope, what's done at FTS is done. It's business. Angie and I talked about it a lot. I grieved. I was letting go of my dream. FearToShred was fun! Just the idea of two skaters building something from scratch—and you! Hope. That jump. Was. Insane!"

Hope nods appreciatively.

"You blew it out of the water, Hope! Three million votes! You did in that jump what all the meetups, and me and Jeff and all the Product Analyst geeks and SEO nerds wanted to do! You nailed it."

"I thought I was going to die!" Hope shakes her head, the pounding worsening.

"Why didn't you tell us? I cannot fucking believe you did that stealth!"

"Why?" Hope tears up at the memory of standing at the precipice with her instructor. How her knees shook, how she was one inch from tearing the suit off when her arms bent forward and she kicked off. "Why? Because I finally realized that I had fears to face. My own demons to liberate." Finally, the knot that was in her stomach all morning loosens and Hope understands that Julie did not call her here to berate her.

Outside, in the fall crisp air, Hope's optimism is restored. A breeze eases the aching in her head. Off of University Avenue, the two walk under the wide sycamores and oaks.

"Julie? Truth? You don't blame me?"

"Hope." Julie takes Hope's arm, faces her squarely. "No blame! You were an employee of FearToShred. You may look like Wonder Woman to us, but you're not. The big boss asks you do something, you do it."

Hope looks at the ground sheepishly. "I could have said no."

"Oh, really?" Julie looks at Hope askance.

"I don't know. Sometimes I wonder if I should have stayed out of it. But then, when they offered us upwards of a hundred million, I thought, hey, I'm going to help make these folks rich. That you and Jeff and Doug would all get good exits."

"We did. We are. Like I said. It's business, Hope."

After a few blocks, reminiscing about silly and horrible FearToShred moments—ice skating, the alley-oop on the wave, Jeff's antics at the barbeque, and the tragic death of the windsurfer in the Indian Ocean— Hope and Julie fall into a friendly silence.

"Wait! Hope! What were we thinking?"

Hope shakes herself out of the dream of her private version of the past six months: Arthur asking her for help, going to YUMI, BASE jumping, kissing Kelly, sleeping with Doug.

"What were we thinking about what?"

Looking skyward, Hope is struck by the purity of huge white magnolia flowers budding from waxy leaves on the thick-limbed trees lining the street. How could she have missed these pristine flowers the size of small footballs?

"Hope Ellson! Forget what happened, and how it happened. That's all in the past. We're going to use our FearToShred winnings. Remember? Megan Smith? Let's do something great." Julie's edict brings her back to the moment.

Julie takes Hope's shoulders in her strong hand. "Let's go help girls. We'll set up an after-school tutoring center to help girls with math and we'll get some young kids to teach them coding. What do you think?"

"I'm there."

The two shake hands on the new deal. Julie is right. Who cares about the past and how they came into money? That was then. This is now.

47

"DID YOU make it?"

"To which *it* are you referring?" Hope sips an icy Cosmopolitan, savoring the lime and vodka with a whisper of cranberry. The Circle Back might be a dive bar, but their bartender rocks it.

"That gaming company, right?"

"Yes, not only did I make it, I jumped." Hope lifts her arm, flexes her bicep.

"You jumped? Off of what?" Dwayne tweaks her bicep, shakes his head in wonder.

"A thousand-foot cliff." Hope grimaces, her stomach clutching at the memory of the BASE jump.

Rifling through her bag, Hope had discovered Dwayne's card stuffed into a side pocket.

"Visit?" she e-mailed.

"Who?"

"Lisa. From the Circle Back. But I'm really Hope."

Hope added a smiley face :) Of all her lies, deceptions, back chan-neling, and withholding of information, Dwayne was by far the most benign infraction.

"No!" Dwayne sips a Blue Moon and nibbles on peanuts.

A sharp slant of late afternoon sun knifes through the Circle Back window and ricochets off the mirror behind the bottles lined up behind the bar. Dwayne squints, angles his stool out of the blinding light. He's dressed for the occasion, a striped button down, black expensive jeans. Hope still didn't know exactly what line of work he was in, but today's rendezvous would answer that. Whether he was potential boyfriend material would take much longer; she wasn't about to jump into anything.

"I almost didn't, after the kid died, but then I decided that I had to do it—for myself." Hope turns off her buzzing phone. "I'll tell you about that in a minute."

Dwayne nods.

Hope excuses herself under the guise of visiting the ladies' room, but it's the phone call she wants to answer.

In the Blue Moon mirror on the wood paneled wall, Hope watches Dwayne turn his attention to the Giants/Dodgers game on the big screen. Has potential, she thinks, slipping into the quiet of the empty restroom.

"Just checking in."

Doug has left a message. His voice sounds stronger, healthier.

Hope texts: "I'm in a meeting. Can I call in an hour?"

"I'm here."

Hope exits the restroom on wobbly legs.

"I was terrified, as you can imagine." She settles back onto the still warm bar stool. Inside, her heart is thumping, her adrenaline pumping. Doug's voice unsettled her. When they parted with "we'll talk" Hope didn't imagine that Doug would actually be reaching out anytime soon. Hope imagined that the next time they spoke, Doug would be in another incarnation, probably a dad, and back to his music. Why not? He'll survive YUMI just like she had survived Manuserve. He'd circle back when life got dull, right? But now? What could Doug want now?

Dwayne is looking awfully handsome, more handsome than she recalled. His sharp cheekbones are accented by a short shock of dark brown hair. His ruddy complexion suggests an outdoor lifestyle— could he be an athlete? Surfer? Biker? Her curiosity is power surging, threatening to short circuit her rational mind. She'll wait. Timing is everything.

"I had a great instructor. Once I was off the ledge it was easy."

Telling Dwayne about that difficult day is almost painless. The fight with James echoes now, along with the memory of how she wanted to, but couldn't bring herself to tell him about the simulation class, how she wanted to jump, and why. By the time James found out, there was no room to tell him any of that; he was too miffed that she had left him out of the loop.

"A good teacher makes all the difference." Dwayne takes Hope's hand again, orders another round.

"It ended up being a really good thing. A kid had died doing one of our challenges; we were being sued. The jump upped our numbers; it pulled us out of a rough spot. But actually, that's not why I did it."

"Tell." Dwayne strokes her hand like a piano player performing a Chopin sonata by heart.

Hope's stomach clutches. Dwayne's touch is as sexy as she remembered, gentle yet strong, kind yet desirous. "At first, I thought that the-jump would show that I was the uber product pro. But you don't jump off a thousand-foot cliff to prove yourself professionally." Hope laughs at the absurdity of her misguided logic.

"Standing on that ledge I came face to face with all my fears. Fear of going for my first tech job, fear of being poor, fear of not measuring up." Damn. Did she really just say that?

Talking to Dwayne might be easier than talking to James, but still she has enough wits about her to not tell Dwayne what got her, finally, to that ledge. What finally got her to the jump was that she realized that her worst fear was feeling nothing. Being numb. BASE jumping was at least less harmful than cutting.

"I jumped out of a plane once."

"To the jumpers!" Hope clinks her drink with his. She is tipsy, in a pleasant way. There's Dwayne's hand, and the dusky bar, money in the bank, and Charlene resigned to her choices, set up in her new condo. There's time. Time has been the biggest perk of the buyout. So much has changed. Her mother is married! Charlene finally went on that cruise. She met her mate, Christian Ferst. They got married as soon as they reached dry land. "Mrs. Ferst," she calls herself now.

And here's Dwayne. Easygoing and gentle, comfortable in his skin. Successful but with no obvious lineage. Kind, but not doting. Her kind of guy, exactly.

Dwayne's face changes from the delight of a shared life experience to earnest. "So why did you call? Oh, and why did you tell me your name was Lisa?"

"I wanted to see you again. I'm sorry. I didn't mean to . . . it was a weird time for me . . . I didn't always tell the truth."

"You've changed?"

Hope holds up her index and middle finger in a salute: "Scout's honor."

It's been a month since she broke with James. Two weeks since the company was sold, and she got off with a free pass. "I thought you were cute," she winks. "But I was busy," Hope says.

"You're not busy now?"

"No, I'm not. Are you?"

"I was. But not now. So, what happened with the company?"

"You first. What do you do?"

"Real estate. Oh, and surfing whenever I can."

"Yeah, I can see that." Hope says, the part of her that worried that he might be some Trustafarian relieved. "Listen, I have to make a quick call. You mind?"

"Nope. Two innings left." Dwayne points at the screen.

She kisses Dwayne's neck. "Don't go anywhere."

"Right here."

In the parking lot, Hope's lips quiver from the warmth of his skin, her hands shake, and her knees are ever so slightly wobbly. Is Dwayne the guy she's been waiting for? A sweet home boy? Not a striver. No pretensions. No Lexus. Comfortable.

She leans against a tree, a slow-moving tilt-a-whirl challenging her equilibrium. Should she call Doug? Why is there no one to ask when she really needs advice? Maybe if she'd asked someone before saying "yes" to marrying James, she could have skipped the drama. Maybe if she'd asked someone before joining FearToShred, she wouldn't be standing here today. Yes, maybe it's time to start asking for advice instead of always trying to figure everything out for herself.

"It's me."

"Thanks for calling back. I know you're busy."

"I'm good." Hope says, her words slurring imperceptibly.

"Listen. I just wanted to apologize."

"Doug Wiser! For what?"

"I don't know. For coming to your place. For making life harder than you expected at the company. Maybe even for losing the company. You know, the rewrite?"

"Doug! You were amazing! And Brett! You guys rocked my world!" Hope paces the parking lot, dust graying her Tom's loafers. "And coming to my place? Hello? Doug? We're adults! Takes two to tango. I should be the one apologizing. I kissed you."

"That was my fault. It was a set-up. That night aside, there's still one question."

Hope sucks a deep breath hoping to clear her mind. There was still one question? There were probably three, or four or a million questions. For instance, why did she allow Arthur to use her? Why did she go to Katie's birthday party, alone? Why did she think bringing Doug to FearToShred was a good idea? Those questions were only the tip of the iceberg that had woken her every night without fail at three A.M.

"Yes?"

"Why did you leave?"

"Leave what? FearToShred?"

"No. Topia."

"I was pregnant." Hope chokes back a tear. Hope's heart beats in an irregular rhythm. "Doug . . . it doesn't matter now, really . . . I'm sorry . . ."

"Wait. What? Pregnant? Hope! Why didn't you tell me? I could have been there for you." Doug's voice is frantic.

"I was scared. I wanted it and I didn't."

Silence.

✳ ✳ ✳

But Doug understands. He always understands. "Doug?"

"Yeah?"

"You know that night? At my apartment?"

"Yeah."

"It got us to the finish line, Doug."

"Oh yeah," Doug says. "It took us all the way to the end."

acknowledgments

Over the course of writing this book, there have been countless advisers, editors, and a global pandemic. Of all the players, no one walked this path with me like my husband, Adam Hertz. He was the inspiration for and co-creator of this book. I am forever indebted.

I'd like to thank my mentors, the patient teachers who believed that I could write a novel when I did not, and the people who believed in this book in particular: Sandy Boucher, Kitty Ross, Judith Thurman, Tom Parker and Peter Miller.

My colleagues were stalwart. There is never anything like the kind words of another writer when you are fraught with doubt about what you are doing with your life and time: Judy Behr, Kelly Sullivan-Walden and Dana Walden, Mary Mackey, Renate Stendhal, Diane Frank, Yvonne Campbell and Kurt Lipshutz. I'd like to also thank my mother, who never said no when I called to rant and rave about the slowdowns, the process, and the challenges of writing a book that was out of my comfort zone.

I'd like to thank Playmatics, the gaming company. Nick Fortungo and Margaret Wallace helped with the game design of FearToShred. My colleagues in the Women's National Book Association, Guy Vincent and Lee Constantine of Publishizer and a special shout out to the friends and family who supported my Publishizer campaign: Debbie Kinney, Kate Greer, Shane Ginsberg, Jay and Sarah Pober, Irene Minkowsky, Ruth Hertz, Emily Klion and George Brooks, Kate Farrell, Ted Barnett and Melanie. I'd like to thank EcoSystms Co-Working space and my friend, Charles Shaw, who welcomed me with warmth and humor.

I also am grateful to my friends who shared their homes and provided quiet places to write: Sue Rushakoff, Kate Greer, Rachelle Zachary and Lea Goldstein, and Brian Greenberg.

I'd like to thank my team of early readers: Andrea Jacoby, Susan Stanger, Mike Morton, Joan Reiss, Elizabeth Block and Brittany Clark.

I want to thank Aaron Sorkin, an exceptional writer who keeps business dramas alive.

Finally, I thank my daughter, Simone Gelfand, who has been with me every step of the way on my writing journey.

Joan Gelfand
January 2020

about the author

Joan Gelfand's reviews, stories, essays and poetry have appeared in over 150 national and international literary journals and magazines, including the *Los Angeles Review of Books, PANK! The Huffington Post, Rattle, Levure littérarie, Voice and Verse, Sycamore Review, Prairie Schooner* and *The Meridien Anthology of Contemporary Poetry.* "The Ferlinghetti School of Poetics," an award winning poem, was made into a short film by Dana Walden. The film has been shown at 20 international film festivals. It won "Best Poetry Film" at the World Film Festival and Certificate of Merit at the International Association for the Study of Dreams. Joan lives with Adam Hertz and two beatnik cats—Jack Kerouac and Lawrence Ferlinghetti.

To schedule readings, book signings, and to invite her to speak to your book club, go to her website: http://joangelfand.com.

books by joan gelfand

Extreme, A Novel

You Can Be a Winning Writer: The 4 C's Approach of Successful Authors

The Long Blue Room

Here and Abroad

A Dreamer's Guide to Cities and Streams

Seeking Center